Strange Shores

Strange Shores

Arnaldur Indriðason

TRANSLATED
FROM THE ICELANDIC
BY
VICTORIA CRIBB

W F HOWES LTD

This large print edition published in 2013 by
W F Howes Ltd
Unit 4, Rearsby Business Park, Gaddesby Lane,
Rearsby, Leicester LE7 4YH

1 3 5 7 9 10 8 6 4 2

First published with the title *Furðustrandir* in 2010
Published by agreement with Forlagið, Reykjavík

First published in the United Kingdom in 2013
by Harvill Secker

A CIP catalogue record for this book is available
from the British Library

ISBN 978 1 47124 695 1

Typeset by Palimpsest Book Production Limited,
Falkirk, Stirlingshire
Printed and bound by
CPI Group (UK) Ltd, Croydon, CR0 4YY

May my poem pass like a breeze
through the sedge by the Styx,
its singing bring solace,
lull to sleep those who wait.

Snorri Hjartarson

CHAPTER 1

He no longer feels cold: instead, a curious heat is spreading through his veins. He had thought there was no warmth left in his body but now it is flooding into his limbs, bringing a sudden flush to his face.

He is lying flat on his back in the dark, his thoughts wandering and confused, only dimly aware of the borderline between sleep and waking. It is terribly hard to concentrate, to grasp what is happening to him. His consciousness ebbs and flows. He doesn't feel unwell, just pleasantly drowsy, visited by a procession of dreams, visions, sounds and places, all familiar, yet somehow strange. His mind plays odd tricks on him, shuttling back and forth between past and present, through time and space, and there is little he can do to control its shifts. One minute he is sitting at his mother's hospital bedside as she slips away; the next, he is plunged into the black depths of winter and senses that he is still lying on the floor of the derelict farmhouse that was once his home. But this must be an illusion.

'Why are you lying here?'

Raising his head, he perceives a figure standing in the doorway.

A traveller must have found his way into the house. He doesn't understand the question.

'Why are you lying here?' the traveller asks again.

'Who are you?' he answers.

He can't see the man's face, didn't hear him enter. All he can make out is his silhouette. The man keeps repeating the same needling question over and over again.

'Why are you lying here?'

'I live here. Who are you?'

'I'm going to stay with you tonight, if I may.'

Then the man is sitting beside him on the floor and appears to have lit a fire. Sensing the warmth on his face, he reaches towards the blaze. Only once before has he experienced such intense cold.

'Who are you?' he asks for the third time.

'I came to listen to you.'

'To listen to me? Who's that with you?'

They are not alone; there is an invisible presence beside the man.

'Who's that with you?' he asks again.

'No one,' says the traveller. 'I'm alone. Was this your home?'

'Are you Jakob?'

'No, I'm not Jakob. Extraordinary that the walls should still be standing. The house must have been well built.'

'Who are you? Are you Bóas?'

'I was just passing.'

'Have you been here before?'

'Yes.'

'When?'

'Many years ago, when there were people still living here. Do you know what became of them – the family who used to live here?'

Now he is immobile in the dark, unable to move for the cold. He is alone again: the fire and the derelict farmhouse have vanished. He is shrouded in freezing darkness, and the warmth is leaching from his face, hands and feet.

Again he hears a scraping noise.

It is approaching from some remote, cold distance, growing ever louder, accompanied by piercing wails of anguish.

CHAPTER 2

He stood in the drizzle by the crags at Urdarklettur, watching as a hunter picked his slow way towards him. They exchanged polite greetings, their words shattering the silence as if broadcast from an alien world.

The sun had not broken through the clouds for several days. Fog lay in a heavy cloak over the fjords and the forecast was for falling temperatures and snow. Nature had sunk into its winter torpor. The hunter asked what he was doing up there; no one went on to the moors these days except a few old-timers like him, culling foxes. He tried to sidestep the question by replying that he was from Reykjavík. The hunter remarked that he had spotted some-body down at the deserted property by the fjord.

'That was probably me.'

The hunter did not pursue the matter but said he had a farm nearby and was out on his own today. 'What's your name?' he asked.

'Erlendur.'

'I'm Bóas.' They shook hands. 'There's a sheep-worrier living in the rocks higher up; a real pest. It's attacked a lot of stock recently.'

'A fox?'

Bóas rubbed his jaw. 'I caught it skulking around the sheep sheds the other day. Got one of my lambs. Put the wind up the entire flock.'

'And you say it has a lair up here?'

'I saw it make off this way. I've seen it a couple of times now, so I reckon I know where its earth is. Are you heading up to the moor? Don't mind if you keep me company.'

He hesitated, then nodded. The farmer seemed content with that; no doubt he would be glad of the conversation. He had a rifle slung over one shoulder and an ammunition belt and worn leather satchel over the other. Under them he was wearing a shabby anorak and dull-green waterproof trousers. He was a vigorous little man, though he must have been well into his sixties. His head was bare and a thick mop of hair hung over his forehead, obscuring a beady pair of eyes. His nose was flattened and bent, as if broken long ago and never properly set, and his mouth was concealed by an unkempt beard apart from when he opened it to talk – he was a chatty fellow and had opinions on everything under the sun. Yet he tactfully refrained from asking Erlendur too much about his movements or why he had chosen to stay in the ruined croft at Bakkasel.

Erlendur had made himself at home in the old house. The roof was still fairly intact, though not watertight, and the rafters were rotten but he had managed to find a dry patch on the floor in

5

what had once been the sitting room. It had started to rain and gust a couple of days ago, and the wind howled around the bare walls, yet they did provide shelter against the wet and he was cosy enough thanks to the gas lantern which he kept on a low flame to eke out the canister. The lamp cast a dim glow where he sat, but all around him the night closed in, black as the inside of a coffin.

At one time the house and land had ended up in the hands of a bank, but Erlendur had no idea who owned them now. In any case no one had ever complained about his camping there on his trips out east. He didn't have much luggage. The rental car was parked out the front, a blue SUV, whose jeep-like appearance belied the heavy weather it had made of the drive up to the house. The track had almost disappeared, overgrown by vegetation that never used to be there. Little by little nature was conspiring to merge the property into its surroundings, gradually obliterating all traces of human habitation.

Visibility grew steadily worse as he and Bóas gained height, until they were enclosed on all sides by milk-white cloud. Once they reached the tops the drizzle gave way to light rain and their feet left a trail on the damp ground. The hunter listened for bird calls and cast around for his quarry's tracks in the wet grass. Erlendur tramped behind in silence. He had never lain in wait by a fox's earth, never stalked an animal or fished a river or lake, let alone felled any larger prey like reindeer. Bóas seemed to read his mind.

'Not a hunting man yourself?' he asked, pausing for a brief rest.

'No.'

'Don't mind me – it's the way I was brought up.' Bóas opened his leather satchel, offered Erlendur some dark rye bread and sliced off a hunk of hard mutton pâté to go with it. 'I mainly go after the foxes these days, to keep the numbers down. The little buggers are getting bolder by the day, though personally I've nothing against them. They've as much right to live as any other creature. But you have to keep them away from the stock – harmony in everything.'

They ate the rye bread. The pâté was very good and he guessed it was probably home-made. Having failed to bring any supplies himself, he had nothing to contribute to the meal. He didn't really know why he had accepted this unsought but civil invitation. Maybe it was a desire for human contact. He had hardly seen a soul for days, and it occurred to him that the same was probably true of this man Bóas.

'What do you do down there in the city?' asked the farmer.

He didn't answer immediately.

'Sorry, I'm such a nosy bastard.'

'No, it's all right,' he replied. 'I'm a policeman.'

'That can't be much fun.'

'No. Though it has its moments.'

They climbed on higher to the moor, and he took care to tread lightly on the heather. From time to time he stooped to brush his hand over the low-growing vegetation, trying to remember if he had ever heard of Bóas as a child. The name didn't ring any bells, though that was hardly surprising – he had lived in the east for a comparatively short period and lost touch with the area after moving to the city. Anyway, guns had been a rare sight in his home. He vaguely recalled a passer-by at his parents' house who had stopped to speak to his father, gesturing down the river with a rifle in his hand. And he remembered that his uncle, his mother's brother, had owned a jeep and used to shoot reindeer. He had worked as a ghillie for city dwellers who came out east to bag a deer, and would bring his family the meat. The fried steaks were a real treat. But he couldn't remember anyone hunting foxes, nor a farmer named Bóas.

'You find the oddest things in foxholes,' remarked Bóas, keeping up a brisk pace. 'They certainly don't go hungry. They'll wander down to the shore and scavenge for drowned guillemots or shellfish and crabs. The cubs will even eat crowberries, as well as the odd field mouse. And once in a while, if a fox gets lucky, it'll find a dead ewe or lamb. But there's the odd sheep-worrier that gets a taste for live meat and then you're done for. Then it's up to Bóas to track the little blighter down and destroy it. But not with any pleasure, mind.'

Uncertain whether the farmer was addressing him or merely thinking out loud, he did not reply. He followed in the other man's footsteps as they waded through deep beds of heather, and enjoyed the sensation of the cool rain pricking his face. He knew the moors well but had put all his faith in the farmer and was no longer sure of their exact whereabouts. Bóas trudged on, carefree and confident, chatting away, apparently unconcerned whether his new companion was listening.

'We've seen a fair few changes around here since the construction work began,' he said, stopping to take a pair of binoculars from his satchel. 'It's had an impact on the environment and maybe the fox has realised. Maybe it doesn't dare go down to the shore any longer because of the factory and all the shipping. What do I know? We should be getting close now.' He replaced the binoculars.

'I saw work under way on the new smelter as I drove up from Reykjavík,' remarked Erlendur.

'That eyesore!' exclaimed Bóas.

'I went and had a look at the dam too. I've never seen anything so huge.'

He could hear Bóas muttering grumpily under his breath as they continued their climb. It sounded like: 'Can you believe they let this happen?' As he toiled along behind, he thought about the foundations that were being sunk for a vast aluminium smelter in the picturesque setting of Reydarfjördur Fjord, and the giant freighters that docked there, transporting construction materials for the plant and the controversial hydroelectric dam at Kárahnjúkar in the highlands. He couldn't understand how on earth an unaccountable multinational, based far away in America, had been permitted to put its heavy industrial stamp on a tranquil fjord and tract of untouched wilderness here in the remote east of Iceland.

CHAPTER 3

Bóas halted in the middle of an expanse of scree and gestured to him to do likewise. Emulating the farmer, he dropped to his knees and peered into the fog.

Minutes passed without his being aware of any movement, until quite suddenly he found himself looking into the eyes of a fox. It stood about fifteen metres away, staring at them with ears pricked. Almost imperceptibly, Bóas tightened his grip on the gun, but it was enough to startle the fox which whisked away up the slope, vanishing from sight in an instant.

'Bless her,' said the hunter, standing up and slinging his gun over his shoulder again before continuing on his way.

'Is that the culprit?' asked Erlendur.

'Yes, that's the little blighter. I know the earths in this area like the back of my hand and I reckon we're close. They return to the same lairs generation after generation, you know, so I dare say some date back a pretty long way – though maybe not quite to the Ice Age.'

They walked on, through the hush of nature,

until they came to a small hide made of heaped stones and moss. Bóas told him to take a breather and remarked that they were lucky with the wind direction, then said he was going to take a look around. Erlendur sat down on the moss and waited. He recalled what he knew about the Arctic fox, said to be the first settler of Iceland since it had arrived ten thousand years ago at the end of the last Ice Age. Judging by the way he blessed it and spoke about it like an old friend, Bóas had a great respect for the beast. Even so, he was prepared to exterminate it if necessary – to snuff out its life and dispatch its offspring as if this were all in a day's work.

'She's here, bless her. All we need now is a little patience,' Bóas announced when he returned, and got down beside him in the hide. He unslung the rifle and ammunition from his shoulder, and put down the leather satchel, producing a hip flask that he offered to Erlendur who grimaced as he tasted the contents. Bóas obviously made his own moonshine and was none too particular about how he distilled it.

'What does a bit of depopulation matter anyway?' Bóas asked rhetorically, taking back the flask. 'The countryside was uninhabited when we arrived, so why shouldn't it be abandoned again when we leave? Why sell the land to speculators to try and halt a perfectly natural process? – tell me that. People come and people go. I ask you, what could be more natural?'

Erlendur shrugged.

'Look at poor old Hvalfjördur on your doorstep,' Bóas continued, 'with those two monstrosities belching out poison day and night. And who for? A bunch of insanely rich foreigners who couldn't even find Iceland on a map. Is that our fate? To end up as a factory for people like that?'

He handed the flask back to Erlendur who this time sipped with extreme caution. Bóas rummaged in his satchel again and removed a large object wrapped in plastic that produced a rancid stench when opened. It was a lump of meat that had gone distinctly high. After chucking it as far as he could in the direction of the fox's earth, he wiped his hands on the moss and reclined again with the rifle at his side.

'Shouldn't take her long to get wind of that.'

They waited quietly in the drizzle.

'Of course, you wouldn't remember me,' Bóas said after a while.

'Should I?' asked Erlendur, coughing.

'No, it would be surprising if you did,' said Bóas. 'After all, you weren't yourself at the time. And it's not as if I knew your parents – we didn't have any contact.'

'When was this? How do you mean I wasn't myself?'

'During the search,' Bóas said. 'When you and your brother went missing.'

'You were there?'

'Yes, I joined the search party. Everybody did. I

13

hear you come out here now and then. Roam the moors like a ghost and sleep in the old croft at Bakkasel. You still believe you can find him, don't you?'

'No, I don't. Is that what people are saying?'

'Us old folks like to reminisce about the past and someone happened to mention that you still go up on the moors. And to prove it, here you are.'

He didn't want to have to explain his behaviour to a stranger or justify how he chose to live his life. This was his childhood home and he came back for a visit every so often when he felt the urge. He did a lot of walking in the area and preferred the ruined farmhouse to a hotel. Sometimes he pitched a tent, at other times he unrolled his sleeping mat on a dry patch in the house.

'So you remember the search?' he said.

'I remember them finding you,' Bóas replied, not taking his eyes off the bait. 'I wasn't with them but the news spread quickly and it came as a tremendous relief. After that we were convinced we'd find your brother too.'

'He died.'

'So it seems.'

Erlendur was silent.

'He was younger than you,' prompted Bóas.

'Yes, two years younger. He was eight.'

They sat there, the minutes ticking by, until Bóas seemed to sense a subtle alteration in their surroundings. Erlendur could not detect it, though he thought it might have been related to the behaviour of the birds. It was some time before Bóas relaxed again and offered him more of the hard mutton pâté and rye bread, and another swig of the hip flask's poisonous brew. The fog settled over them like a white eiderdown. From time to time the piping of a bird reached their ears; otherwise all was quiet.

He couldn't remember any member of the search party in particular. When he came to, they were hurriedly carting him down from the moor, his body rigid as a block of ice. He remembered warm milk being trickled between his lips on the way, but after that he had lost consciousness and was aware of nothing until he found himself lying tucked up in bed with the doctor leaning over him. Hearing unfamiliar voices in the house, he knew instinctively that something bad had happened but couldn't immediately recall what. Then his memory returned. His mother hugged him tight, telling him his father was alive – he had made it home against all the odds – but they were still out looking for his brother, though they were bound to find him soon. She asked if he could help at all, by telling the search party where to look. But all he could remember was the screaming, blinding whiteness that had battered him to his knees over and over again until he couldn't take another step.

He saw Bóas's knuckles whiten as the fox emerged without warning from the fog and picked her way warily towards the bait. She moved closer, sniffing the air, and before he could ask Bóas if it was really necessary to kill her, the hunter had fired and the vixen crumpled to the ground. Bóas rose and went to fetch the carcass.

'Like some coffee?' he asked as he brought his prey into the hide. He took a Thermos from his satchel and unscrewed the two lids that served as cups. One of these he passed to Erlendur, full of steaming liquid, and asked if he took milk. Erlendur declined, saying he drank it black.

'You have to take milk, it's unnatural not to!' Bóas exclaimed, rooting around in the bag, unable to find what he was looking for. 'Blast it! I've only gone and forgotten the bloody stuff.'

He took a mouthful of coffee and declared it undrinkable. Then, clearly agitated, he glanced around, slapping the pockets of his coat as if he might have secreted a carton of milk in one of them. Finally his gaze was arrested by the carcass.

'Probably pointless,' he remarked, seizing the animal and groping under her belly for her teats, only to discover that they were empty.

CHAPTER 4

Erlendur walked slowly up to the house in Reydarfjördur and observed a woman sitting by the window, facing in his direction. One might have thought she had been waiting there all day expressly for him, though he had given no warning of his visit and was still unsure if he was doing the right thing. In the end, however, curiosity had overcome his reservations.

As they descended from the moors, Erlendur asked Bóas about a story he had heard as a child, which had stayed with him ever since. His parents and most of their neighbours had known the tale back then, and it may well have been a motivating factor behind his decision to come out to the East Fjords this autumn.

'So you joined the police?' Bóas said. 'What do you do down there? Direct the traffic?'

'I was in the road division for a while, but that was years ago,' he answered. 'I don't know if you've heard but we have something called traffic lights these days.'

Bóas smiled at the jibe. He was carrying the vixen over his shoulder and his coat was dark with her blood. He had wiped it off his hands as best he could on the wet moss. Originally, his plan had been to spend the night on the moors but the hunt had gone better than anticipated, so he reckoned they would make it back to civilisation before dark.

'You've lived in this part of the world all your life, haven't you?' said Erlendur.

'Never dreamt of living anywhere else,' replied the hunter. 'You won't find better people in Iceland.'

'Then you must have heard the story of the woman who set out to cross the Hraevarskörd Pass and never came back.'

'Sounds familiar,' said Bóas.

'Her name was Matthildur,' said Erlendur. 'She made the trip alone.'

'Oh, I know her name all right.' Bóas stopped and looked at Erlendur. 'What did you say you did in the police?'

'I investigate cases.'

'What kind?'

'All kinds: serious crime, murder, violent incidents.'

'The seamy side of life?'

'If you like.'

'And missing persons?'

'Those too.'

'Do you get many?'

'Not really.'

'Once my generation's gone, there'll be no one left to remember Matthildur's story,' said Bóas.

'I first heard it from my parents,' Erlendur told him. 'My mother knew her slightly and I've always found it . . .' He groped for the right word.

'Mysterious?' suggested Bóas.

'Interesting,' said Erlendur.

Bóas put down his burden, straightened his back and peered down through the gloom to the village nestling by the sea. They were nearly back at Urdarklettur; it was growing chilly and the light was fading. Bóas shouldered the fox again. Erlendur had offered to carry it but the farmer had declined, saying there was no call to muck up his clothes too.

'Of course, you would be interested in that kind of thing,' Bóas commented, his mind still running on missing persons. He spoke more to himself than to Erlendur and looked thoughtful for a while, then resumed his journey downhill over the screes and heathery slopes. 'Then you'll know the story of the British soldiers who got caught in a storm out here on the moors during the war? Members of the occupation force, stationed in Reydarfjördur.'

Erlendur said he had heard about the incident as a boy and later read up on the circumstances, but this did not prevent Bóas from rehashing the story. His question had been rhetorical; he was not about to be denied the pleasure of telling a good tale.

A group of about sixty young British servicemen had planned a hiking expedition from Reydarfjördur to Eskifjördur via the Hraevarskörd Pass, but had got into serious difficulties on the way. The route over the pass had turned out to be too dangerous due to icy conditions, but instead of going back the way they came, they had headed further inland, along the Tungudalur Valley, then down over Eskifjördur Moor. It was late January; the weather had deteriorated drastically during the day and the skies had turned black, thwarting their original aim of reaching their destination while it was still light.

That evening the farmer from Veturhús at the head of Eskifjördur Fjord had been battling his way through the gale to his stable when he stumbled across one of the soldiers, overcome with exhaustion and cold. In spite of his weakened state, the man was able to communicate to him that there were more people in danger, and the labourers from the farm had gone out with oil lamps to search for them. Almost immediately, they found two other soldiers at the foot of the home field, and one by one their comrades had trickled down from the moor until forty-eight were safely accounted for. It transpired that torrential rain had swelled the rivers that flowed between their party and the village, blocking the route. Some of the men, who had made it across while the water was low, were now trapped on the other side, and their cries for help could be heard from the farm. Four died of exposure, but a handful of their companions made it all the way down to the village, arriving in a desperate state. When morning brought a slight improvement in the conditions, the farmer went up the Eskifjördur Valley with the corporal and recovered still more of the soldiers, some alive, others dead, including their captain. One body was found in the sea: the man was believed to have fallen into the Eskifjördur River and been washed down to the fjord. One way or another all the British turned up in the end. The disaster was discussed at great length locally, where it was generally agreed that things would have turned out much worse had it not been for the courageous and timely efforts of the Veturhús folk.

'Plenty of people have heard of the British soldiers but not many remember Matthildur nowadays,' said Bóas, walking ahead of Erlendur with the fox nodding over his shoulder. 'She disappeared in the same storm. According to her husband, she was planning to hike over to Reydarfjördur on the same path as the soldiers, via the pass. It was a route she'd taken before. But when they asked the British if they'd seen her, they swore they hadn't.'

'Shouldn't they have run into each other?' asked Erlendur.

'They were in the same area at the same time, caught up in the same storm. And they were approaching from opposite directions, so by rights they should have met. Then again they were busy fighting for their lives, so maybe they missed her. The soldiers were all accounted for in the end but no trace of Matthildur was ever found. A search party was sent out when they discovered she hadn't arrived in Reydarfjördur. But that was later.'

'What did her husband have to say?'

'Just that her mother lived in Reydarfjördur and Matthildur had decided to visit her by a path she reckoned she knew. He said he'd tried to dissuade her but she'd been adamant. The way he described it, you'd have thought she was fated to go.'

'Why didn't he go with her?'

'I don't know. But he told people where she was headed before the news broke about the British soldiers. He wasn't aware they were in the same area.'

'Did he say she'd gone missing?'

'No, just that she'd set out on the journey.'

'Is that significant?'

'Like I said, you'd have expected the soldiers to have run into her or at least seen her, though of course visibility may have been too poor. But when people asked her family in Reydarfjördur if they'd been expecting her, they had no idea she was planning a visit, either then or at any other time.'

'Why didn't she go by boat or car?' asked Erlendur. 'There was a perfectly good road between Eskifjördur and Reydarfjördur by then.'

'She wanted to walk. Apparently she'd been talking for some time about making the trip. The British too; they were bored and the expedition was meant to liven things up during a quiet period. They didn't have any particular business in Eskifjördur, but it's a beautiful walk in good

22

weather, as you'll know. And there was nothing to suggest a storm was brewing.'

'So she'd mentioned her plans to her husband?'

'Yes.'

'Did she discuss it with anyone else?'

'I don't know. I doubt it.'

They gazed down at the village slumbering by the peaceful fjord.

'What do you think happened then?' asked Erlendur.

'Search me,' said Bóas. 'I haven't the foggiest.'

After Erlendur had knocked several times and waited in vain for the woman in the window to answer, he opened the door and walked in uninvited. He didn't know why she had failed to respond but it occurred to him that she might be incapacitated somehow. He found the door to the sitting room. The woman had not moved from her post by the window and when he greeted her, she didn't answer, merely continued to contemplate the view.

He moved closer and said good day again, at which she turned her head and glared up at him, looking outraged.

'I didn't invite you in.'

'I'm sorry,' he said. 'I should have rung beforehand to let you know I was coming.'

'What do you want?'

'I'm sorry, I'll leave.'

The woman perching on the cushion was tiny

and grey-haired; around eighty, he guessed, with piercing eyes that were now fixed sharply on him. She was holding a pair of binoculars. He thought he had gone too far; he shouldn't have barged in like that. He had no business intruding on people's private lives. When she didn't answer the door he should have left her to her own devices.

'I have no intention of selling this house,' she announced. 'I've told you people a thousand times. A thousand times. I'm not going to be packed off to a nursing home and I'm utterly opposed to these developments. You lot can just clear off back to Reykjavík and take all your rubbish with you! I want nothing to do with aluminium barons!'

He paused in the doorway. 'But I don't want to buy your house. I'm not involved with the smelter.'

'Oh. Who are you then?'

'I wanted to talk to you about your sister, Matthildur – the one who died.'

The woman studied him. She obviously hadn't heard the name for years and couldn't hide her astonishment that a complete stranger should have entered her house and asked about Matthildur.

'We get no peace from Reykjavík hotshots wanting to buy everything up around here,' she said at last. 'I thought you were one of them.'

'Well, I'm not.'

'There's no end to the strange goings-on these days.'

'I can imagine.'

'Who did you say you were?' she asked.

'I'm a police officer from Reykjavík. I'm on holiday and –'

'How do you know about my sister?' the old woman interrupted.

'I heard about her.'

'How?' she asked sharply.

'When I was a child,' said Erlendur, 'and I was talking about her the other day with a fox-hunter I met on the moors. His name's Bóas. I don't know if you're acquainted with him.'

'I ought to be – I taught him when he was a lad. The naughtiest boy at the village school. But what's Matthildur to you?'

'As I said, I was told her story when I was young, so I asked Bóas about her and . . .'

Erlendur didn't know how to explain his long-standing fascination with the fate of this woman who had once lived near his home but had no other connection to him. After all, he was an outsider, no relation, and only ever came out east on flying visits, years apart. Although he had grown up here until his early teens, he didn't know any of the locals, hadn't kept in touch with anyone or come back until he was an adult. Whether he liked it or not, his life was in Reykjavík now.

Yet part of him would forever belong to this place, a witness to the helplessness of the individual when confronted by the pitiless forces of nature.

'. . . I'm interested in stories about ordeals in the wilderness,' he finished bluntly.

CHAPTER 5

The woman's demeanour changed. She asked his name and he told her, saying he was just passing through, only stopping in the East Fjords for a few days. She shook his hand and introduced herself as Hrund. As he took in the view from the window, he realised that far from watching, let alone waiting for him, she had been spying on the progress of the enormous pylons that were being erected above the town to connect with the smelter further down the fjord. At her invitation, he sat down on an old sofa that creaked in protest, while she took a chair facing him, neat and, now that some kind of understanding had been established between them, inquisitive. He elaborated on his interest in accidents in the mountains, easing the conversation round to Matthildur's disappearance in the great storm of January 1942, when the British servicemen had famously come to grief.

There had originally been four sisters, daughters of a couple who had moved to Reydarfjördur in the 1920s, fleeing a miserable living on a small croft in the northern district of Skagafjördur. Their father, who came of an East Fjords family, had taken over a relative's smallholding, but according to Bóas he was a heavy drinker who made a mess of running the place and was killed in an accident some years after the move. His wife, left on her own with four daughters to support, had managed to turn around the fortunes of the farm with the help of her neighbours, married a local man and saw her daughters safely into adulthood. The two eldest had left, moving right across the country to Reykjavík, while Matthildur had married a fisherman from Eskifjördur, the neighbouring fjord. At the time she went missing they had been together for a couple of years but had no children. Hrund, the youngest of the sisters, had got hitched to a local and stayed on in Reydarfjördur.

'They're all dead, my sisters,' Hrund said. 'I didn't have much contact with the two who moved to Reykjavík. It was years between their visits. We did exchange the odd letter but that was it really, though Ingunn's son moved out here as a young man and still lives in Egilsstadir. He's in a care home now. We're not in touch. As for Matthildur, I have nothing but good memories of her, though I was only thirteen when she died. She was considered the prettiest sister – you know how people talk – perhaps because of what happened to her. As you can imagine, her loss was a terrible tragedy for the family.'

'I gather she'd been planning to walk over here to see your mother.'

'That's what her husband Jakob said. She got caught in the same storm as the British soldiers. Maybe you know the story?'

Erlendur nodded.

'They had no luck finding Matthildur, though they made a huge effort, both here in Reydarfjördur and over on the Eskifjördur side where she started out.'

'I hear there was torrential rainfall,' Erlendur said, 'and the rivers were in spate. They think one of the British soldiers drowned in the Eskifjördur River and got washed down to the sea.'

'Yes, that's why they combed all the beaches. Maybe she was carried out to sea. It seemed by far the most likely explanation to us.'

'They say it was a miracle that so many of the soldiers survived,' Erlendur commented. 'Maybe people thought they'd exhausted the store of good luck. Did anyone else know of her plan to go over to Reydarfjördur? Aside from her husband, that is?'

'I don't think so; at least, she didn't warn us she was coming.'

'And no one saw her? She didn't stop anywhere along the way? There were no witnesses who spotted her heading up to the moor?'

'The last time anyone saw her was when she said goodbye to Jakob. According to him, she was well prepared, and had a packed lunch as she expected the walk to take all day. She left at the crack of dawn because she wanted to get to Reydarfjördur in good time, so there wouldn't have been many people about when she left. And she wasn't planning to stop anywhere either.'

'The British claimed not to have seen any sign of her.'

'No.'

'Though she was on the same path.'

'Yes, but they would hardly have been able to see a thing in that weather.'

'And your mother didn't know she was coming, did she?'

'Bóas *has* done a thorough job of filling you in.'

'He told me the whole story, yes.'

'Jakob was . . .'

Hrund looked out of the window, as she did all day every day, sitting at her post, armed with her cushion and binoculars. When dusk fell, the glow from the construction site lit up the landscape. She gave a wry smile.

'What extraordinary times we're living through,' she said, with an abrupt change of subject, and started talking about the local developments that she simply could not come to terms with: the aluminium smelter, the huge dam at Kárahnjúkar, the destruction of a majestic canyon in order to build a reservoir that was to become the largest man-made lake in Iceland. Erlendur understood that she welcomed none of it. He automatically thought of Bóas and his hostility to the transformation. During their descent from the moors, the farmer had told him of the suspicions

29

that had arisen at the time of Matthildur's disappearance and lingered on in the memories of the
locals. Though most of them were pushing up the
daisies by now, according to Bóas, or had grown
old and peculiar.

'Jakob Ragnarsson didn't have an easy time of
it,' Hrund said, taking up the subject again after
her digression.

'In what way?'

'Well, as the months went by, various rumours
started to do the rounds. People even claimed she
haunted him – persecuted him until he died. Such
a pack of nonsense. As if my sister would come
back as a ghost.'

'What did your family think? Was there any
reason to doubt his story?'

'There was never any investigation,' said Hrund.
'But when Matthildur's body failed to turn up,
people became suspicious that Jakob was hiding
something, as you might expect. There were dark
mutterings that she'd been running away from him
when she went out in that storm – that she'd never
meant to go to Reydarfjördur. That he'd driven
her out of the house. I expect Bóas probably laid
it on a bit thick to you.'

Erlendur shook his head. 'He didn't mention
that. What happened to Jakob? He was killed in
an accident, wasn't he?'

'He drowned and was buried in Djúpivogur.
That was several years after Matthildur vanished.

His boat capsized in Eskifjördur Fjord during a storm and both men on board died.'

'So that was the end of that.'

'I suppose so,' said Hrund. 'Matthildur was never found. And years later a young boy went missing on the moor. He was never found either. It's an unforgiving country.'

'Yes,' Erlendur said. 'That's true.'

'Are you looking into that case as well?'

'No.'

'People said she haunted Jakob and dragged him to his death – they even blamed her for his accident. Utterly absurd. But Icelanders love making up ghost stories. Things went so far that one of the pall-bearers at Jakob's funeral claimed to have heard him moaning as he was lowered into the grave. Complete codswallop, of course. And that wasn't all.'

'I once heard some talk about the British,' Erlendur prompted.

'Yes, there were rumours that she'd been involved with them. That she was pregnant – she'd been having an affair with a soldier and secretly fled the country with him. She was supposedly so ashamed that she never even wrote home.'

'And died abroad?'

'Yes, or died shortly after leaving the country. They questioned the troops stationed in the area but no one had heard a thing. Because it was rubbish, of course – preposterous.'

'Are there any surviving friends or relatives of Jakob that I could talk to?'

'They're pretty thin on the ground. He came from Reykjavík, you know; lived with his mother's brother in Djúpivogur to begin with, but the uncle died years ago of course. Maybe you should have a word with Ezra. He was a friend of Jakob's.'

CHAPTER 6

He is enveloped by cold and darkness, assailed by a flood of images of people and past events that he cannot hold back. There is no distinguishing time and place – he is everywhere and nowhere at once.

He lies in his room, a strange sense of serenity easing through his body after the injection. Although he tries to resist, it is futile; his blood has ceased to flow and a mist has shrouded his thoughts.

The doctor tells him what he is going to do but he can't take it in, and continues to writhe and thrash his limbs until hands seize him and subdue him. The doctor consults his mother and she nods dully. He sees the syringe in the man's hands, feels a sharp prick in his arm, then little by little the fight goes out of him.

His mother sits on the edge of the bed, stroking his forehead, her expression infinitely sad. He would give the world to change it.

'Is there anything you can tell us about your brother?' she whispers.

The minor patches of frostbite on his hands and

feet do not trouble him unduly. He can remember nothing before waking up in the arms of a member of the search party, who was trying to pour hot milk down his throat. They took it in turns to carry him home from the moor, desperate to get him into the warmth as soon as possible. His mother took over for the final stretch and delivered him to the doctor, who examined him and tended to his frostbite. They told him that his father was safe. Why shouldn't he be? he wondered. His mind was blank. He gazed around at the strangers who filled the house, the men milling around in the yard, armed with walkie-talkies and long poles. They stared back at him as if they had seen a ghost. Gradually he regained full consciousness and snatches of what had happened after they left home began to reassemble themselves in his mind, fragmentary at first, then merging to form a coherent picture. He gripped his mother's arm.

'Where's Beggi?'

'He wasn't with you,' she replied. 'We're searching the area where they found you.'

'Hasn't he come home?'

His mother shook her head.

It was then that he went berserk. Reared up and fought to get out of bed while she tried to hold him down. This only made him more determined and he succeeded in tearing himself from her grasp and running out into the passageway, straight into the doctor and the two men who had carried him down to Bakkasel. Despite his frenzied struggles they hung on to him, trying to talk sense into him, to calm him. His mother clasped him in her arms and explained that a large group was out looking for his brother Bergur; he would soon be found and all would be well. Ignoring her, he bit and scratched, straining to reach his boots and anorak. When they prevented him from going outside he lost his head completely. In the end the doctor had no choice but to sedate him.

'Can you give us any clues about Beggi?' his mother asks again as he lies in bed, too weak to resist any more. 'It's urgent, darling.'

'I was holding Beggi's hand,' he whispers. 'I held on to it as long as I could, then suddenly he wasn't there any more. I was alone. I don't know what happened.'

'When? At what point?'

He senses the effort she is making to maintain her composure, in spite of the terrible strain. She has recovered two out of three alive from the storm but the thought that Beggi might be lost is unendurable.

'I don't know,' he says.

'Was it still light?'

'Yes, I think so. I don't know. I was so cold.'

'Have you any idea which way you were heading? Were you going uphill or down?'

'No, none. I kept falling over and everything was white and I couldn't see. I remember Dad saying we must turn back at once. Then he vanished.'

'That was more than twenty-four hours ago,' his

mother tells him. 'I'm going back up to the moors, dear. They could do with more helpers. You rest. It'll be all right – we'll find Beggi. Try not to worry too much.'

The drug is taking effect and his mother's words soothe him a little. He falls asleep and for several hours is dead to the world. When he stirs again it is strangely quiet; a sinister silence has fallen on the house. He feels as if he is waking from a long, harrowing nightmare but understands at once that this is wrong; he has a sudden vivid memory of the events of the last thirty-six hours. Still groggy from the sedative, he climbs out of bed and staggers into the passage. The door to his parents' room is shut. When he opens it, he finds his father alone on the edge of the bed. He doesn't see the boy but sits motionless, his head sunk on his chest, hands in his lap. Perhaps he is asleep. The room is dark. He doesn't know of his father's terrifying ordeal; how he crawled the last few metres to Bakkasel on hands and knees, frostbitten, hatless and almost out of his mind after his battle with the elements.

'Aren't you out looking?' he asks.

His father doesn't answer, just stares down at his lifeless hands. Moving closer, he puts a hand on his father's knee and repeats his question. His father seems to have aged many years: the lines in his face have deepened, the light in his eyes has been extinguished, leaving them cold, remote and indifferent. He has never seen his father so far

36

gone before, so desolate and alone, as there in that shadowy room. He stands before him, filled with dread and horror, and offers up the feeblest excuse of all:

'I couldn't help it,' he whispers. 'I couldn't help it.'

CHAPTER 7

Erlendur found Ezra outside in a shed that stood diagonally down the slope from his house. After knocking in vain at his front door, Erlendur had followed the sound of hammering to a ramshackle shelter with slatted sides, built from offcuts of timber and corrugated iron. The door, from which hung a piece of string to fasten it, was standing ajar when Erlendur approached, revealing a bowed figure sitting on a stool with a heavy mallet in his hand. Ezra had placed a fillet of dried haddock, or *hardfiskur*, on a grimy stone slab and, holding it by the tail, was beating it rhythmically to tenderise the flesh, sending up a puff of crumbs with each blow. The old man did not look up from his task or notice Erlendur, who waited in the doorway, watching him work. Drips kept forming at the end of Ezra's nose and every now and then he wiped them away with the back of his hand. He was wearing woollen mittens with double thumbs, an oversized leather hat with ear flaps that covered his cheeks, brown overalls and a traditional Icelandic jumper. A straggly beard sprouted from his unshaven jowls and he was muttering under his breath through a swollen lower lip, scarred from an ancient injury. His eyebrows jutted in tufts over small, grey eyes that seemed to be perpetually watering. Ezra was certainly no looker: his face was abnormally wrinkled, with a massive, powerful chin and fleshy nose, yet he had obviously once been a man of presence.

When he finally took a rest from beating the fish, he glanced up and saw Erlendur standing in the doorway.

'Have you come to buy *hardfiskur*?' he asked in a hoarse, threadbare voice.

'Have you got any to spare?' Erlendur felt as if he had briefly stepped back into the nineteenth century.

'Yes, a little,' Ezra replied. 'Some of this is headed for the shop but it's cheaper to buy direct from me.'

'Is it good?' Erlendur asked, moving closer.

'I should say so,' said Ezra, his voice gaining strength. 'You won't find better anywhere in the East Fjords.'

'You still use a mallet?'

'For small quantities like this it's not worth investing in machinery. Anyway, there'd be no point as I'm bound to kick the bucket any day now. I should have gone a long time ago.'

They agreed on an amount and exchanged small talk about the weather, the fishing season and, inevitably, the dam and smelter – a subject that clearly bored Ezra.

'For all I care they can destroy the environment,' he said.

Hrund had told Erlendur that Ezra had always been a recluse, never married or had children – at least not as far as she knew. He had lived in the village for longer than the oldest residents could remember, largely keeping himself to himself and respecting other people's privacy. He had done a variety of jobs on land and sea, mostly working in solitary occupations. Recently he had slowed down a bit; it was unsurprising, given that he was nearly ninety. Well-meaning neighbours wanted him to go into a home but he was having none of it. Ezra had no qualms about discussing his imminent death with all and sundry, and gave the impression that he looked forward to meeting his end. He had been trotting out the same old excuse for putting things off for years – that he would die soon, so it would all be a waste of time. Hrund said it was the oddest form of apathy she had ever come across.

Erlendur gradually steered the conversation round to tales of ordeals in the wilderness as Ezra resumed his pounding of the *hardfiskur*.

'I've been doing a bit of research into stories about people who've got into difficulties in the mountains around here.'

'Oh yes?' said Ezra. 'Are you a historian?'

'No, it's just a hobby really,' Erlendur replied. 'I

was reading about the British servicemen who were planning to cross the Hraevarskörd Pass. I suppose that would be, what, more than sixty years ago now?'

'I remember it well,' said Ezra. 'I met some of them. Fine lads. They got caught in a freak storm. Some of them died but they were all found in the end, dead or alive. Which is not always the case, I can tell you.'

Erlendur agreed.

Ezra touched his mitten to his nose and asked if Erlendur would like a coffee while they were settling up. Erlendur thanked him and they went up to the house and into the kitchen where Ezra put on an old percolator that belched and hissed but produced good, strong coffee. The kitchen was neat and tidy, with an old-fashioned fridge and an even more ancient Rafha cooker. From the window the head of the fjord and the brooding swell of Eskifjördur Moor were visible. Ezra fetched two cups and poured the coffee, dropping four sugar lumps into his, then offering the bowl to Erlendur who declined. After they had talked about the tragedy of the British soldiers, the conversation moved on to the young woman who had disappeared the same night.

'That's right,' Ezra said with slow deliberation. 'Her name was Matthildur.'

'I gather you were friends with her husband, Jakob.'

'Yes, we knocked around together. In those days.'

'So you knew her too, you knew both of them?'

'I did indeed.'

'Did they have a good marriage?'

Ezra had been methodically stirring his coffee but now he stopped, tapped his spoon several times against the cup and laid it on the table. 'I'm not the first person you've discussed this with, am I?'

'No,' Erlendur admitted.

'Who did you say you were again?'

Erlendur had not introduced himself but did so now, explaining that he lived in Reykjavík but had been born here and had a special interest in stories of people who got lost in the wilderness and died of exposure, especially people who were never found and whose fates remained a mystery. When Ezra grasped that his visitor had local roots, he immediately wanted to know where Erlendur had lived and the names of his parents. Erlendur duly gave them and Ezra said he certainly recalled Sveinn and Áslaug from the tenant croft which had always been known as Bakkasel.

'Well, you know all about me then,' said Erlendur. 'So, what can you tell me about Matthildur?'

'They had to move,' Ezra said, leaning forward over the kitchen table. 'Sveinn and Áslaug. They couldn't face staying on in the shadow of the moors. Not after all that. I gather you come here from time to time and go walking up there.'

'That's right,' said Erlendur. 'I've made several visits.'

'They're both buried here in the churchyard, aren't they? Your parents?'

'Yes.'

'Fine, upstanding people,' the old man remarked, sipping his coffee. 'Good people. He taught music at the school – occasionally, anyway, if I'm not mistaken. Played the fiddle too. Dreadful what happened. Someone said you'd become a policeman in Reykjavík. Is that why you're asking about Matthildur?'

'No,' said Erlendur. 'I'm just curious on my own behalf. I'm interested in that sort of case.'

Ezra sat lost in thought, his eyes on the distant moor. It was still cloaked in the same cloud as when Erlendur had arrived several days earlier, having driven the entire journey from Reykjavík non-stop. He had felt the urge to head out east that autumn after reaching a dead end in his investigation of the alleged suicide of a woman at Thingvellir. The case had hinged on hypothermia and this had had the odd effect of stirring up memories of his brother perishing in the mountains above Eskifjördur.

'Jakob wasn't quite what he seemed,' Ezra said at last. 'I don't judge people. I'm in no position to – I'm far from perfect myself. But Jakob had some quality that put people on their guard. I wouldn't call it dishonesty, exactly, but he was a tricky customer. And people sensed it. They all knew him. But then everybody knows everyone else around here. I suppose Reykjavík's grown so big you don't even know your own neighbours.'

Erlendur nodded.

'Over the years all sorts of rumours circulated,' Ezra continued. 'That he'd thrown her out of the house, driven her away and so on. You'll have heard them, of course.'

'Some.'

'Then he drowned in the fjord here and that was that. He didn't marry again after Matthildur died. Took to drink and let himself go to seed. Then he had the accident – his vessel went down. They managed to drag Jakob and the other man ashore but the boat was smashed to pieces.'

'And that was here in Eskifjördur?'

'Over on the other side of the fjord, there. They were coming home in a terrible gale and the boat capsized. It was the middle of winter.'

'Tell me one thing – is it possible that someone didn't want Matthildur to be found?'

'I expect you'd have a better idea about that than me,' Ezra said, regarding him with small, watery eyes.

Erlendur smiled suddenly. 'What did people guess had happened?'

'They didn't have far to look for an explanation. The rivers were running high – both branches of the Thverá – and the Eskifjördur River had turned into a raging torrent. It's possible she was washed away. Maybe you know that one of the British soldiers was found in the sea after being carried downstream. They only discovered his body by chance.'

'Yes.'

'I suppose she must have gone the same way,' Ezra said, his eyes wet. 'It seems the most likely explanation to me.'

CHAPTER 8

As Erlendur listened to the old man, he remembered what Hrund had said about him living alone all his life. Erlendur could have guessed as much as soon as he entered the house. The signs of a recluse, which he knew only too well, revealed themselves in the few, spartan possessions, the worn furnishings and lack of ornaments, the absence of everything required to make a place homely. At that moment a cat wended its way into the kitchen and rubbed against Erlendur's leg, before slipping under the table and jumping onto Ezra's lap where it made itself comfortable, observing them curiously.

'So people didn't approve of Jakob?' Erlendur said.

'No, I don't suppose they did,' Ezra replied hesitantly, stroking the cat absent-mindedly. 'There was gossip, as I said. It wasn't taken seriously . . . well, not too seriously, but mud sticks and the rumours dogged him until he died. And still do, I gather,' he added, glancing up.

'What did you think?'

'Me? I don't know what difference my opinion would make.'

'Weren't you friends?'

'Yes, we were.'

'Was she going to leave him?'

'I wouldn't know.'

'Did you ask him?'

'No,' said Ezra. 'And I don't know if anyone else did either, because there was no reason to.'

'I've heard it said that she used to haunt him,' Erlendur continued. 'Have you any idea what they meant by that?'

'Well, that's a load of rubbish, obviously. You'd have to believe in ghosts for a start. An educated man like yourself would hardly do that. Though it's true he wasn't the same afterwards. He changed – started avoiding people. Maybe he felt responsible somehow. Maybe he was haunted by her memory. But the idea that she appeared as a ghost in their house and then dragged him to his death in the shipwreck is utter nonsense. Nothing but old wives' tales.'

'You mean people implied she caused the shipwreck?'

'That was one story, yes. You can judge for yourself how much truth there was in that.'

Erlendur nodded again. He knew that despite the popularity of such yarns, few genuinely believed them. They were part of the old Icelandic story-telling tradition that had peopled the landscape with ghosts, elves, trolls, magic stones and unseen beings, linking man to his environment with invisible bonds. In the past people had lived more closely with nature and their lives had depended on it. Respect for the land and the forces latent within it was the theme of many a folk tale, and implicit in them was the warning that no one should underestimate the power of nature. That was also the substance of many of the stories of calamities in the wilderness that he had read and reread until he knew them by heart.

'But what did you think? About the stories people told about Jakob?'

'They were nothing to do with me.'

'Did you grow up together?'

'No, I'm not from around here. Neither was he. We were about the same age – he was a couple of years older. He came from Reykjavík originally but didn't talk about it much.'

A pause developed.

'Do you think you'll be needing any more fish?' asked Ezra. He was still caressing the cat but abruptly it sprang to the floor and tore out of the kitchen. It was in such a hurry that Erlendur assumed it must have spotted a mouse.

'No, thank you, this'll do,' he said, rising. 'I've taken up enough of your time.'

'That's all right,' said Ezra.

'There was some rumour that she'd met a British soldier and fled the country with him.'

'I know the stories but they're damned lies. Matthildur wasn't involved with any soldier – that's a ridiculous idea.'

As Erlendur was on his way out of the kitchen

he caught sight of a small object amid the clutter on top of the fridge by the door. He stared at it before moving closer for a better look. It had once been a toy car that would have fitted in a child's hand but was now faded and weathered, missing its wheels and base so that only the hollow chassis remained.

'Where did you get this?' he asked, his eyes fixed on the toy.

'I found it.'

'Where?'

'Let me see. By a foxhole, probably. Somewhere on Hardskafi, I think.'

'Hardskafi?'

'Yes, probably. Donkey's years ago now. I'd forgotten all about it. It's been sitting there ever since – I was reluctant to throw it away for some reason. It struck me as a bit funny at the time.'

'Have you any idea when this was?'

'Goodness, it would have been a long time ago,' said Ezra. 'I have a feeling it was around 1980, though I couldn't swear to it. I expect I was out after foxes. They used to pay a decent price for the tails back then but there's no market for them nowadays, so people don't bother to hunt much and the foxes are growing very bold as a result.'

Erlendur couldn't take his eyes off the car. 'Can I touch it?'

'Touch it?' echoed Ezra in surprise. 'Of course you can. This isn't a museum.'

Picking up the toy, Erlendur turned it over in his fingers.

'You're welcome to keep it,' said Ezra, noticing the powerful effect the small object had on his visitor. 'I've no use for it. It doesn't matter to me – I'm not long for this world anyway.'

'Are you sure?'

'My dear lad, keep it.'

'Did you find anything else in the hole?' asked Erlendur, pocketing the car.

'Not that I recall.'

'Have you any idea how it might have got there?'

'A fox could have picked it up or maybe a bird nabbed it and dropped it there. Impossible to say.'

'And you think this was on Hardskafi?'

'Yes, I'm fairly sure.'

'Thank you,' said Erlendur, as if in a daze. He walked out of the house, climbed into his car and drove away, still in shock. In the rear-view mirror he saw Ezra step outside and watch him leave, as Bóas's words rang in his ears: 'You find the oddest things in foxholes.'

CHAPTER 9

Erlendur sat in his car until evening fell, lighting one cigarette after another and keeping the driver's window open a crack to prevent the interior from filling with smoke. Ezra's dried fish lay on the passenger seat but he had no appetite. He had driven down to the shore and, as daylight merged into dusk, he watched a giant container ship glide up the fjord and pondered how heavy industry was transforming people's lives. Houses and shops were springing up all over the place, served by a network of new roads, and the local economy was booming. The few villagers who had passed the time of day with him – shop-keepers, dockworkers, the boys at the petrol station, all East Fjords born and bred – shared none of Bóas's and Hrund's misgivings. They were pleased with the developments. They saw the situation changing so fast it took their breath away.

'The place was dying on its feet,' he was told. 'Now times have changed for the better.'

'They've certainly changed,' he replied.

His thoughts wandered back to Matthildur, and to the British servicemen who had been fighting

51

for their lives on the moors that night. The pass at Hraevarskörd had been blocked. It was there that their journey had taken a turn for the worse and the soldiers' death march had begun. Unfamiliar with the climate and terrain, they had ploughed on instead of turning back, climbing ever higher, unwilling to surrender to this remote, alien land to which war had brought them. But in the end they had been forced to admit defeat.

Matthildur had been better prepared, although she should never really have set out. There were countless stories of people who embarked on journeys against their instincts, ignoring all advice and common sense. Was that what Matthildur had done? Such trips often began well, with no hint of imminent danger: the weather pleasant, the going underfoot good and the prospect of a reasonable day's journey. They would head off full of confidence, only to find themselves halfway along and abruptly confronted with death. Perhaps that was what had happened to Matthildur.

She had been a robust woman, according to Ezra, and would have equipped herself well. She had food and intended to stop at least once. After saying goodbye to her husband early that morning, she had marched off with a high heart. At much the same time the British had been readying themselves to leave. No doubt they had sought local advice and been directed to take the shortest route over the pass. When the storm struck, with a ferocity that stunned them, the group was scattered and each man was forced to fend for himself. Matthildur would have found herself in the same predicament. Perhaps she had tried to retrace her steps down from the moors, only to fall in a river and be washed out to sea, which would explain why her body was never found.

But it was also possible that she had never left home in the first place.

The idea was hardly novel. Bóas and Hrund had both hinted as much, going on no more than fickle rumour. But their words had not fallen on deaf ears. Erlendur had an old theory that among the many and various incidents of people going missing in the Icelandic interior, more than one crime had gone undetected. He knew of an example from the Second World War, which bore out his belief. Several years ago he had investigated the discovery of human bones in the Reykjavík suburb of Grafarholt which was then being built. A family man had been murdered and buried in a shallow grave not far from his own front door. His wife, the victim of years of domestic abuse, had stated that he had gone missing in bad weather – she had not heard from him since he set out on foot to cross Hellisheidi, the mountain road between Reykjavík and Selfoss. The matter had not been investigated at the time; he had simply been presumed dead. Then decades later his grave had been uncovered close to where the couple's house had stood, and the truth had come to light.

Erlendur stubbed out his umpteenth cigarette, delved in his jacket pocket for the broken hunk of metal that had once been a toy car and balanced it on the dashboard. He had postponed a closer inspection, uncertain whether it would be of any use, but now he sat and contemplated the almost unrecognisable object.

He distinctly remembered a toy car of the same make, which had once been a bright red, with windows through which a child's eye could make out a front seat and a minute steering wheel. The tyres had been white. The car had belonged to Bergur. Erlendur recalled the day it had come to Bakkasel. Their father had been playing the violin at a dance in Seydisfjördur and bought them each a gift. Erlendur had been given a lead soldier holding a rifle with a bayonet on the end. The soldier was painted green, apart from his boots which were black and a pale pink splash where his features could be discerned. It was not the best figure he owned. The colour of the soldier's face had leaked onto his helmet, his hands were green like his uniform and it was hard to make him stand up. Bergur was presented with the car and immediately fell in love with its small, shiny perfection and miniature steering wheel. Although Erlendur was pleased with his soldier and propped it up in the vanguard of his toy army, Beggi's car left him feeling oddly resentful.

Lighting up again, he sat and drew on his cigarette, contemplating the piece of metal on his dashboard, dwelling on those long-ago events. The massive freighter had sailed past through the autumn darkness, lights ablaze like a Christmas tree, bringing new prosperity to this remote spot.

He had tried to persuade Beggi to swap his car for the lead soldier but his brother had refused point-blank. He had offered him three soldiers for it, but Beggi just shook his head and carried on playing with the little red car, from which he would not be separated. On one occasion Erlendur had picked it up, looked it over and started playing with it tentatively, but Beggi had immediately demanded its return. They never used to quarrel: this was the only time any rivalry ever reared its head. Erlendur had deliberately flung the car at Beggi so hard that he couldn't catch it, and it fell on the floor with a clatter. It had startled them both and they had checked it together for any damage. So Beggi had kept his car, in spite of the generous offer, and Erlendur had had no choice but to accept the fact.

He ground out his cigarette. He had not left the engine running, and the car was now cold and dank. Condensation had formed on the windows, obscuring his view. He coughed from the sour reek of smoke and wiped his mouth. He couldn't say for sure whether this toy had once been Beggi's. These things were impossible to prove, as he knew better than anyone. But if this battered scrap of metal that Ezra had found by a fox's lair on Hardskafi had once been Bergur's shiny red car, it would be the first ever clue to his fate on the moors.

Their quarrel had taken place only two weeks before the disaster. At the time he had still been feeling envious of Bergur's car.

CHAPTER 10

He has crept into his parents' room in search of comfort and reassurance but his father is unresponsive. He sits impassively on the edge of the bed, stony-faced, mute and withdrawn. It sometimes happens like this. Minutes pass.

'It'll be all right,' Erlendur says timidly.

He feels much calmer than during his earlier frenzied struggle to return to the moors. His fingers and toes are still aching from the worst patches of frostbite but otherwise he is remarkably well and has suffered no harm from his night in the snow.

There are times, when his father is in one of his moods, that he is afraid to disturb him. Beggi too. Then the brothers sense that their father needs to be left in peace, spared the noise and commotion that children bring. When the black cloud is upon him, he tends to withdraw into the sitting room, where they are seldom allowed to set foot, and will practise the violin for hours. He also has two mouth organs, and can play other instruments, such as the accordion. As a result he is much in demand for parties and dances, though he rarely obliges since there is nothing he detests more than rowdy, drunken behaviour. Far more to his taste is standing in for the church organist when he is ill. He also derives a quiet satisfaction from teaching music to the primary-school children, though the opportunity doesn't often arise. Recently he has established a small string orchestra with musicians from all over the eastern districts. One of them plays the guitar which Erlendur finds much jollier than his father's violin, particularly since the man in question runs a small record shop and stocks all the latest hits.

His father keeps his violin in a handsome case in the bedroom wardrobe, from which he takes it out most days, together with his sheet music, before retiring to the sitting room. His practice sessions vary in length and the boys are occasionally allowed to watch, but he is unpredictable: at other times he will throw them out and shut the door. The instrument emits squawks and squeaks as he tunes it and warms up the strings, making the boys clamp their hands over their ears. Often the violin is alive under his touch and the strings vibrate to a jaunty tune, filling the house with the purest notes. But there are other days when he can call forth nothing but a sound of dark, plangent yearning, as if for courage and fortitude.

Some days are better than others and Erlendur is learning to recognise his father's moods, but it is only with hindsight that he can see that he was in the grip of a severe depression. He tries to introduce his sons to the world of music and teach them to play their own instruments and but soon discovers that neither has any real aptitude. They learn a few basics but lack the determination and passion to continue. He doesn't force them, conceding that there is no point, though he hopes they will eventually learn to appreciate music.

He had grown up to the sound of the accordion and male-voice choirs, then, inspired by the acquisition of a harmonica in his teens, he headed north to Akureyri to study music. Such opportunities were rare in the Depression years but in the event he had to abandon his studies prematurely and return home. He played mainly on borrowed instruments, even at music school, but long cherished the dream of ownership. Over time he saved up enough for a second-hand violin that he had learned was for sale at Höfn, down in the southeast. That was just after Beggi came into the world.

The Bakkasel family have little money to spare and seldom permit themselves any luxuries. Thrift is a necessity. Their farming is on a small scale but the music lessons he gives bring in extra cash and the boys' mother ekes out their income by working in the fish factory when needs must. Presents are for Christmas and birthdays only, but once in a while the sun breaks through the clouds and their father is in such high spirits that he buys the boys little gifts to make up for the bad times. These are nothing special, just cheap toys, but worth their weight in gold in the eyes of his sons, for whom it is the thought that counts.

In his worst bouts of depression, their father takes to his bed and will not leave his room. They are forced to creep around the house on tiptoe. His condition is usually most severe around Christmas and New Year, in the blackest depths of winter when it feels as if the sun will never return. Long, dark days succeed one another and the violin lies untouched in its case, both its celebrations and its dirges silenced.

His father is aware that one of his sons has been found alive but the knowledge is not enough to pierce his isolation or mitigate his anguish. No one knows the violence of the storm better than him: he came close to dying himself. So he does not respond to Erlendur, although the boy has come in need of consoling. His younger son is still missing and the single thought that fills his head is fear that the boy is already dead.

Erlendur stands at a loss beside his father, whose indifference fuels his growing sense of dread that he must somehow be to blame. Trying not to think about what exactly he has done, he longs instead for reassurance that he is mistaken, that he couldn't have behaved any differently. But his father is unreachable. He will not respond, will not even look at Erlendur. The fact that this son at least is safe does not appear to afford him any solace. The silence stretches out unbearably. It is almost worse than lying in the snow.

'I'm sorry,' he says, so quietly that the words are barely audible. 'I didn't mean to . . . I shouldn't have . . .'

His father raises his head and looks at him.

'What have you got there?'

'You gave it to me: it's a soldier,' he says, opening his fist to show him. 'Beggi got a little car.'

'What are you talking about?'

'You gave me the soldier and Beggi the car.'

'Did I?'

'He had the car with him. It was in his glove.'

CHAPTER 11

He lay awake in the ruined farmhouse for much of the night, reliving the sequence of events that had led up to the brothers' departure with their father on their ill-fated journey. Now and then he would doze off in his warm sleeping bag but never for very long. He felt stiff and unrested when he got up in the morning. Huddling over the lantern, he ate three oat cakes and poured himself a coffee in the plastic lid of the Thermos. He had acquired the coffee at a convenience store in the village late last night, from a cheery but rather brash young man who had made determined efforts to force him into conversation.

'Here in connection with the smelter, are you?' he had asked, noticing that Erlendur was not local.

'No,' Erlendur had answered curtly. 'And three packets of Viceroy, please.'

The young man, who was wearing ripped jeans and a slashed T-shirt, had fetched the cigarettes from a drawer and laid them on the counter.

'Working on the dam, then?'

'No. Could I have some coffee for my Thermos?'

'Help yourself,' the young man had said, gesturing to a coffee machine with a half-full jug that stood on a rather dirty table in the corner. 'It's free. What do you do, then?'

Erlendur had filled his flask and paid for the cigarettes. The shop assistant had followed his every move. Realising more questions were imminent, Erlendur had made his way quickly to the door.

'Are you the bloke up at the deserted . . .?' he had heard the young man ask as the door slammed behind him.

'Pushy little sod,' Erlendur had muttered as he left.

After finishing his frugal breakfast, he set out to drive the fifty or so kilometres to Egilsstadir, the administrative centre of east Iceland. To begin with, he followed the coast road around the headland at the foot of Mount Hólmatindur and caught glimpses of the feverish activity around the construction site in Reydarfjördur. Then, leaving the fjords behind, he drove inland where the road clung to the steep, gully-scored mountainside, before descending into the Fagridalur Valley and following the river in its rocky gorge, which brought him down to Egilsstadir in no time at all. Driving conditions were good but the stream of heavy-goods vehicles hammering in both directions, destroying the peace of the morning, meant he kept to a sensible speed.

He managed to locate the care home and asked

the receptionist for Kjartan Halldórsson. He was directed to speak to one of the attendants, who escorted him to a small TV lounge where a man of about seventy sat watching cartoons. The girl bent to his ear.

'You've got a visitor, Kjartan,' she announced in a loud, sing-song voice, as if addressing a small child.

The man straightened up in his chair, mumbling.

''E wants a word with you,' the girl bellowed.

Erlendur thanked her and greeted the man, who had thick grey hair and bony, work-worn hands. He seemed surprisingly frail and arthritic for his age. In the ensuing small talk Erlendur discovered that the man had a degenerative disease which had cost him the sight in one eye.

'Yes, I'm almost blind on this side,' Kjartan explained.

'That's too bad,' said Erlendur, unsure how to react.

'Yes, it's a bit of a nuisance,' agreed Kjartan, 'especially since the other eye is going too. They thought it would be best to stick me in here in case I had an accident. I can hardly even make out the screen any more.'

Erlendur assumed he was referring to the television. They talked about visual impairment for a while, before he was finally able to get to his purpose, saying that he was researching cases of people going missing in the mountains, and had heard that Kjartan's aunt Matthildur had vanished when walking from Eskifjördur to Reydarfjördur in January of 1942.

A radio was playing somewhere, and the poignant strains of a 1960s pop song – 'Spring in Vaglaskógur' – carried to where they were sitting.

'Yes. Yes, that's quite right,' Kjartan said, apparently pleased to be of assistance, in however minor a way. 'She was my mother's sister, you know, though I never met her.'

'Do you have any memory of the incident?'

'No, I can't say I do. I was very young when it happened and we were living in Reykjavík. But I clearly remember hearing about it. I must have been seven. My mother was the eldest sister. She moved to Reykjavík as a young woman and I was born there.'

'I see.'

'I left home early myself, you know. Started a family. Went to sea. We used to be able to catch what we liked in those days. Now it's a rich man's game, thanks to all these quotas.'

'So you moved out east?'

'Yes, my wife was from these parts. But I've never really been in touch with my relatives here. Hardly know them.'

'Matthildur went missing the same night some British soldiers got into difficulties,' said Erlendur.

'That's right,' said Kjartan. 'There was a terrible storm on the moors – hurricane-force winds, they said. People couldn't stand upright. Incredibly dangerous conditions.'

'Did the search last long?'

'Several days, from what I heard. But it was hopeless, of course.'

'Do you remember if your mother talked much about the accident? Was there any aspect that struck you as out of the ordinary?'

'Not that I recall.'

'What about Matthildur? Did your mother mention her at all? How she was? Or whether they got on?'

'They didn't have much contact. My mother was in Reykjavík, and the roads were dire in those days.'

'I was wondering if you had any papers connected to Matthildur that belonged to your mother or aunts,' said Erlendur. He had put the same question to Hrund, who said she had nothing herself but that Matthildur might have corresponded with her other sisters, though if she did Hrund couldn't remember hearing about it.

'A few bits and bobs,' Kjartan said, after wrinkling his brow.

'Did she and your mother write to each other in those days – that you know of?'

'My sister sent me a trunk after our mother died, saying I could chuck it out if I liked. There was all sorts of rubbish in there: rental contracts, old bills, tax returns. As far as I can remember, she'd kept a whole pile of newspapers as well. Our mother never threw anything out. I don't know why my sister sent it to me. I didn't have any use for it. There were some letters too but I never did more than glance at them.'

'So you've never read them?'

'Good heavens, no. I had quite enough on my plate without wasting time on that sort of thing.'

'Do you still have the trunk?'

'I think so,' said the old man. 'My son looks after the few belongings I've hung on to. You could talk to him. Are you writing about the storm, then?'

'I may do,' said Erlendur non-committally.

CHAPTER 12

It was after midday by the time Erlendur pulled up outside the house belonging to Kjartan's son, Eythór. It was a large, detached villa, not far from the Egilsstadir sixth-form college. Eythór, who had popped home for lunch, worked for a firm of contractors involved in the dam project in the highlands. Erlendur repeated his spiel about researching stories of accidents in the mountains and mentioned that he had just come from visiting Eythór's father, who had given him permission to look at some old papers in a trunk his son was keeping for him.

Intrigued, Eythór asked more about Erlendur's research and whether he was writing a book. Erlendur managed to dodge the question without telling an outright lie. Eythór said he hardly knew why he was keeping the trunk: he had got rid of lots of his father's junk when the old man went into the home, and should by rights have binned that too. He had taken a look inside but it contained nothing but papers. Next time he cleared out the garage it would probably go to the dump.

'How was the old boy, anyway?' Eythór asked,

and it took Erlendur a second or two to realise that he was enquiring after his father.

'Fine, I believe,' he replied.

'His sight's not getting any better.'

'So I gather.'

'I haven't been able to look in on him for ages. That's what happens when you're building the biggest dam in Europe – it takes up all your time. Speaking of which – you couldn't come back this evening, could you? I'm already late.'

'I'm afraid I've got to head back to Reykjavík,' said Erlendur, on the off chance that this ploy might work, 'so it'll just have to wait.'

The man wavered. His phone rang. He checked to see who it was, then ended the call.

'OK, come on then,' he said.

The trunk was in the garage, buried under all kinds of junk that Eythór had to push aside: summer tyres, paint pots, garden tools. He didn't know what the papers related to and had no time to hang around, but if Erlendur needed any help, he said, his youngest son was at home. A sixth-former who was 'out to lunch', if Erlendur had heard correctly. He thanked Eythór for being so obliging, apologised for bothering him and said he would not take long.

The man climbed into his four-wheel drive and departed, leaving Erlendur behind in the garage with the door open and the trunk at his feet. It started to rain. He took out a large brown envelope containing tax returns for the years 1972 to 1977, and placed it on a work bench. Two extremely dog-eared hymn books followed. He flipped through the pages before laying them on top of the envelope. Next he unearthed three copies of *Reader's Digest*, together with a sizeable bundle of yellowing newspapers.

'What do you think you're doing?' he heard a voice behind him ask, and turned to see the sixth-former.

'Good afternoon,' he said. 'I'm researching missing-persons' cases in the East Fjords.'

'In our garage?'

'One of the stories concerns your aunt who disappeared on the moors.'

'On the moors?'

'Yes.'

'What was she doing up there?'

'She was climbing over a pass and presumably had an accident.'

'Oh.'

The boy shuffled past him and sauntered off down the street back to school, a gawky figure, his trousers worn deliberately low to reveal his boxer shorts. 'What is the world coming to?' Erlendur thought, watching the boy until he vanished round a corner.

He resumed his task of removing papers and pamphlets from the trunk, and finally came across a sheaf of letters which he stopped to read. Some were from Ingunn's sisters, others from her mother or friends. Matthildur had last written to her sister about three months before she went missing. She reported the local news and described the weather in some detail: it had been unsettled that autumn and now winter was just round the corner. But she was looking forward to Christmas and was busy making herself a dress for the festive season. The earlier letters also stuck to generalities, giving no hint of her relationship with her husband. Erlendur knew he should not necessarily attach any significance to this. People didn't always commit their private thoughts to paper.

I went to a dance with Ninna, she had written in a letter dated two years before her disappearance, *and we had a smashing time. The band was local and played a mix of new tunes and old favourites. Ninna and I danced till we dropped. To begin with, the boys were really shy about asking us up. Jakob – the one you used to know – was there and we had a long talk after the dance. He's living in Eskifjördur these days.*

Having gone through the whole trunk without becoming any better acquainted with either Jakob or Matthildur, Erlendur began to replace the contents, trying to put them back in the same order. It occurred to him that it might be worth looking at the newspapers, so he started turning the pages. He couldn't imagine why Matthildur's sister should have kept so many copies of this particular rag, the mouthpiece of the Progressive Party. Reports of heated political squabbles and resolutions passed by the Farmers' Association were interspersed with news items about the

71

lambing and hay harvest. But one issue contained a story about the disaster that had befallen the British soldiers, as well as a small piece on Matthildur's disappearance the same night.

In another issue he found an obituary of Jakob. As far as Erlendur could gather the writer, one Pétur Alfredsson, had been a friend. The article traced Jakob's family to Hornafjördur in the east and to Reykjavík, where he had been born. After the customary enumeration of his virtues, it was stated that Jakob had lost his young wife in a tragic accident, after which he never remarried. Finally, there was a brief description of how he had drowned in a storm while returning from a fishing trip and how his body and that of his companion had been pulled from the sea and, prior to their funerals, stored in the old ice house in Eskifjördur.

But it was not the contents of the obituary that attracted Erlendur's attention so much as the word, still perfectly legible, that had been scrawled across it in thick black pencil:

BASTARD.

CHAPTER 13

As before, Hrund was sitting at her window, gazing over to where the pylons would soon be rising. The glare from the floodlit building site brightened the sky behind the house but the smelter itself was hidden from view. She saw Erlendur arrive in his car and this time when he knocked, she rose from her chair, opened the door and invited him in. He followed her into the sitting room where she resumed her customary post.

'The evenings are so lovely at this time of year,' she said.

'They certainly are,' Erlendur agreed, taking a seat. There were no lights on. Hrund had been sitting in semi-darkness, wrapped in a blanket. The street lamps cast her shadow on the wall behind her and Erlendur found himself watching her silhouette in fascination. Hrund seemed uninterested in the reason for his visit, as if taking it for granted that they should be sitting there, two strangers, in companionable silence.

'I went over to Egilsstadir today,' Erlendur said eventually.

'Oh?' said Hrund. 'Do you want to tell me about

it? You're welcome to help yourself to coffee, by the way. There's some in the pot, and you'll find a cup in the cupboard above the sink.'

Erlendur went into the kitchen. When he came back, Hrund had turned away from the window and was waiting expectantly.

'I suppose you're still after information about Matthildur.'

'That's right.'

'Then you must have been to see my nephew. Did you go to the home?'

Erlendur nodded.

'I've never really known him well. It just worked out that way.'

'That's common enough,' said Erlendur, thinking about his own family. 'He's on good form. Well, having said that, he's lost the sight in one eye. He let me have a poke around in a trunk that belonged to your sister Ingunn, and I found some old letters and stuff like that.'

'Were they useful?'

'No, not really.'

'I'm afraid I don't have any letters from Matthildur, if that's what you're after.'

'No, you told me. Actually, I was wondering if any of Matthildur's belongings, her personal effects, were still around. Or if you had a photograph.'

'I don't know about any of her things, but I do have a picture of us sisters, if only I knew where to lay my hands on it.' Hrund rose and went into her bedroom. Erlendur felt guilty about putting her to this trouble, but consoled himself with the thought that she was lonely and that a bit of company, however unexciting, would probably do her good.

Hrund returned carrying two shoeboxes, sat down in her chair and started to sift through them.

'It's not in an album,' she said. 'I've never bothered to sort these pictures out properly. My husband's dead – did I tell you that?'

'No,' said Erlendur. Bóas had informed him that Hrund was a widow with two sons who had gone away to study in Reykjavík and stayed there, only coming home for visits.

'There are photos of him here that I'd forgotten all about. And here's one of us four sisters during the haymaking.'

She handed Erlendur a curling, black-and-white picture with a yellowing back, stained with what might have been coffee. The four sisters were standing in a meadow, holding rakes. It was a brilliant summer's day and they stood there beaming at the camera, all wearing dresses, and two of them headscarves, lined up in a row for the photographer. There was no mistaking their happiness, even so many years on.

'Our mother took the picture,' said Hrund. 'The camera belonged to her second husband, Thorbjörn. That's me on the far left, the baby of the family – the afterthought. Then that's Ingunn, with the headscarf, and Matthildur beside her and then Jóa – poor old Jóhanna.'

Their faces were not particularly clear but Erlendur could make out Matthildur's features: deep-set eyes and a determined expression. He looked for a date but couldn't see one.

'I think it was taken about eight years before she went missing,' said Hrund, as if reading his mind. 'During the Depression.'

'Ingunn and Jóhanna moved to Reykjavík, didn't they? Did they go at the same time?'

'No, Jóhanna went first, then Ingunn followed. Shortly after the picture was taken, in fact. Everything changed so quickly. One minute we were all living at home, having a whale of a time. Next thing you know, we'd scattered to the four winds. It all seemed to happen at once and nothing was ever the same again.'

'Do you remember a friend of Matthildur's, known as Ninna?' Erlendur asked.

'Yes, I do. A sweet girl. I believe she's still alive. You should check. Ninna's her real name – not a nickname.'

'Has she lived in the East Fjords all this time?'

'Yes. She and Matthildur were great friends – childhood friends.'

'Maybe I'll look her up,' said Erlendur, rising to his feet. 'Anyway, I don't want to keep you up all night.'

'That's all right,' said Hrund. 'I'm not going anywhere. I just don't understand why someone who didn't know the family should be so interested in Matthildur. Are you writing a book?'

'No,' Erlendur said, smiling. 'There'll be no book. By the way, did Ingunn and Jakob know each other before he got together with Matthildur?'

'Ingunn and Jakob? Why do you ask?'

Erlendur wondered if he should tell her about the letter from Matthildur that he had found in Ingunn's trunk, and the word 'bastard' scrawled across Jakob's obituary. There was no telling whether Ingunn had written the word herself. The paper may not even have been hers: someone could have sent it to her.

'Just a thought,' he said. 'Good-looking girls like you must have had dozens of admirers.'

'What have you found out?' asked Hrund, brushing aside Erlendur's attempt at flattery.

'Nothing,' he said hastily, sensing an abrupt change in her mood.

'You're not . . . spying on our family, are you?' she asked.

The conversation was taking a disastrous turn but Erlendur could think of no way of rescuing the situation. After a bad night's sleep and a long drive he was not at his sharpest.

'No, of course not,' he assured her, realising how unconvincing he sounded.

'Well, let me tell you that I'm far from happy with your prying. Far from happy. I don't like the way you come here and start interrogating members of my family like a . . . like a policeman. I won't have it!'

'No, of course not,' Erlendur repeated. 'I'm very sorry if I've offended you in some way –'

'What are you up to?' Hrund asked, thoroughly riled by now. 'What are you trying to dig up? What's all this got to do with people going missing?'

'Nothing,' Erlendur said. 'Really. You said yourself that rumours had been going around about Jakob – that people used to claim Matthildur haunted him.'

'I told you that was just gossip. Surely you're not taking it seriously? Gossip from half a century ago?'

'No, but –'

'And I don't believe in ghosts.'

'Neither do I.'

'I think perhaps you should leave.'

Erlendur said a hasty goodbye and went out to his car without looking round, aware of her presence at the window, her eyes boring into his back.

He parked by the aluminium smelter to watch all the activity. The construction of the huge sheds for the reduction pots was well advanced, a crowd of labourers swarming over the site, day and night, racing to finish on time. Floodlights lent the surroundings an unearthly appearance in the dusk. All this relentless progress was such a striking contrast to the tranquillity of the narrow fjord and the snow-capped mountains reflected in its mirror-like surface.

CHAPTER 14

Again he is overwhelmed by the odd feeling that he is lying on the floor of the derelict farm, haunted by an unseen presence. He must be hallucinating. He knows he is no longer at the old house. He must have left, or he wouldn't be able to see the stars in the night sky.

But perhaps that is part of the hallucination.

He turns his head to where the door should be but sees nothing but inky blackness. Reaching out his arm, he touches the rough, damp render of the wall. He has a torch somewhere. He gropes for it and switches it on. The beam is weak: it casts a feeble glow over the surroundings – the empty doorway to the hall, the broken windows through which the cold air is streaming, the ceiling that has collapsed here and there. He has a powerful sense of a presence but can see no one.

'Who's there?' he calls. There is no answer.

Rising to his feet, he picks his way across the room by the beam of the torch. He can see no sign of the traveller he remembers standing in the doorway, then later lighting a fire on the floor and talking to him as if they were acquainted. The vision has gone, yet he has the bizarre impression that the event has yet to happen.

He has made up a bed for himself in the sitting room where the couch was in the old days. It consists of a thin mat, two blankets to cover his sleeping bag and a rucksack for a pillow. Next to it are his scuffed hiking boots and a bin bag containing a few scraps of food. He has made an effort to keep the place tidy, helped by the fact that he doesn't have much luggage. The house may be nothing but a bleak ruin, open to the wind and weather, but he moves around the room with the respect for the home that was instilled in him as a child.

'Is anybody there?' he asks in a low voice.

His only answer is the moaning of the wind, accompanied by the squeak of a door still hanging stubbornly from its hinges, and the creaking of two sheets of corrugated iron which cling with extraordinary tenacity to the roof. He steps into the hall and shines his torch outside into the yard before entering the kitchen. As the beam gradually fades, the night closes in around him. The faint circle of light flickers over the bare shelves. The table used to stand under the window facing the byre and barn, and beyond them the moor and mountains. Every new day would begin at that table and end there in the evening.

'Is anybody there?' he repeats in a whisper.

He continues his search, out of the kitchen and down the short passage to the bedrooms. He can't get into his parents' room because the roof has fallen in over the door and part of the passage. There his father had sat after his descent from the moors, inconsolable, aware that his two sons were still out there; sure that they were lost. He had known better than anyone what conditions up there were like and his collapse had been total. There were ugly patches of frostbite on his face as he sat there while the rescue party gathered in the kitchen.

'Is anybody there?' he whispers a third time. The torch beam fades still further and begins to gutter. He bangs it on his palm and the light grows momentarily brighter. The battery is almost dead. He proceeds to the room he once shared with his brother and illuminates the place where their beds used to stand, separated by a night table. There was a small wardrobe in the corner and a thick rug to protect their toes from the icy floor. Now the room contains nothing but darkness.

The realisation finally hits him that there is no one else in the house. The presence he felt was merely an illusion. There is no one left but him. He turns and makes his way back past the kitchen and hall to the sitting room, where the torch conks out. When he thumps it again it sheds a weak light on the wall opposite. The shadow of a man plays over the rough surface and for an instant he sees a figure with back turned and head bowed, as if in defeat. The vision startles him so much that he drops the torch and it goes out again.

Stooping, he fumbles for it, then knocks it on the floor three times until the bulb comes on, lighting up the room with an instant of brilliance before finally dying for good. He looks around frantically but the man has vanished.

'What do you want from me?' he murmurs into the night.

He is lying in the cold, eyes half open, unsure how long it is since the involuntary shivering ceased. He can't feel his hands or feet, is no longer aware of being frozen. He knows he will soon fall asleep but struggles against the drowsiness. It is vital to stay awake as long as possible but his strength is dwindling. He remembers seeing the stars as he lay in the snow.

Through the brain-numbing cold it occurs to him that he is no longer in his right mind.

CHAPTER 15

As Erlendur bumped slowly up the track to the farm, he saw Bóas emerge into the yard to greet him. He had not called on him before because they were to all intents and purposes strangers, in spite of the hunting trip. But now he felt he had personal business with this man who had tried to extract milk from a dead vixen.

Bóas had seen him coming and hurried out in slippers and shirtsleeves, with a stump of pipe in his mouth. He had recognised the blue four-wheel drive from seeing it parked outside the old place at Bakkasel over the last few days. Erlendur got out and they shook hands.

'I don't understand how you can rough it in that ruin,' the farmer remarked as he invited him indoors. 'The nights are getting damned chilly.'

'Oh, I can't complain,' said Erlendur.

'I'm not used to entertaining guests, so I'm afraid you'll have to make do with coffee.' Bóas explained that his wife was visiting relatives in Egilsstadir. His tone revealed that he was not sorry to miss them.

They sat down together in the spotless kitchen.

Bóas put two cups on the table, filled them with coffee and added such a generous splash of milk to each that they turned pale brown and tepid. Then he puffed on his pipe and started grumbling about the industrial developments and those bloody capitalists making fools of the politicians.

'Discovered any more about Matthildur?' The question came from out of the blue. It made it sound as if Erlendur was conducting an official inquiry into her disappearance more than sixty years ago.

'No,' said Erlendur, lighting a cigarette to keep Bóas company. 'There's nothing new to report. She must have died in the storm. It wouldn't be the first time that had happened.'

'No, I'm afraid you're right there.' Bóas slurped his milky coffee. 'Not the first time by a long chalk.'

'Do you know any more about her sisters? Two of them moved to Reykjavík. And there's the one who lives in Reydarfjördur.'

'I know Hrund quite well,' said Bóas. 'A fine woman. Have you spoken to her?'

Erlendur nodded.

'Oh, so you *are* interested, then.'

'Did you ever hear any gossip about Matthildur and Jakob's marriage? About her sisters' attitude to him, for example?'

'What have you discovered?' Bóas demanded, with unabashed curiosity.

'Nothing.'

84

'You're lying, of course,' said Bóas. 'I don't remember hearing that. Did they disapprove? Which ones? Why?'

'I'm asking because I don't know,' said Erlendur. 'Are you familiar with the name Pétur Alfredsson? I imagine he'd be dead by now.'

'Yes, I remember him. He was a fisherman. Died years ago. What about him?'

'Pétur wrote an obituary for Jakob in the farmers' paper. It was the only one printed. I checked at the library in Egilsstadir. He described him as an all-round good bloke and mentioned that he'd lost his wife several years before.'

'Did he now?'

'Did this Pétur have any children?'

'Yes, three, I think. One of his daughters used to live in Fáskrúdsfjördur. Probably still does. She was involved in local politics. I assume his other kids must have moved to Reykjavík because I haven't heard their names for years.'

'What about a woman called Ninna? It's not a nickname, by the way. She was Matthildur's friend, mentioned in one of her letters. They went to a dance together and Jakob was there.'

'I don't recall any Ninna,' Bóas said. 'Is she supposed to have lived in Eskifjördur?'

'I don't know. She's probably not important – just a name in a letter. But she may have been present the evening Matthildur and Jakob got together. I spoke to an old friend of Jakob's too – Ezra.'

'You're obviously not at all interested,' said Bóas, grinning. 'I'd be better off asking who you haven't talked to. Seems I really got you going.' He sounded pleased with himself.

'Do you know Ezra?'

'Ezra's getting on, and his health's not what it was. You'd never guess to look at him now but in his day he was a titan: hardy, brave and good in a fight, as they used to say in the sagas. And never beholden to anyone.'

There was no mistaking Bóas's admiration. Sitting up eagerly, he embarked on a long speech about how they didn't make them like Ezra any more: the last of his breed, indomitable, a man of true grit. He was the best hunter and fisherman Bóas had ever known: fox, reindeer, ptarmigan and geese, cod and haddock – none of them stood a chance. Finally breaking off his eulogy, he asked: 'What sort of welcome did he give you?'

'Not bad,' said Erlendur. 'I bought some first-rate dried fish off him.'

'No one makes better *hardfiskur*,' said Bóas. 'Did he mention the dam business at all?'

'No.'

'No, that's just it. I don't know where he stands on it. He's not one for showing his hand, Ezra. Never has been.'

'Did he ever go out fishing with Jakob?' Erlendur asked.

'I don't know – I'd have to ask around. Ezra's done so many jobs. He was foreman at the ice house in Eskifjördur for years. Started work there during the war, I believe.'

Erlendur vacillated for some time before changing the subject. Now that it came to it, he wasn't sure he really wanted to find the answers he had been seeking for so long. Noticing his preoccupation, Bóas held his tongue for once. In the end, Erlendur took from his pocket the scrap of metal that Ezra had found by a fox's earth on the slopes of Mount Hardskafi.

'You said the oddest things turned up in foxholes.'

'That's right,' said Bóas.

Erlendur showed him the toy.

'Ezra came across this up on Hardskafi. I believe my brother may have owned one like it.'

'I see.'

'In view of what you said, and because you're a fox-hunter and know the mountains like the back of your hand, it occurred to me to ask if you've ever come across any other objects like this? Or any tatters of clothing, that sort of thing?'

Bóas took the toy.

'You think this belonged to your brother?' he asked.

'Not necessarily. I know he had a car like it that my father gave him. I wondered if you could keep your eyes open for me. I don't mean right this minute, or today or tomorrow, just next time you're staking out an earth. See if you notice any unusual bits and pieces.'

'Like this, you mean?'

Erlendur nodded. 'Or remains,' he added.

'Bones?'

Erlendur took the car back and returned it to his pocket. He had tried to banish the thought. Every time it entered his mind, he visualised the disembowelled corpse of a lamb that he had once found on the moors; the empty sockets in its skull where the ravens had pecked out its eyes.

'Would you get in touch if you find anything of interest, however small?'

'If that *is* your brother's car, there are several possibilities,' said Bóas. 'He could have lost it earlier – dropped it outside your house, for example, where a raven snatched it and flew with it up the mountain. That's one way it could have ended up by the fox's earth. Or he could have been carrying it with him when he went missing and a fox found it and his body at the same time.'

'I know he had it with him,' said Erlendur.

'How do you know?'

'I just know. Will you get in touch?'

'Of course I will, no question,' said Bóas. 'Though I've seen nothing of the sort so far, if that's any comfort.'

They sat without speaking until Bóas eventually leaned forward and asked: 'What are you expecting to find up there?'

'Nothing,' said Erlendur.

Back at the ruined farm, trying to warm himself over the lantern, Erlendur took out the newspaper obituary that he had appropriated from the trunk in Egilsstadir. He reread the piece carefully, pausing at the mention of the ice house in Eskifjördur. After Jakob drowned, his body and that of his companion had been stored there. He recalled what Bóas had said about Ezra, who might therefore have been working at the ice house at the time – who might even have taken in and kept vigil over the dead men.

CHAPTER 16

At noon the following day, Erlendur reached the small village in Fáskrúdsfjördur, having driven the long way round via Reydarfjördur Fjord and the headland at the foot of Mount Reydarfjall. He could have taken the new road tunnel, opened that summer, which linked the two fjords, but preferred the old route. The mercury had dropped sharply in the night and the ground was white right down to the shore. It was the first snowfall of the autumn and brought with it the customary alien quietness, muffling the houses and landscape in a soft, white quilt. The flakes continued to fall all morning in the still air, clogging the roads and making for treacherous going.

He knew that if the wind picked up, causing the temperature to plummet still further and the snow to drift, it would no longer be feasible for him to stay in the abandoned farm. The old house would soon begin to fill with snow. He might as well be sleeping out in the yard for all the shelter it would provide. It crossed his mind to call it a day and go home to Reykjavík. Winter was closing in, after all. But he had a nagging sense of unfinished business, as if there were something he had yet to achieve here, though he wasn't sure what.

He drove to a garage, filled the car with petrol and asked the assistant at the till if she knew Gréta Pétursdóttir. There were three girls working behind the counter and even so they could hardly keep up with demand. The shop and café were packed with lorry drivers and labourers, while two men in suits sat hunched over their laptops. Erlendur had read that the volume of traffic using the tunnel connecting Fáskrúdsfjördur to the smelter site in Reydarfjördur had exceeded even the most optimistic expectations. He wanted no part in it.

'Sorry, no,' said the girl. 'But hang on a minute while I ask the others.'

She squeezed a thick line of mustard onto a hot dog laden with all the trimmings, handed it to a customer, did some rapid mental arithmetic, called out to ask another girl if she knew Gréta, received an answer, told the hot-dog customer how much he owed, then turned back to Erlendur.

'Sorry, I was mixing her up with someone else. The Gréta you want works at the swimming pool.'

Erlendur nodded and thanked her. He drove round the village through the thick curtains of snow until he located the pool. Unusually for Iceland, it was an indoor one, and he was struck by the smell of chlorine as he entered the reception area. A fleshy woman with greying hair, probably in her early sixties, was sitting at the desk, looking at a news site on the Internet. The noise of children screaming carried from the pool. Erlendur was immediately transported back to school swimming lessons.

'For one?' asked the woman, looking up. She wore a small name badge which said 'Gréta'.

'What?' said Erlendur.

'Do you want a swim?' asked the woman.

'No,' he replied. 'I'm here to see Gréta Pétursdóttir.'

'That's me.'

Erlendur introduced himself and explained that he had a special interest in stories of accidents in the interior and was currently researching the incident involving the British servicemen from Reydarfjördur. He had discovered that a young woman from Eskifjördur, called Matthildur, had also died on the moors the same night. She had been married to Jakob, a friend of Gréta's father Pétur, who had later written his obituary.

The woman regarded him placidly as he repeated this rigmarole and Erlendur realised she was not following him.

'Who did you say you were?' she asked.

'I'm researching examples of this kind of incident here in the East Fjords,' he said, and started again on his explanation about the long-ago events until finally the woman seemed to twig. She served a couple of children who came in; others began to emerge in dribs and drabs from the changing rooms. When it had quietened down again, she asked Erlendur if he would like a coffee, and he accepted. They sat down at a small table in the reception area. A man wearing white trousers and clogs came over and she asked him to stand in for her, using strange words and a good deal of gesturing.

'He's Polish,' she explained.

'Oh,' said Erlendur. 'I suppose you get a lot of foreigners working out here.'

'Not just here but all over. Reykjavík too. You can't move for them. I think I know what you're talking about,' she went on, pausing to take a sip of watery coffee. 'But it was before my time, so I don't know if I can be much help. I'm amazed you were able to track me down.'

'Do you have any memories of Jakob?'

'Not really. He died around 1950, didn't he? I was just a little girl. But Dad used to talk about him a lot. They were good friends and often worked together – they were both fishermen. I think I've got a copy of that obituary you mentioned. Dad wrote several and kept them all. It appeared in the farmers' paper, didn't it?'

'Yes. Were they roughly the same age?'

'Yes, my father may have been slightly younger, but not much. He often told the story of Jakob's shipwreck. There was a violent storm. People watched helplessly from land but in the end all they could do was bring the men's bodies ashore.'

'I gather they were stored in the ice house,' Erlendur said. 'In Eskifjördur.'

'That sounds likely. They were buried only a day or two after they died, according to Dad. It all happened very quickly, but then I think Dad said neither of them had any dependants.'

'Did your father ever mention Matthildur?'

'Not very often.'

'Or their relationship?'

'You mean Jakob and Matthildur? Not that I recall. There were rumours but my father dismissed them as nonsense. That she'd come back to haunt him and even caused the shipwreck.'

'What triggered them, do you think?'

'Search me. Isn't it typically Icelandic? All that superstitious claptrap about ghosts and elves and trolls. Isn't it all the same thing?'

'I suppose so.'

'And of course she was never found – Matthildur, I mean – which only fuelled the gossip.'

'That must have made things worse,' agreed Erlendur, who had no time for coincidence or superstition.

'You don't believe in any of that, do you?' asked Gréta, touching a silver cross that she wore on a chain round her neck.

'Not really,' said Erlendur.

The screaming from the pool had abated. Through an open door, Erlendur caught a glimpse of a young female instructor kneeling beside the water, teaching backstroke.

'Not everyone learned to swim in the old days,' Gréta remarked after he had been watching the lesson for a minute. 'I seem to recall Dad saying Jakob couldn't swim.'

'What else did he say about him?'

'Once he said Jakob's worst fear had come true. He recited those lines from the *Hymns of Passion*.'

'Which lines?'

'Oh, how do they go again?' Gréta thought. '"The fate he feared most of all / would in time upon him fall."'

'And he was talking about Jakob?'

'Yes. Apparently he suffered from severe claustrophobia. I don't even know if they used the word back then, but from the way Dad described it that's what it was. Apparently you could hardly close the door when he was in the room. Dad didn't know why but his worst nightmare was to be trapped somewhere and suffocate.'

'Are you saying he actually got locked in somewhere?'

'Yes, at least once. He and Dad worked together when they were young – this was in Reykjavík. They were taken on by the slaughterhouse for a few months, no longer. That's where they met. Times were hard and they were grateful for any job they could get. Jakob worked in the smokehouse.'

'Smoking meat?'

'Yes. And got locked in.'

'In the smokehouse?'

Gréta nodded. 'Dad said it was one of his mates

having a laugh – he didn't know about Jakob's phobia.'

'Perhaps no one did.'

'No, probably not. Anyway, Dad said he went completely berserk. When they eventually opened the door he attacked the first man he could lay his hands on and they thought he was going to kill him. They had to hold him down. His fingers were all bloody from where he'd been clawing at the door. It was made of steel, Dad said.'

'Sounds pretty nasty.'

'Dad had never seen anything like it. Jakob refused to discuss it afterwards. Dad once tried to ask him what had happened but he clammed up.'

'Did your father ever learn any more about Matthildur's disappearance?' asked Erlendur. 'Did he mention it at all?'

'No, he didn't. It was just one of those tragedies.'

'Do you know how Jakob reacted?'

'Well, I gather he was devastated,' said Gréta. 'Of course, they organised a big search party, not just for her but for the British soldiers too. Every able-bodied person in the district took part, including Jakob and Dad. Dad spent a lot of time with him afterwards but he felt Jakob had changed. He became very edgy – quick-tempered and diffi-cult to be around. Not the same man.'

'I heard Jakob wasn't all he seemed,' said Erlendur, remembering Ezra's words.

'That's not the impression I got. At least, Dad never described him like that.'

'It must have been a terrible strain,' said Erlendur. 'By the way, do you know a woman called Ninna? She'd be pretty old by now, if she's still alive. I gather Ninna's her Christian name, but I can't find her listed in the phone book.'

'The only Ninna I know around here lives in the nursing home,' said Gréta. 'I used to work there. I don't know if it's the same woman, but the one I'm thinking of is ancient.'

CHAPTER 17

The snow was coming down ever more heavily as Erlendur parked in front of the nursing home in Fáskrúdsfjördur. Instead of getting out, he lit up and watched the flakes floating lazily to the ground. There was not a breath of wind.

As he sat there, taking his time over the cigarette, he relived the walks he had been on since arriving in the east. Clad in his old boots, waterproof trousers and a thick down jacket, with a small rucksack on his back, he had hiked from the head of Eskifjördur up to the moor, along the foothills of the mountains, then high up their flanks. It had been returning from one such trip that he had bumped into Bóas by the Urdarklettur crags. His expeditions generally lasted from early in the morning until dusk, though on one occasion he had slept rough on a carpet of moss, alone with the birds. He enjoyed lying on his back, head propped on his rucksack, gazing up at the stars and reflecting on the theory that the universe was expanding into the void. There was something strangely soothing about pondering such incomprehensible distances, as if a reminder of the greater context provided a temporary relief from petty terrestrial concerns.

It was not the first time he had bedded down in the heather, listened to the birds and contemplated the sky. He had a clear memory of his first trip back east after the family had moved to Reykjavík. It was following the death of his father, whose last wish had been to be laid to rest in his home ground. Erlendur and his mother had flown with his body to Egilsstadir and driven from there to Eskifjördur on rough gravel roads, with the coffin in the back of an open pickup truck. He remembered thinking what an undignified homecoming it was. He and his mother had sat in the cab, listening to the driver gassing away, music blaring from his radio. Erlendur had wanted to ask him to show a little respect, but his mother had seemed indifferent. There was a short ceremony in the church, attended by a handful of locals. It was the middle of the week, the funeral had only been announced once on the radio and there were no obituaries. In the end mother and son had been left standing alone by the open grave. A white cross bearing a black metal plaque lay beside them, waiting to be driven into the ground.

'God bless you,' he heard his mother whisper.

Later that day he took her to visit the croft at Bakkasel, which had been standing empty ever since they moved to Reykjavík. The house was already looking very dilapidated, the doors wide open, windows broken and signs of animal activity inside. At first, his mother had wandered from room to room in a daze, as if their life there had belonged to another world, a world that was gone forever. Until now, her resilience had surprised him. She had shown no emotion when his father died long before his time, merely busied herself with organising his funeral the way she knew he would have wanted it. She had not shed a tear on the journey or expressed any irritation at the garrulous driver, and had stood in the graveyard speaking only those three whispered words: 'God bless you.' But now, confronted by the evidence of decay and neglect, and remembering the time when they had all lived there together, she seemed to have woken from her stupor. At last a crack appeared in her calm facade.

'What's happened here?' she whispered.

'Let's go,' he said.

'I can't,' she said, so quietly he could hardly catch the words.

'Come on.'

That night, after his mother had gone to bed at the guest house, he had hiked up onto the moor. It was summer, the sky still brightened by the midnight sun, and he had walked right to the foot of Mount Hardskafi, where he had stretched out on the moss and gazed up at the heavens. He had been a child when they moved away and it was with mixed emotions that he returned now as an adult. The visit to the abandoned croft had dredged up memories long forgotten or suppressed. Deep down he knew that he had been avoiding this place, not just physically but in his mind. The light Arctic night offered no comfort. On the contrary, it illuminated with painful clarity all that was most difficult and distressing about this homecoming. He was convinced there and then that he would never be a happy man – not that it really mattered in the great scheme of things.

Erlendur stubbed out a second cigarette. He watched the snow turning the earth a pristine white, like the promise of a new beginning, and inwardly cursed the cruelty of fate.

Ninna, a tiny old lady of eighty-five, was reading the Bible in her room when Erlendur, with the help of an attendant, tracked her down. He had been keen to avoid any awkward attempts to explain his visit to the staff, but in the event he was directed to her room without query and had no problem finding it.

'Who are you?' she asked in a clear voice.

'My name's Erlendur and I'd like a word with you, if that's all right.'

'I rarely get any visitors,' Ninna said. She was sitting on the edge of her bed, the Bible in her hands and her long grey hair trailing loose down her back. 'Though a girl came here the other day and started rabbiting on about traditional farming methods. She said she was collecting recordings of old folks like me for the National Museum. I

101

said, look, dear, I have no time for nostalgic twaddle like that and absolutely no intention of being an exhibit in the National Museum. You can put me there when I'm dead!'

'Ninna – it's an unusual name, isn't it?' said Erlendur, testing the waters. She had few personal belongings in her room; no photographs of relatives or ornaments to cheer up her surroundings apart from two old prints on the walls. Her bed was neatly made and a half-full glass of water stood on the bedside table.

'So what if it is?' said the old woman, closing the Bible with a snap. 'What do you want with me, young man?'

Erlendur abandoned the attempt to ingratiate himself.

'I'm investigating what happened on the night in January 1942 when the British soldiers were caught in a storm on Eskifjördur Moor. Do you remember it?'

'Of course I do.'

'That night a woman died as well. I believe she was a friend of yours.'

'Yes, Matthildur. Poor, dear Matthildur. Know all about her, do you?'

'Not really, no.'

'Matthildur was a wonderful girl,' said Ninna. 'We were great friends and it was a terrible loss when she died. Someone spread the rumour that she'd committed suicide but I always regarded that as tosh.'

'Oh?' said Erlendur. This was new.

'They put it about that she must have thrown herself in the sea – that she'd never been near the moors or the British soldiers would have run into her. Absolute tosh. The soldiers couldn't see a thing and didn't have a clue where they were. That was one rumour and a malicious one too.'

'That she'd killed herself, you mean?'

'She'd never have done that in a million years,' declared Ninna firmly. 'She had no reason to. None whatsoever. I knew her better than that. The suggestion was ludicrous.'

'So what do you think happened?'

'I expect she died in the storm. It wouldn't be the first time in this country.'

'Did you know Jakob well?'

'I was with her the first time they met. He came from Reykjavík. Lived in Djúpivogur for a while. They didn't really know each other that well.'

'What kind of man was he?'

'Frankly, I thought she could have done better,' said Ninna. 'Though I never said as much to her face. Or his, for that matter. After all, it was none of my business, even when the truth came out. She was my friend and I'm in no position to judge her. I ended up with a wrong 'un myself – though I don't wish to speak ill of my Viggó.'

Ninna's old eyes regarded him. 'When those good-for-nothings drink, then you've really had it.'

Erlendur smiled to himself. 'The truth came out?' he repeated.

103

'Yes.'

'What came out?'

'That they'd been with the same man.'

'Who?'

'Not at the same time, of course. Matthildur met him later.'

'Hang on a minute – Jakob knew her sister.' Erlendur recalled Matthildur's letter to Ingunn.

'Jakob and Ingunn had been stepping out but it didn't last and was over by then. I remember Matthildur telling me her sister had been dead set against her marriage. By then Ingunn had moved south to Reykjavík. I reckon she moved because of Jakob. But what would I know? It had nothing to do with me.'

'Bastard' had been scrawled in bold letters across the obituary in Ingunn's possession. It had obviously been written in anger. Although that did not necessarily mean Ingunn had written it herself, it did seem highly likely if what Ninna said was anything to go by. Ingunn and Jakob had known each other before she moved to Reykjavík to start a new life, and later fate had decreed that he should marry her sister. Judging by the letter, Matthildur had been aware that Ingunn and Jakob were acquainted, but apparently not how intimately.

'Did Matthildur know about their relationship?'

'Know! It only came to light after they got married. The consequences only emerged then.'

'Consequences?'

'Well, it was never common knowledge. I was in

on the secret, and maybe a few others. After all, Ingunn had moved away and seldom came home.'

'What secret?'

'About the baby,' said Ninna. 'Ingunn had a child by Jakob. Matthildur was distraught when she found out. Quite distraught.'

CHAPTER 18

Ingunn told no one about her condition. Nor did she ever reveal the identity of the child's father. When she discovered she was pregnant, she decided to move to the city. At first she had considered an abortion and was put in touch with people who could organise one, but when the time came she decided against it. Instead she took a job at a fish factory and had a tough few months as a single mother until she met and married a fishery foreman, going on to have three more children with him. She never looked back and never returned to Reydarfjördur or anywhere else in the east while Jakob was alive.

She had gone to see him shortly before moving to Reykjavík, to inform him that she thought she was pregnant and that the baby was his, which Jakob immediately cast doubt on. They had met when Ingunn took a summer job at the same fish factory in the village of Djúpivogur and had slept together once, towards the end of the season. She had fallen in love with him, believing him to be a good, decent man, but the truth had turned out to be different. After sleeping with her, he quickly lost interest and eventually told her bluntly to stop chasing him around. Their relationship was over almost before it began. When she went to see him to tell him about the baby, he lost his temper and declared that she could never prove it was his, then called her a slut and said he wanted nothing more to do with her. She had better not dare name the child after him, were his final words.

Shattered and humiliated, Ingunn chose to remain silent. She had often talked about wanting to go and live in Reykjavík, so no one was particularly surprised when she acted on her impulse. Most of her belongings fitted into a single suitcase. Some months later she gave birth to a son and, once they got together, her husband took the place of the boy's father.

'Matthildur knew all about it,' Ninna said, looking Erlendur straight in the eye. 'I heard the story from her. But Ingunn didn't tell her until too late. She didn't speak out when she first learned they were seeing each other – probably couldn't bring herself to – but you can imagine how she must have felt. At first I don't suppose she wanted to believe it. Perhaps she hoped it wouldn't last. It wasn't until later that she summoned up the courage to send Matthildur a letter describing what had happened between her and Jakob.'

Ninna glanced out of the window at the snowflakes drifting to the ground.

'I never blabbed about this and I hope you won't

either,' she said sternly. 'Though I can't imagine who'd be interested. Not many people knew them at the time and I don't suppose anyone would remember them nowadays.'

'You said Matthildur was distraught when she heard,' said Erlendur.

'Jakob had never told her about his relationship with Ingunn – I suppose it's not surprising. He'd never been to the sisters' house, so he didn't really know the family. That business between him and Ingunn happened in Djúpivogur. Ingunn must have been horrified when she found out who Matthildur had married.'

'Matthildur too, surely?'

'Devastated. Told me so herself. When she confronted Jakob, he didn't deny he'd known Ingunn but he refused point-blank to acknowledge the child.'

'Could it have driven her to do something desperate?'

'You mean did she kill herself over it? I don't believe that for one minute. She wasn't the type. She got the letter from her sister a year before she died, so she'd had plenty of time to recover. No, I think she meant to leave him.'

'To divorce Jakob?'

'Yes.'

'Over this?'

'It's all I can think of.'

'Could there have been another motive?'

'That's the only one I'm aware of.'

Ninna relapsed into silence and stared down at her gnarled hands. Then she sighed and began to tug absent-mindedly at her grey hair, as if from habit, apparently lost in reverie. Time passed. It was very quiet in the nursing home. Outside, the houses across the road were barely visible. Ninna's eyes were trained on the window but she was staring past the snow, buildings and mountains to something far beyond.

'I wonder if I'll live to see the spring,' she remarked distractedly.

Erlendur did not know how to answer. He wanted to say that of course she would but knew he had no grounds for thinking so.

'Haven't we had enough?' said Ninna. 'Enough of these interminable winters?'

'Do you think Ingunn might have sent the letter in a deliberate attempt to destroy Matthildur's marriage? As a way of taking revenge on Jakob?'

'Why do you say that?'

'Because I have reason to believe she wrote elsewhere that he was a bastard. She seems to have nursed a real grievance against him.'

'Do you want to see her letter?'

'Are you . . . You mean you have it?'

'Matthildur showed it to me and asked me to keep it for her. She was afraid Jakob might destroy it. See that chest? There's a small box in the bottom drawer. Could you bring it to me? I'm a bit rickety on my pins these days.'

Erlendur got up, found the carved wooden box

in the chest, and brought it over to Ninna. She opened it and rummaged around among photographs and letters until she found what she was looking for. Putting the box down, she held up the letter and studied the address briefly before handing it to Erlendur.

'I've kept it ever since,' she said.

He opened the envelope carefully. The letter consisted of a single sheet, written in a feminine hand, and dated in Reykjavík, a year before Matthildur's disappearance.

Dear Matthildur,

What I have to tell you is something I never meant to reveal to anyone, and I wouldn't do so now if it weren't for the unusual circumstances we find ourselves in. You must have wondered why I was against your relationship with Jakob from the start. I'm afraid that what I have to tell you is not very pleasant. I do hope you can forgive me.

I don't know how best to put this into words, so I'll just come straight out and say it: Jakob is the father of my son. He'll deny it but it's true. It happened when I was in Djúpivogur over the summer. When I realised I was pregnant with his baby I told him, but he questioned what I said as if I was some kind of whore and insulted me in ways I can never forgive him for. So I moved here to the city and met Halldór. He's a lovely man and I have a good

life with him. I didn't tell Mum or the rest of
you at the time but since then I've confided in
Jóa. She's been a real brick. Jakob's son is a
bouncing boy who takes after his father.

I'm not one to tell tales but I felt I had to
let you know the truth. Jakob made such ugly
threats against me that I'm afraid of him. Since
then I've heard that he beat up a woman he
was seeing in Höfn in a fit of jealousy. He told
me that if I didn't leave him alone he would
spread all kinds of filthy lies about me, and I
know he'd already started before I left. He
threatened to batter me too and used words I
shan't repeat here.

Dearest Matthildur, you can hardly imagine
my shock when I heard that you two had got
together. I couldn't believe my ears and maybe
I've dithered for longer than I should before
telling you the whole story. I suppose I'm still
ashamed of letting him seduce me. I'm still angry
with myself. I wish I had some advice for you
but I don't know what to say. Maybe he's
changed, but I doubt it. Matthildur, dear, I'm
so sorry to have to tell you that Jakob is not an
honourable man. He's not a good man.

Please forgive me for this terrible letter.
Your loving sister,
Ingunn

Erlendur folded the letter again, replaced it in the
envelope with care and handed it back to Ninna.

'Did she show this to Jakob?' he asked.

'Of course she did,' said Ninna. 'He denied it, as I told you. Denied the whole story, then and always.'

'Matthildur must have been in a real quandary. Did she want to leave him?'

'I think that became obvious as time went by.'

'But perhaps not in the way she did?'

'I couldn't say.'

'I gather Jakob didn't have a very good reputation around here,' said Erlendur. 'Do you think it could have been because of this? Because the secret had got out?'

'I haven't a clue,' said Ninna. 'Look, I'm getting rather tired of this. It's high time you were leaving.'

'Just a minute. Jakob and Ingunn's son – where is he now?'

'He used to live here in the east. I gather he's in a home in Egilsstadir now, since losing the sight in one eye. He's called Kjartan after the girls' father.'

'Kjartan Halldórsson!' exclaimed Erlendur, his mind leaping to the old man in Egilsstadir who had allowed him access to his mother's trunk.

'He adopted his stepfather's patronymic,' explained Ninna. 'Naturally, Ingunn didn't want the boy to be named after Jakob. Have you met him?'

'Someone I know sent me to see him and now I understand why.'

CHAPTER 19

In one of his more lucid spells, he recalls reading about a simple method of diagnosing hypothermia. It gives him an odd sense of déjà vu, although he can't recollect ever having put it to use before.

He tries to touch his little finger with his thumb, but can't do it. He tries again. His hand won't respond; his claw-like fingers are lifeless. None of them will move, let alone touch one another. He can't even raise an index finger. The message has frozen somewhere on the neural pathway from brain to hand. He quickly abandons the attempt, unable to remember at what stage of hypothermia he would become incapable of this movement.

There are three stages. He has often read up on hypothermia and how exactly it causes unconsciousness, which is followed by a slow death as the brain gradually shuts down.

The loss of one or two degrees Celsius of body heat triggers involuntary shivering and numbness in the hands. He can't tell if he has gone beyond that stage. He tries to focus his fuzzy mind on the question as he struggles in vain with the simple action of touching his little finger to his thumb. The capillaries in the outer layer of his skin have contracted to reduce heat loss in a classic defence mechanism. Goose pimples are another such mechanism.

He remembers having gooseflesh, as if it were weeks ago.

He also recalls being assailed by a bizarre impulse to tear off all his clothes, but how long ago that happened is a mystery to him. He associates this urge with progressing from the first to the second stage of hypothermia. It felt as if the heat were rushing to his skin and extremities, making him suddenly boiling hot, though this could have been a delusion. He has read about cases where the victims stripped themselves, convinced they were suffocating. There are two theories explaining the symptom: one is that the region of the brain that regulates body temperature malfunctions and sends out the wrong messages to the skin; the other is that the muscles which cause the blood vessels to contract in order to prevent heat loss and ensure the blood supply to essential organs, such as the brain, simply stop working. This releases a flow of blood to the skin and as a result the victim experiences an unexpected hot flush.

During this second stage, when the body temperature can drop by as much as four degrees, the lips, ears and fingers turn blue.

During the third stage, the body temperature falls below thirty-two degrees Celsius. Shivering ceases, speech and thought are impaired and the victim feels drowsy. The skin turns blue and mental functioning and sensations become increasingly irrational. Eventually, the organs fail and clinical death ensues. Yet brain death is not instantaneous as the cold impairs cell deterioration, slowing the damage to the cerebral tissue.

He has read studies about the human ability to endure cold; about victims of shipwrecks in the Arctic winter who managed to survive the most extreme conditions; about people who were given up for dead after being lost in Iceland's frozen interior but survived against all the odds. And now he has proof that such accounts are true. In recent days he has seen with his own eyes how the will to live can exceed all expectations.

He tries once again to touch his little finger to his thumb, but to no avail. He can't even feel his hand, let alone see if it is turning blue and developing frostbite.

Some of what he knows about man's ability to endure the most hostile conditions is linked to the missing-person case he has been investigating since he came out east. His knowledge of the subject has progressed as he has dug up more about the locals, about their strange family ties, friendships, lies, and Matthildur's fate.

Earlier he could see the sea of stars spreading over the night sky. Now he can see nothing.

He knows that the scratching he can hear from below the ground is imaginary; the distant cries that reach his ears exist only in his own mind. He knows where they come from and is not afraid of them.

His consciousness fades out again.

Other sounds assail him: his own words uttered an eternity ago that have stayed with him ever since. Words he should never have spoken.

Words at once so trivial and yet so immeasurable.

CHAPTER 20

He drove back the same way, once again avoiding the tunnel between Fáskrúdsfjördur and Reydarfjördur. The going was slower than it had been that morning but his four-wheel drive negotiated the road over Vattarnesskridur without any difficulty. He was aware that the drop to the sea in these parts was known, appropriately enough, as Manndrápsgil, or 'Death Gorge'. Below him, he could just make out the islands of Skrúdur and Andey.

Daylight was fading and the misty radiance from the smelter site cast a ghostly light over Reydarfjördur Fjord. He wondered if he should visit Hrund now, while Ninna's information was still fresh in his mind, and decided there was no reason to delay. As he drove up to her house, however, he noticed that she was not at her usual post by the window.

He approached the front door, knocked, waited, then knocked again. Hrund was not at home. Not daring to barge straight in again, he did a circuit of the house, trying to peer in through the windows. No lights or movement were visible.

When he returned to the front door and gripped the handle, he discovered that it was unlocked, so he stepped cautiously inside, calling Hrund's name. No answer. Closing the door behind him, he groped his way to the sitting room where the chair stood by the window, then suddenly got cold feet, struck by the fear of appearing rude. Hrund had probably just gone out to the shops and would be back any minute: he did not want to be caught in her house. Returning to the front door, he opened it and was about to make a quick exit when he happened to glance down the hall to the kitchen. In the faint glow from the street lights, he saw Hrund's legs stretched out on the floor. Hurrying into the kitchen, he found her lying on her side, her eyes shut. He laid his fingers on her neck and detected a weak pulse, then located her phone and dialled the emergency number. Afterwards, he fetched a blanket from the sitting room and laid it over her but was afraid to touch her otherwise. She was unconscious. The door had been unlocked when he arrived but he had not been aware of anyone else near the house and did not suspect foul play.

Hearing a weak moan, he knelt beside her.

'What happened?' he asked.

Hrund opened her eyes and looked around in confusion.

'Are you all right?'

She tried to sit up but he told her to lie still; he had rung for an ambulance and it would be here very soon. He asked if she had a pain in her chest or head but she indicated that she did not.

'Diabetes,' she croaked.

'You mustn't try to talk,' Erlendur said. 'You're burning up. Where can I find sugar?'

'In the cupboard . . .'

He stood up.

'I suppose I'll have to . . . go to hospital . . .'

Erlendur found a sugar lump and fed it to her, then fetched a cushion from the sofa, placed it under her head and tucked the blanket better around her. He went outside in search of the ambulance. Though the regional hospital was thirty kilometres away in Neskaupstadur, with any luck they would have an ambulance stationed in the village because of the construction work.

Hrund was still in the same position when he came back. She asked him to help her up off the floor and he was hesitant at first, unsure if he should move her. Eventually, at her insistence, he helped her to sit up on a kitchen chair.

'I should have known. It starts like the flu, then just gets worse. All it takes is the slightest scratch and I end up with blood poisoning.'

'They should be here shortly. What can I do to help?'

'Why do you keep coming here?' she asked, her voice low and breathless, drained of all strength.

'Perhaps you should lie down till they arrive,' Erlendur suggested.

'Tell me what you've found out,' she persisted

weakly. 'You haven't stopped sniffing around, have you?'

'No,' he admitted.

'Ah . . . I thought not. What's the latest?'

'Isn't there someone I could call?' asked Erlendur. 'Don't you have any family?'

'They've all moved away.'

'Friends?'

'There'll be plenty of time for that. Tell me what else you know.'

Headlights lit up the house and blue flashes bounced off the walls. Erlendur went outside to meet the ambulance. Two men, dressed in thick, reflective overalls, climbed out and followed him into the house.

'Diabetes again, is it?' one of them asked Hrund.

'I'm such a blasted nuisance,' she said, trying to stand.

'Easy now,' said the man. 'Haven't you been doing your injections regularly?'

'Yes, I have, but I think my leg's infected. I burnt myself on the oven door the day before yesterday, then started feeling very ill, and the next thing I know he's found me on the kitchen floor,' she said, gesturing at Erlendur.

The men fetched a stretcher, eased her onto it and carried her out. It had stopped snowing and she lay staring up at the stars until they slid her into the back of the ambulance. Erlendur stood by and watched as they closed the doors, then climbed into the cab and drove off. But they had not gone far before he saw the reversing lights come on as they backed up to the house again. One of the men jumped out.

'Can I ask who you are?' he said.

'Does it matter?' asked Erlendur.

'She wants you to come with her.'

'Really?'

'There's plenty of room.'

'All right,' said Erlendur and, climbing into the back, perched on a seat beside Hrund who had apparently fallen asleep. When they set off again, however, she opened her eyes and studied his face.

'Why won't you give up?' she asked huskily.

'Give up what?'

'Stirring up ghosts that have nothing to do with you.'

'Do you want me to stop?'

Hrund did not answer.

'They'll give me antibiotics,' she said at last. 'As soon as I get to hospital. A massive dose to kill all the infection in my body. That's how they beat it. Otherwise I'll die. Not that I should care, really. I'm old and tired and ill, and I don't suppose anyone'll miss me. But it's not a tempting thought. Not for me. I may be an old cripple but I don't want to let go. I really don't want to let go.'

The ambulance skidded and bumped over a snow-drift that lay across the road. Erlendur was thrown off his seat, almost falling against the rear door.

'Sorry,' called the driver from the cab. 'It's like a skating rink.'

'Why are you investigating Matthildur's story?' asked Hrund, returning to her theme. 'What have you found out?'

'Why didn't you tell me about Ingunn and Jakob?'

'It was none of your business. Why are you raking up what's long forgotten? Why can't people rest in peace?'

'It's not my intention to disturb anyone,' said Erlendur.

'Who've you been talking to?'

'Matthildur's friend.'

'Ninna?'

'Yes.'

'What do you know? I want to hear.'

'Nothing you don't already, I suspect,' said Erlendur. 'Ingunn didn't tell anyone she'd given birth to Jakob's child and he refused to acknowledge that he was the father. Their son is the man you sent me to see in Egilsstadir. Later, when Ingunn learned that Matthildur had married Jakob, she wrote her a letter telling her the whole story. A year after that Matthildur died.'

'You *have* been busy,' Hrund remarked.

'I sometimes get the feeling . . .' Erlendur began.

'What?'

'I get the impression – though I may be wrong – that you're on my side, in spite of everything, and that you've been guiding me. But you're in two minds. You find it hard to admit it to yourself, so you react badly because you don't really feel it's appropriate for strangers to rummage through your family's dirty laundry. I think your objections are a pretence, but I understand. I think you're trying to encourage me to take a second look. You've been searching for answers for years and you reckon it's about time somebody uncovered the truth – which is where I come in.'

'You think you know it all,' said Hrund in a faint voice.

'Well, I know why you sent me to see Kjartan in Egilsstadir, but why did you want me to meet Ezra?'

He thought Hrund had lost consciousness again. Her eyes were closed and her breathing had grown oddly peaceful. The ambulance men were driving with great care through the snowy night. In his ignorance about diabetes, he wondered if he should alert them.

'You said you were a policeman,' said Hrund suddenly.

'Yes.'

'I've always . . .' She drew a deep breath, apparently at the end of her strength.

'What?'

'I've always . . . felt Matthildur's disappearance was a matter for the police.'

CHAPTER 21

Hrund slept for the rest of the journey and the ambulance drew up outside the hospital in the small town of Neskaupstadur late that evening. Erlendur accompanied Hrund into a ward and stayed with her until the doctor started the treatment that had been used on her before, administering a dose of strong antibiotics to deal with the infection in her leg. The merest graze could fester and, if unchecked, result in these serious complications.

The doctor informed him that Hrund would need a good night's sleep, and only now did it dawn on Erlendur that he didn't have his car. He hadn't given any thought to how he was to get back to Hrund's house to retrieve it. It was too late to get a lift to Reydarfjördur, and in any case he wanted to talk to Hrund when she woke up in the morning. He asked if the doctor could recommend a decent guest house and was directed to a cheap B & B near the hospital, with the warning that all the construction work meant it was generally full.

Erlendur was in luck, however: they had a

vacancy, and he found himself sharing the place with exhausted engineers, buoyant salesmen up from Reykjavík, American management consultants and Chinese labourers. A middle-aged man, one of the engineers, struck up a conversation, informing him that he had in the past worked on avalanche barriers in the West Fjords and in the remote town of Siglufjördur in the north. His family came from the East Fjords, though, from an ancestral farm with a name that sounded like Strókahlíd. His conversation quickly degenerated into a rant about all the fuss over the dam and the smelter, and he was still grumbling about his brother's views when Erlendur wished him a curt goodnight.

The following morning he returned to the hospital to see Hrund, who had slept well and was much brighter. She was sitting propped up in bed and the burn on her leg had been properly dressed.

'The drugs are starting to work,' she announced as Erlendur took a seat beside her. 'Thank you for your help. I'm such an ass not to have called the doctor sooner. I must have passed out on the kitchen floor, though I can't really remember much.'

'It didn't look good,' said Erlendur.

'You needn't have come all the way with me.'

'It was the least I could do.'

She adjusted the blankets on her bed.

'I remember some of our conversation yesterday evening, but maybe not all.'

'Well, if I understood you right, you suspect there may have been another explanation for Matthildur's death than the one Jakob gave at the time.'

'Yes, you're right,' she said, as if with relief. 'I know it's terrible to be so cynical but it's been bothering me for years. I've always thought it strange that her body was never found. All the British soldiers were accounted for, even though some of them had wandered way off course. I've felt for a long time that she should have been found too.'

'One of the soldiers had been washed out to sea after falling in the river.'

'I know – I can't get that out of my head either. Perhaps she went the same way and was carried out by the tide. Perhaps she did die on the moors after all.'

'I had a long chat with Ninna yesterday and she mentioned a rumour about suicide. Did that never occur to you?'

'Of course. But the problem's the same. Why wasn't she found? No one's been able to answer that. And I doubt anyone could after all these years.'

'You're not in touch with your nephew Kjartan?'

'No. He may be my nephew but we're not close. We're aware of each other's existence, but that's all. Of course, he didn't grow up around here, just moved out east as a young man and he's kept pretty much to himself. I'm not in touch with Ingunn's other children either. They're all in Reykjavík, as far as I know.'

126

'Why didn't you tell me about Ingunn and Jakob?'

Hrund hesitated. 'Why should I?' she said eventually. 'I didn't know you at all. When you told me you were in the police, it set me off dredging it all up again. But I couldn't make up my mind, so I'm afraid I lost my temper when you came back. It was uncalled for and I hope you'll forgive my rudeness.'

'There's no need. I know I'm an outsider,' said Erlendur.

'You must realise it's not easy to talk about.'

Erlendur nodded. 'So you knew about Ingunn and Jakob?'

'I didn't grasp what had gone on until I was older,' said Hrund. 'My mother didn't like to talk about it. I only really picked it up from whispered hints much later on. By then both Matthildur and Jakob were dead. I gather she was shattered by Ingunn's letter. That must explain what happened afterwards.'

'Do you think she was intending to leave Jakob?'

'It seems likely.'

'Is there any reason to believe Ingunn was lying?'

'Why should she?'

'It crossed my mind that Jakob might not have been the father. That there was someone else.'

'I find that highly unlikely. Though I never saw the famous letter. Goodness knows what happened to it.'

'Ninna's got it,' said Erlendur. 'Maybe you

127

should speak to her. Ingunn claims in it that Jakob's the father.'

'So you've read it?'

Erlendur nodded.

'I don't believe there was anyone else in the picture,' said Hrund. 'Then, by complete coincidence, Matthildur went and married him. It was just one of those things. Life's like that – coincidences happen.'

'But that doesn't necessarily mean Jakob was to blame. He didn't cheat on Matthildur. His relationship with Ingunn, whatever form it took, was over before he and Matthildur moved in together. Everybody has a past.'

'Of course.'

'So if she was lying about Jakob being the father, Ingunn must have had some other reason for wanting to destroy the marriage.'

'Jakob treated her shabbily,' Hrund pointed out.

'I know, Ingunn says so in her letter.'

'I don't know what she said, but he made all sorts of threats when she told him the news and asked him to acknowledge the baby. He threatened to beat her. Maybe he actually did it. And warned her he'd put it about that she was a . . . was no better than a common tart. It was because of him that she fled to Reykjavík, I'm sure. My mother was convinced he'd hit her, though Ingunn refused to discuss it.'

A nurse came to the door and asked if Hrund needed anything. She shook her head. The woman removed an empty water jug from the bedside table and said she would fill it.

'Ring the bell if you do need anything,' she added with a friendly smile.

'Mother had a go at him when Matthildur didn't turn up,' Hrund continued, once the nurse had gone. 'Asked Jakob straight out if he'd hurt her. If he'd hit Ingunn. He denied everything. Claimed he'd never laid a finger on either of them. There wasn't much my mother could say to that.'

'Matthildur must have been stunned when she discovered her nephew was her husband's son,' Erlendur remarked.

'All I know is that Ingunn managed to wreck their marriage with that letter,' said Hrund. 'Perhaps that was her intention all along.'

'What do you mean?'

Hrund did not answer.

'What happened?'

She looked him in the eye. There was a clacking as someone walked past wearing clogs. Outside a lorry started up noisily.

'What did you mean when you said that must explain what happened afterwards?'

'What?'

'You implied that Ingunn's letter had an impact on what happened afterwards. Were you referring to Matthildur's disappearance?'

'No,' said Hrund. 'That was later . . . No. Matthildur turned to Ezra. She had an affair with Jakob's friend.'

'Ezra?'

'Yes. They started meeting in secret. Didn't you visit him?'

'Yes, I did.'

'And he didn't tell you?'

'No.'

'Well, it's hardly surprising,' said Hrund. 'He's never opened up about it – except the once. He's kept it secret all these years and no doubt he'll take it to his grave.'

CHAPTER 22

Erlendur sat in silence while Hrund's words sank in. The clogs clomped along the corridor again, and gradually the rumble of the lorry's engine faded away. Hrund stroked the white quilt. Erlendur noticed that someone had brought her a book with a worn brown spine. The title looked like *Man and Dust*.

'I suppose you want to know more,' Hrund said, after an awkward pause.

'You call the shots,' said Erlendur. 'At least you have so far.'

To the best of Hrund's knowledge, Ezra and Matthildur had been acquainted – though no more than that – before Matthildur received her sister's letter. Ezra used to work on a fishing boat with Jakob. They got on well enough, having first met several years earlier in Djúpivogur, though Hrund didn't know the circumstances and had no idea what had brought them both to Eskifjördur after the war. Ezra had never married, nor, as far as Hrund was aware, had he ever been involved with a woman before. Jakob was clearly much more experienced.

Ezra was a loner. He had been that way as a young man and had never changed. People knew next to nothing about him except that he was not local but came originally from the other side of the country. Before meeting Jakob in Djúpivogur he had been living out west, in Stykkishólmur and Borgarnes, where he may well have been born and brought up, though it had never occurred to anyone to ask. It was the fishing that had drawn him to the East Fjords, where he had settled down to work on the sea.

Although he was a solitary man, little given to talking about himself, showing his feelings or getting involved much in local affairs, he was by no means unpopular. He was hard-working and always ready to oblige if asked for help. Clean-living and abstemious too. Despite his powerful frame, though, he had never been considered much of a looker, with his low brow, small eyes, prematurely wrinkled face and the odd blemish on his lower lip that might have been from a fight – not that anyone had ever asked him. Some joker had once quipped that his face looked like a rug that had been kicked into a corner. Maybe that accounted for his shyness and diffidence where women were concerned. Until, that is, he met Matthildur.

Their acquaintance had begun when she and Jakob first started seeing each other. In his shy way Ezra had noticed her before, but only got to know her properly when he and Jakob started crewing a three-tonne motor vessel whose owner ran a fish-processing factory in the village. The boat was christened *Sigurlína* after the man's wife. They used to head out at the crack of dawn and return to the harbour in the afternoon or early evening, sometimes manning the boat on their own when the captain had other business. Ezra would wake up in the early hours and drop by to fetch Jakob, by which time Matthildur would be up and about, and they would exchange a few words while Jakob was getting ready. Then the two men would set off down to the harbour while she stood watching from the doorway. Jakob never looked back but Ezra would sometimes snatch an unobtrusive glance over his shoulder, capturing the image of Matthildur to take with him out to sea.

Once when they came ashore, Jakob announced that he had to go over to Djúpivogur for a few days. He did not explain his business, merely told Ezra that he would have to man the boat with the owner in the meantime. The following morning, as he walked past the house, Ezra noticed that Matthildur was up and about. Jakob had made an early start and she had woken to say goodbye to him but couldn't get back to sleep. The door was open, so Ezra greeted her and they had a brief chat as usual.

The next day Ezra passed the house again and saw that Matthildur had the door open, as if waiting for him. She came out and said hello, and he lingered longer than the day before, enjoying a more leisurely conversation. Matthildur was just as much in the dark about what had taken Jakob to Djúpivogur. He had discussed buying a share in a fishing boat and she thought he might be looking into opportunities. Ezra nodded. Jakob had once suggested they club together to buy a stake in a vessel, but Ezra had poured cold water on the idea because he was broke. 'We'll take a loan, mate,' Jakob had said. 'Who do you think would lend money to the likes of us?' Ezra had retorted.

He and Matthildur stood by the door in the early-morning quiet and he asked if she needed anything. She did not.

'Thanks, anyway,' she said.

The third morning he dawdled even longer and the owner was fuming by the time he finally turned up to work. Matthildur had not been up when he passed the house, so he had hung around until he heard a noise inside and plucked up the courage to tap on the door. She had smiled as she opened it, still in her nightie.

'I prepared some lunch for you last night,' she said, handing him a small parcel. 'It's so kind of you to drop by in the mornings.'

He accepted the food in surprise.

'There was really no need,' he said, without wishing to sound ungrateful.

'Oh, no, it's nothing special,' she said, amused at his astonishment.

'Thank you very much.' He put the packet in his bag. 'Jakob's back tomorrow, isn't he?'

'I'm expecting him this evening,' Matthildur replied. 'He'll go out with you in the morning.'

On the fourth day he walked up to Matthildur's house. He had not heard from Jakob but assumed he would have returned home the night before, so he knocked on the door as usual. He turned towards the harbour: fog lay over the fjord but he hoped it would disperse during the morning. The door opened and Matthildur appeared. It was immediately clear that she had been crying.

'What's the matter?' he asked. 'What's happened?'

She shook her head.

'Has something happened to Jakob? Is he here?'

'No,' she said. 'He's not here. I don't know where he is.'

'Wasn't he meant to come back yesterday evening?'

'Yes, but he didn't show up, and I don't know when he's going to.'

She seemed extremely agitated and disappeared into the kitchen, returning with a letter that she brandished in his face.

'Did you know about this?' she demanded.

'About what?'

'What sort of man he is,' she retorted and slammed the door in his face. Ezra stood there at a loss. He hesitated, wondering if he should knock again. The boat was waiting: he could not stay. In the neighbouring houses people were waking up.

He vacillated for a while longer before eventually setting off down the hill, but kept pausing in case the door opened again. Nothing happened. He had never seen her so distressed and couldn't bear to think of her alone in that state.

When Ezra came ashore later that day his eyes went straight to the house but it was dark and appeared empty. He walked home, preoccupied, and opened his door which, like everyone else in the village, he always left unlocked. As he put down his bag he was startled to see Matthildur sitting at his kitchen table in the gloom. He reached for the light switch.

'Do you mind not turning it on?' she asked.

'All right.'

'I'm sorry about the way I behaved this morning,' she said. 'I've been worrying about it all day.'

'Don't worry,' he said, looking around to see if Jakob was with her. 'I hope you're feeling a bit better.'

'I am.'

'Are you alone?'

'Yes, I'm alone. I wanted to talk to you. Is that all right?'

'Of course,' said Ezra. 'Of course. Are you hungry? Would you like some coffee?'

'No, thank you,' she said. 'Don't go to any trouble. That's not why I'm here.'

'Why are you here?'

Matthildur did not answer immediately. He joined her at the table. He was glad she was there, glad she had been waiting for him when he came home, though he had no idea what was going on.

'Is Jakob back?' he asked.

'Yes, he came home late this morning.'

'But he's not with you now?'

'You needn't worry – no one saw me come in,' said Matthildur. 'Not that I'd care if they did. I couldn't care less.'

'What . . . what's the matter, Matthildur?' he asked. 'What happened this morning?'

'I had a letter yesterday evening from my sister Ingunn.' She took an envelope out of her pocket. 'She moved to Reykjavík a while back and we haven't written much. I knew she was against me marrying Jakob but until now I didn't know why. You can read it if you like.'

She handed it to him and he read it twice before putting it down on the table.

'What does Jakob have to say?'

'Nothing,' said Matthildur. 'He remembers Ingunn from Djúpivogur; he admits that much. But he reckons there's no way the baby's his. Says he's told Ingunn before but she's got this crazy idea. He claims she's off her rocker.'

'And you knew nothing about this?'

'Ingunn never told me till now. I knew she had a child in Reykjavík but I never for one minute connected it to Jakob.'

'Was he aware that you and Ingunn were sisters when you met?'

'Yes, and I knew they were acquainted,' said

Matthildur, 'but that's all, nothing about the baby or what sort of relationship they'd had. He never mentioned it, never mentioned the affair. He still won't talk about it. Refuses even to discuss it. He just told me to shut up. He hit me, then stormed out of the house. Where he is now I don't know.'

'He hit you?'

'Yes, on the head.'

'Are you all right?'

'Yes, it just gave me a bit of a shock.'

'Do you believe your sister?'

'Yes.'

'What are you going to do, then?'

'I don't know,' said Matthildur. 'I don't know what to do. I wanted to see you because I had to know if you were aware of this. Did you know he'd had a child with my sister?'

'I had no idea,' Ezra assured her.

'So he never mentioned any of it to you?'

'Not a word.'

'He could have children all over the place for all I know. He's probably been chasing skirt in Djúpivogur all this time!'

She reached out for the letter and before he knew what he was doing he had laid his hand shyly over hers. The gesture was almost instinctive. Instead of snatching back her hand, she met his gaze.

'I'm sorry,' he said, releasing her hand. 'It's not . . . I'm sorry. You're upset.'

'It's all right.'

'I've never experienced this before,' he whispered.

'Don't be ashamed,' she said. 'I feel happy when I'm with you.'

He glanced up again and their eyes locked.

'You're a good man, Ezra.'

'You can't imagine how I've been feeling. The way I feel.'

'Perhaps I can,' she said.

'You don't mind?'

In the darkness he saw her shake her head.

'What about Jakob?' he whispered.

'He can go to hell,' said Matthildur.

CHAPTER 23

A doctor entered Hrund's room, examined the drip and enquired how she was feeling. After a curious glance at Erlendur, who did not say a word, he briskly took his leave. Hrund asked Erlendur to arrange her pillows more comfortably and refill her glass. He poured her some water from the jug and Hrund took a sip, then set the glass down again.

'My mother got the story out of Ezra years later,' she said. 'After Jakob died. Ezra never meant to tell her and of course he never would have done if she hadn't pestered him. But I can well believe she only learned a fraction of the truth. Ezra's a very dark horse, though I've always had a soft spot for him.'

'I've only met him the once,' said Erlendur. 'Naturally, he didn't say a word about any of this.'

'No, I don't suppose he'd tell you,' said Hrund.

Concerned that she might be tiring, Erlendur asked if he should come back later when she had had a rest.

'A rest?' exclaimed Hrund. 'I don't know how I'm supposed to rest any more than I'm doing right now, lying flat on my back in hospital.'

'I don't want to be a nuisance.'

'You're not. It isn't often I get the chance to reminisce like this, and, anyway, there's always the possibility you'll turn up something new. You've certainly made the old pulse beat a bit faster.'

Erlendur couldn't deny that Hrund was looking better and seemed livelier and more talkative than before. He wondered how much this was down to the antibiotics. Apart from an episode of arrhythmia a few years back, he had never been ill himself; never spent a day in bed in his life.

'Well, I'm all ears,' he said. 'What happened next?'

'Nothing for a few months, though Ezra and Matthildur grew closer all the time. He carried on fishing with Jakob, but increasingly took days off sick. It's remarkable they managed to keep their affair secret in such a small community. They knew they'd have to tell Jakob at some point – better it came from them than from somebody else. But Matthildur was reluctant. She was worried he'd make life difficult for them.

'Do you think Matthildur could have started an affair with Ezra to get even with Jakob?'

'I've asked myself that. She gets the letter, reacts furiously and turns to another man for comfort.'

'What did your mother think?'

'She couldn't really say,' said Hrund. 'But she knew Matthildur went into things wholeheartedly. However it may have started, she was genuinely in love with Ezra. He was in the best position to know, after all, and he told my mother.'

The hardest part was meeting in secret. There were limits to how many days Ezra could take off work. On the other hand, he didn't want to put too much pressure on Matthildur to leave Jakob. She had already postponed the evil moment twice. Although she felt she had good grounds to divorce him, Jakob denied that her sister's child was his, and she was frightened of how he would react to her leaving. Finally, finding it increasingly difficult to associate with Jakob and hating the furtiveness and deceit, Ezra invented an excuse to stop working on the boat with him. News of his meetings with Matthildur must not get out, but he knew it was inevitable sooner or later.

One night, as he lay awake thinking about their predicament, he heard a light tap on the door. When he opened it, Matthildur darted inside and he closed it hastily behind her.

'I've missed you so much,' she whispered, flinging her arms around him.

He crushed her to him, kissing her, then carried her into the kitchen where they kissed until she tore herself away.

'Let's leave,' said Ezra. 'Together. Tonight. Right now.'

'We can't just leave, Ezra,' she protested. 'I have to talk to him first. *We* have to talk to him. You're his friend, after all. And I want him to admit he was a sod to my sister.'

Ezra stared at her as she stroked his forehead. Jakob had gone to Reydarfjördur and was planning to stay there overnight.

'All right,' he said. 'We'll talk to him, tell him the truth. If that's the way you want it, I won't object. It'd be for the best. But we'll do it together. You mustn't do anything on your own. We'll face him together.'

'You know how jealous he is.'

'I can imagine – especially where you're concerned.'

There was no sign of her the next day. He hadn't stirred from the house since waking because of a howling gale that had blown up out of nowhere, but late that evening there was a rapping at his door. It was Jakob, in a frantic state. Ezra expected the worst, but not in the form it took.

'Matthildur's out in the storm,' Jakob gasped. 'I came to ask if you could help – help me find her.'

Ezra could hardly believe his ears. He had just been thinking how dangerous it would be to go outside in weather like this. Not in all the time he had lived out east had he experienced such ferocity. In the worst gusts he had feared the roof would be torn off.

'She was going to see her mother,' Jakob explained. 'She's on foot. I'm gathering a search party. Can you come and help?'

'Of course,' Ezra replied. 'Are you saying she's out in this weather?'

'You haven't seen or spoken to her at all?' Jakob asked.

'No.'

'She said she might look in on you.'

'Really?' said Ezra, and nearly blurted out that she hadn't mentioned any Reydarfjördur trip to him. He caught himself in the nick of time.

'She said she wanted a quick word with you,' said Jakob.

'I can't imagine what about,' Ezra replied. He gaped at Jakob in feigned surprise, trying to pretend it was out of the ordinary for Matthildur to want a word with him, as if she were not constantly in and out of his house. As if there were nothing between them; she had never talked of leaving Jakob; they were not planning to run away together. As if they had not made love here in the kitchen, right where Jakob was standing.

He forced his features into an expression of puzzlement to conceal all these lies.

'No, well, perhaps we'll find out,' said Jakob.

In desperate haste, Ezra pulled on his waterproofs and left with Jakob. He could detect no sign that Jakob had learned of their relationship. If he knew or suspected, he hid the fact. As far as Ezra could tell, Jakob was genuinely anxious about Matthildur. They were going from door to door, recruiting searchers, when they discovered that a rescue party was already assembling to look for a group of British soldiers from Reydarfjördur who had failed to return from a hike. The farmer at

Veturhús had raised the alarm and already rescued a number of the men.

Ezra and Jakob joined the search party, and news soon spread that Jakob believed his wife had been intending to cross the moors by the shortest route to visit her mother in Reydarfjördur. He believed she had been making for the Hraevarskörd Pass and might even have reached it before the storm peaked. The wind was still gusting with hurricane force, and conditions were hazardous for the rescue party, but neither Ezra nor Jakob were deterred.

'Why didn't you get in touch sooner?' Ezra yelled to Jakob once they were staggering up the path to Hraevarskörd. They could hardly make any headway against the wind.

'I fell asleep. I've been dead to the world all day and by the time I woke up this evening the storm was already raging. I'd never have let her go if I'd known the weather was going to turn like this.'

'Are you sure she hasn't made it over to the other side?'

'Yes. I phoned. They're getting another search party together in Reydarfjördur.'

'Oh God, we have to find her,' exclaimed Ezra.

'I'm sure she'll make it,' Jakob shouted back.

They ploughed on through the downpour, their calls lost in the screaming gale. But before long they were driven back by the savagery of the weather, as were the searchers on the other side of the pass. They had managed to struggle only a few hundred metres before realising they would have to wait out the storm if they were not to put their own lives at risk.

The wind had lost much of its force by the time the search parties met on the pass the following day, having seen no sign of Matthildur. They continued combing the highlands for the next few days but to no avail.

Hrund asked Erlendur to help her sit up a little.

'That's the story, more or less, as Ezra told it to my mother and she passed it on to me. So it should be pretty accurate. She described how shattered Ezra was by Matthildur's disappearance and how he suffered from not being able to confide in anyone about what they meant to each other.'

'Ezra knew Matthildur was planning to leave Jakob at the time she vanished,' said Erlendur thoughtfully, 'but no one else was aware that she and Ezra were lovers?'

'Not a soul. They kept it absolutely secret.'

'And he never let on?'

'No, never, according to my mother. He didn't want to drag Matthildur's name through the mud by admitting that she'd been having an affair with him before she went missing, and take the risk that people would speak ill of her. Given how things had turned out, he didn't feel their relation-ship was anyone else's business. But it's possible someone had noticed their visits and heard gossip about the child Ingunn claimed was Jakob's. Because as time went by Jakob's reputation took a hammering – not that it had been all that good to start with.'

'Hence the rumours that she haunted him and caused his shipwreck?'

'Yes.'

'What about Ezra? What did he think?'

'He was convinced she'd died in the storm. In his opinion, there was no other explanation.'

'And your mother believed him?'

'Yes. She had no reason to doubt him.'

'But Matthildur had told him Jakob was jealous. Ezra must have had his suspicions that she'd revealed all to Jakob and that trouble had come of it.'

'It's possible. But if so, he didn't tell my mother,' said Hrund. 'For some reason he was positive that Jakob would never have done her any harm. He accepted what had happened and mourned Matthildur. Still mourns her to this day.'

'How could he be so positive?'

'I really don't know. Jakob was the only living soul who could have shed light on Matthildur's fate. Once he was gone, all hope of solving the mystery was almost certainly lost.'

'But you've never been satisfied with Jakob's explanation.'

'Not for a minute.'

CHAPTER 24

His mother returns from the moor in a state of utter exhaustion. The blizzard has intensified again, bringing a complete whiteout, and so much snow has fallen that it is impossible for the searchers to continue. They gather at Bakkasel to wait out the worst of the storm.

The sedative the doctor gave him has worn off but he is quieter now and stays in bed in the room he shares with Bergur. He is still assailed by fits of shivering, as if coming down with the flu. The doctor looks in on him, takes his hand, examines his frostbite and feels his forehead. Then nods, apparently satisfied, and says he will soon be himself again.

His mother enters and sits down on the edge of the bed, her waterproof trousers, thick jumper and lace-up boots still caked with snow and ice. Water drips from her clothes onto the floor. She is ready to head back into the mountains the instant the weather lets up and can't relax. She has only come to pay him a brief visit before making a meal for the rescue party. She wants to share her knowledge of the land above Bakkasel with the leaders.

'How are you, dear?' she asks. She radiates energy, decisiveness and dogged determination, but tries to appear calm so as to avoid making him agitated again.

'How's it going?' he asks in return.

'Well so far, but we need a rest,' she answers quickly. 'Then we'll be able to carry on with twice the strength. Have you spoken to your father?'

He nods. He spent some time in his father's room but they barely exchanged a word. He has picked up on the fact that his parents are not speaking. His mother has made little effort to rouse his father from the crushing depression that has him in its grip.

'You will find Beggi, won't you?'

'Yes, we'll find him,' his mother reassures him. 'It's only a matter of time. We'll find him, you can rely on that.'

'He must be cold.'

'Now, we mustn't think like that,' says his mother. 'I know we've asked you a hundred times already but can you remember anything that might help us? Could you see any landmarks? Do you have any idea what direction you were going in?'

He shakes his head. 'I never saw a thing after we lost Dad. Just snow. I could hardly open my eyes. I don't know if I was walking uphill or down. Sometimes I had to crawl. I didn't see any land-marks. I didn't see anything at all.'

'They say the position they found you in suggests you might have been heading away from home, driven by the wind. The storm seems to have blown you further than we would have dreamed possible. You were so high up it was sheer luck we found you. Since then we've been searching even higher. Do you think Beggi could have gone that way?'

'He was supposed to stick with me. I was holding his hand all the time but suddenly he wasn't there any more. I kept shouting and calling his name but I couldn't even hear my own voice.'

He is struggling to suppress his tears.

'I know that, dear,' says his mother. 'I know. Thank God we found you, my darling.' She hugs him tight.

'Beggi took his little car with him,' he says.

'What car?'

'The one Dad gave him.'

'The little red one?'

'Yes.'

'The one you wanted?'

'I didn't want it,' he says quickly.

'But you two quarrelled over it.'

'I only asked him to swap it. For some soldiers.'

'But he didn't want to?'

'No.'

'And he had it with him when you left home?'

'Yes.'

He is on the verge of telling her what he said to his father before they set out on the fateful journey. He only mentioned the car because he wants to unburden himself, but he can't bring himself to. He doesn't know why. Perhaps because there is still hope that all will turn out well. That Beggi will be found and then it won't matter any more.

'We'll find him,' repeats his mother. 'Don't worry. As soon as the storm dies down. They say it's bound to blow itself out soon. When it does, we'll be ready and we'll find Beggi. There are more people coming to help and we'll be able to organise ourselves better. We'll find him, you can count on that.'

He nods.

'Now, try to get some rest, dear. Try to sleep as much as you can. You need it.'

Then she is gone and he is left alone with his thoughts, the roaring of the wind still echoing in his ears. It batters the house as if it wanted to rip it up from its foundations and blow it to kingdom come. He tosses and turns for an eternity, then falls into an indeterminate state between sleep and waking, before fatigue finally overwhelms him and plunges him into evil dreams.

He is alone in the house, unprotected against the elements. He might as well be lying outside on the ground. The doors swing loosely on their hinges, the windows are broken and all life has vanished from within; all furniture, light and colour. Inside it is dark, dreary and dead. Water trickles down the bare, clammy walls as if they were weeping.

Glancing down, he catches sight of a man lying

on the floor in a sleeping bag with a blanket over him. He stoops and is about to prod him when the man suddenly turns over and stares right through him. He gets a terrible shock. He has never seen the man before and his heart is filled with fear.

He is woken by the sound of his own screaming. He screams for all he is worth, till his lungs are ready to burst, till his face is scarlet and swollen. Screams and screams as if his life depended on it, until his mother comes in with the doctor and they manage to give him another shot of sedative.

CHAPTER 25

In the event, Erlendur had no trouble arranging a lift from Neskaupstadur back to Hrund's house. Having retrieved his car, he drove home to the ruined croft as evening fell. As he brought in more blankets, he saw to his satisfaction that his camp in the old sitting room was still dry. He lit the gas lantern and the room soon began to warm up around him. After two cigarettes and a cup of strong coffee, he took out the takeaway he had purchased on his way home. It was wrapped in an insulating bag so should still be lukewarm. To his surprise, he discovered that he was hungry and polished off most of the meal of lamb in thick brown gravy with mashed potato and a small pot of jelly. He washed it down with more coffee and smoked another couple of cigarettes. Then he picked up his book, a history of Icelandic students in Copenhagen in the nineteenth century. From time to time as he read a smile rose to his lips and once he even laughed out loud.

While his eyes were following the words, however, his attention began to stray back to Hrund and to the fate of all those left behind when their loved ones depart this life without warning, leaving the survivors to wrestle with feelings of bereavement and even guilt. When someone disappeared, all the focus was on the lost person, on the circumstances of their life and possible explanations for what had happened. But Erlendur's interest went further. He had said as much to Marion Briem, his colleague of many years, whom he missed more than he cared to admit. Marion had known how to listen; known, perhaps better than anyone, about loss. Erlendur attributed this to Marion's childhood experience of tuberculosis, which had led to prolonged sojourns in sanatoria in Iceland and Denmark. On the whole Marion had been reluctant to speak of it, but occasionally over the years, at Erlendur's prompting, had opened up enough to give an impression of those times: the rows of patients lying in the wards, coughing up blood; the grim surgical procedures like collapsing the infected lung or removing ribs. These accounts had been tinged with a sense of grief that Erlendur guessed was connected to a lost love, though Marion never said so.

'What exactly do you mean?' Marion had asked once when he tried to explain this reaction.

'I'm telling you that as a professional, as a police officer, my main objective is to find out what happened, who disappeared, how and why.'

'Yes,' Marion had said. 'That's obvious.'

'But then I start wondering: what about all the others?'

154

'Others?'

'The ones left behind.'

'What about them?'

'The people I pity are the ones left to cope with the fallout. Who have to endure the sadness for the rest of their lives. It's them I'm concerned with.'

'Policemen can't be responsible for men's souls, Erlendur,' Marion had said. 'That's what priests are for.'

'But I can't stop thinking about it.'

'And trying to help.'

'If I can. But there's so little one can do.'

Erlendur stared blankly into the black void of the house and listened to the moaning of the wind. Eventually, he put down his book and enjoyed a dreamless night's sleep in the warmth of the gas lantern.

The road through the Fagridalur Valley had been snowploughed by the time Erlendur drove along it at lunchtime next day. He parked outside the care home in Egilsstadir and thought about all those who remembered the story of Matthildur and Jakob. Most were getting on; some, like Ninna and Ezra, were very elderly. Soon their tales would be forgotten, along with their lives and fates, their sorrows and triumphs. They would all vanish into the eternal silence, laid to rest under the green turf of the graveyard, where in the end their only visitor would be the wind in the grass.

Kjartan recognised him immediately in spite of

his poor eyesight. He asked if Erlendur had found anything useful in his mother's trunk. Erlendur nodded: actually he had discovered a letter from Matthildur that had provided a promising lead.

'Well, that's good,' said Kjartan, after they had sat down together in the otherwise empty lounge. 'So you're back again, are you? I don't know what more I can do for you. Did you say you were going to publish it in a book?'

'I don't know. It's mostly to satisfy my own curiosity. I've spoken to a few locals and they've all been very kind. It's extraordinary how much they remember.'

'Yes, they're good folk round here,' agreed Kjartan. 'I haven't a bad word to say about them.'

Erlendur nodded again. On the drive through the Arctic landscape he had been debating how to bring up the subject of Kjartan's father tactfully, and wondering whether the old man knew his true paternity. He used a different patronymic, after all. And judging from what people said, Jakob could be an awkward subject to broach with anyone – particularly his supposed illegitimate son. As both a stranger and no relation, Erlendur had absolutely no right to go around interrogating people about the past, and it was doubly despicable to talk to them under false pretences. He wanted to come clean; he abhorred using duplicity and underhand methods when dealing with honest people.

'I'm not sure I've explained my interest in

Matthildur's death or disappearance properly,' he said after a pause. 'The subject came up recently when I was talking to a man called Bóas, but actually my fascination with the story of Matthildur and Jakob and their families goes back a long way.'

Kjartan fixed his unseeing eyes on him, puzzled as to what Erlendur was implying.

'I'm a policeman from Reykjavík, on holiday out here. As it happens, my family comes from these parts and I first heard about Matthildur when I was a boy. Her story intrigues me. But I'm not trying to expose anyone. This is in no way a police investigation.'

'Why didn't you tell me this before?' asked Kjartan. 'You didn't mention it, did you? If you did, I don't remember. I was under the impression you were a historian.'

'No,' said Erlendur, 'I'm not a historian. I felt it was better you understood before we talked any further – if you still want to, that is.'

Kjartan considered this. Erlendur waited patiently. He couldn't predict how the old man would react.

'I've had to put up with a lot because of my family history,' Kjartan said at last. 'But I don't believe it's any business of the police. I'd be grateful if you'd be on your way.'

Erlendur hesitated, at a loss as to how to retrieve the situation. As he dithered, the opportunity slipped from his hands.

'Good day,' said Kjartan, standing up.

'There's a chance I might be able to find out

what happened to Matthildur,' Erlendur inter-
jected hastily. 'With your help, that is.'

'Good day,' repeated Kjartan and stalked out of
the lounge and down the corridor towards his
room.

Erlendur sighed. He watched Kjartan's retreating
back. The man's objections were only fair: Erlendur
had no right to interfere in his life. Yet he couldn't
leave it at that. Even if Kjartan wasn't concealing
any knowledge that would help uncover further
details about Matthildur's fate, the fact remained
that he was an important link in the story.

A member of staff came in and asked if he could
help him, and Erlendur explained that he was on
his way out. He traipsed down the corridor, past
Kjartan's room. The old man had left his door
ajar and Erlendur paused outside. For an instant
he considered testing the old man's patience still
further, but in the end decided to leave well alone.

'Are you still there?' came Kjartan's voice.

Erlendur pushed the door open. Kjartan was
sitting on the bed, his eyes on the floor.

'There's not much to do here but listen for footsteps,' he said.

'I'm leaving,' said Erlendur. 'I just wanted you
to know that I'm not prying. I'm not some sort
of ghoul. And I'm not here in any official capacity.
I'm simply looking for answers. I've been in
contact with your aunt Hrund.'

'Yes, well, I don't know her.'

'So I gather.' Erlendur lingered in the doorway.

158

'What do you think happened to Matthildur?' asked Kjartan.

'I don't know,' said Erlendur, beginning to ease his way into the room. 'She probably died of exposure on the way to Reydarfjördur.'

'My mother and I didn't get along,' said Kjartan, 'so I left home as soon as I could. I know it sounds harsh but there it is.'

'Was that in part because you were aware of your father's identity?'

'Yes.'

'When did you find out it was Jakob?'

'Why do you need to know that?'

'I need to understand the bigger picture,' said Erlendur, choosing his words with care. 'Everything matters, especially details that seem trivial.'

'I've known ever since I was old enough to understand,' said Kjartan. 'I feel like I've always known. But I moved out east long after he died, so I never met him or heard from him as a child. I suppose I moved here partly because my parents used to live in the east and my mother always spoke well of the people here.'

'So she told you about Jakob?'

Kjartan nodded. 'Apparently he always denied being my father. I don't know why. Perhaps it was to do with his past. I've often wondered. I don't think my mother was lying. She didn't really know much about him – could hardly utter his name. She was full of bitterness, hatred even. It's not a very pleasant subject for me, as you can imagine.'

'No, I can understand that,' said Erlendur. 'You call yourself Halldórsson.'

'My mother was very lucky to meet such a decent man in Reykjavík. He was always kind to me.'

'Did your mother have any further contact with Jakob that you're aware of?'

'No, none,' said Kjartan. 'That would have been unthinkable. He rejected her, rejected her child. I can't blame her.'

'What about Matthildur then? They wrote to each other.'

'Did they? I wasn't aware of that, but then she died very young.'

'She didn't know about your mother's relationship with Jakob until your mother wrote her a letter telling her the whole story. By then she and Jakob had been married for some time. Naturally, the letter had repercussions. What did your mother say when Matthildur vanished? What did she believe had happened?'

'Have you uncovered something new?'

'No,' said Erlendur. 'Nothing.'

'She didn't know any more than the rest of them,' said Kjartan, his vacant gaze still on his threadbare felt slippers. 'Naturally she was beside herself with grief – I can remember that – but it goes with the territory when you live in Iceland. People accept it. At least, that was the attitude in those days. Still is, I believe.'

'There were rumours.'

'Yes, I know. I heard some of them when I came

160

out here. Aren't they just part of the whole syndrome? All this endless gossip? My mother never paid it any attention, nor did her sisters. I gather Jakob wasn't a very . . . how shall I put it? . . . easy man to get along with. The family were just sad not to be able to give Matthildur a proper funeral. I heard my mother say once that they'd have liked to have been able to bury her.'

'How did your mother react when Jakob drowned?'

'"Good riddance." That's all she ever said.'

Kjartan raised his eyes in the general direction of Erlendur's face.

'Since you're asking about reactions . . .'

'Yes?'

'I once looked up that aunt of mine who's always lived here. I had some idea about wanting to meet my relatives.'

'You mean Hrund?'

'Yes. It was the first and only time I met her. She was very cold. Said I must take after my father in looks, and she didn't mean it as a compliment. She claimed she couldn't see any resemblance to her family, then told me not to bother her again. I expect she must have been listening to gossip.'

'You never know.'

'I'm aware it sounds childish but . . . I've always felt hurt by that.'

Erlendur thought.

'I found an obituary of your father in the trunk.

His friend found plenty of kind things to say about him.'

'Was that the piece with "bastard" written across it?'

'Yes.'

Kjartan smiled bitterly. 'That was the start I got in life.' He turned to face Erlendur again. 'I'd like you to go now,' he said. 'And please don't bother coming back.'

CHAPTER 26

Erlendur left Egilsstadir towards evening. He was impatient to confront Ezra with Hrund's claims about his affair with Matthildur but decided it was rather late to pay him a visit and resolved to wait until the following morning. The question preoccupying him was whether Jakob had learned of their secret and, if so, how he had reacted. Had he found out before Matthildur went missing or had he remained in ignorance? Years later Ezra had told Hrund's mother the story of their relationship, but only after much pleading. Could he have told anyone else? Who else was in the know? Erlendur felt a certain trepidation, guessing that Ezra was unlikely to be cooperative. But he knew his insatiable craving for answers would overwhelm his doubts.

He stopped at the petrol station in Eskifjördur, where he bought a sandwich, filled his Thermos with coffee and topped up his supply of cigarettes. Then, on an impulse, he left the car where it was parked and strolled over to the graveyard which he had often visited on his trips here. It was situated on a slope on the outskirts of the village: an oasis of silence, enclosed by a handsome stone wall. Now, in the twilight, a thin dusting of snow lay on the ground but the grave inscriptions were still legible. As always he admired the austere, orderly beauty of the place, the hushed atmosphere, filled with the spirits of the departed.

Many years after that journey east with his father's coffin, his mother had passed away after a short spell in hospital. He had been at her bedside; had not left it since the day she was admitted. They had hardly spoken, but towards the end she sensed his presence and it was enough. She had always talked of being buried beside her husband Sveinn, in the plot that awaited her in Eskifjördur. So Erlendur had flown out with the coffin and, repeating his father's last journey, his mother was transported over the final stretch by lorry. The roads had improved little in the intervening years and by some extraordinary stroke of fate it was the same driver that had transported Sveinn to his last resting place. He was no less talkative now.

'Didn't you have your mother with you last time?' the driver asked. He was a brash, thoughtless man; all his actions were accompanied by the maximum noise and fuss. They had been lifting the coffin onto the back of the lorry when he made this remark.

'Yes,' Erlendur had replied. 'This time too.'

'Eh?' The driver looked puzzled.

Erlendur maintained a stubborn silence until the penny finally dropped.

'You mean . . .?' he asked, embarrassed and unable to complete the question. He drove much more considerately over the rough gravel roads than before, and they sat without speaking for most of the way.

The vicar who conducted the service was a genial man. Erlendur had never met him but they had discussed the main events of his mother's life over the phone. There were few mourners in church – just a handful of people who had known his parents or else distant relatives who were virtual strangers to Erlendur.

At last the coffin was lowered with slow ceremony into the ground.

'Make sure you take care of yourself,' his mother had said. She had been delirious until then, failing to recognise him: this was a brief moment of lucidity.

Erlendur had nodded.

'You don't look after yourself properly.'

'Don't worry about me,' he had said.

'Goodbye . . . my darling boy . . .'

She had fallen asleep with these words on her lips, only to wake up again shortly afterwards. Seeing Erlendur sitting at her side, she had tried to smile, then asked if he had found his brother.

'Bury him with us . . . if you find him.'

Less than a minute later she was gone.

He walked without haste across the small cemetery, leaving a trail of footprints in the soft snow. The headstone he had raised over his parents' grave was carved from basalt, its polished face inscribed with their names and dates. Beneath was a simple prayer or plea, depending on your point of view, for mercy: 'Rest in peace'. Erlendur still kept the old cross that had once marked his father's grave at his flat in Reykjavík. He had no idea how to dispose of it. Even after all these years he had never been able to bring himself to do so.

Lichen had grown on the headstone before him, birds had perched there, it had been weathered by northerly gales and caressed by southerly breezes to a worn, blurred grey. Time spares no one and nothing, thought Erlendur, running a hand over the ice-cold basalt. The stone would always bind him to this place.

He had transported it here from Reykjavík in his own car, following the unmetalled roads all the way east. It had taken him two days, with an overnight stay in the northern town of Akureyri. As it had always been his intention to erect a joint memorial to both his parents, he had never put up a temporary cross over his mother's grave. He had nothing but his own dilatoriness to blame for the shameful length of time that elapsed before guilt finally drove him to contact a stonemason. But there was a reason for his negligence. Deep down, he dreaded returning; the emotions his old home stirred up were too painful. When he did eventually brace himself to make the journey, however, it was as if he had broken a spell and since then he had visited at regular intervals, for shorter or longer periods. He had accepted now that he could never flee his past.

He had tried in vain for years to recall memories of their life before tragedy had struck. But after Bergur vanished the past had been obliterated, as if their life had not really begun until then. As the days turned into years, however, his recollections of the time before the disaster began to return with increasing frequency. Some were fleeting snapshots that he had difficulty pinning to a specific time or context. Others were clearer. Occasions like Christmas: his father wearing an Icelandic Yule hat; the tree they had decorated together; listening to a radio serial on a winter's evening. The images glimmered before his mind's eye like the dim flickering of a candle. An excursion to Akureyri. A boat trip to the island of Papey; his fear of the water. Summer days. Sitting on a horse; his mother's hand on the leading rein. The hay harvest. Men drinking coffee and smoking outside the house. He and Bergur playing in the sweet-scented hay in the barn.

Some of these memories aroused a sensation of profound loss that would return again and again to haunt him. As he stood by his parents' grave, he heard the far-off notes of a mournful refrain that he recognised as his father's violin, and saw his mother standing in the sitting-room doorway, her eyes half closed. A long summer's day behind them, their faces ruddy from the sun, the boys nodding off on the sofa. His father's hands moving with such sensitivity over the instrument. She tilted her head as she listened, her eyes on her husband.

'Play something cheerful now,' she said.

'The boys are falling asleep,' he protested.

'You can play quietly.'

Changing tempo, he embarked on a muted rendition of a spirited waltz. She listened smiling from the door, then went over and pulled him to his feet. He laid the violin aside and they danced together in the quiet room.

Bergur was dead to the world beside him, but Erlendur woke him so they could surreptitiously watch their parents treading the steps in silence, wrapped in each other's arms. They were conversing in whispers so as not to disturb the boys and his mother smothered a giggle. She found it easy to laugh. Bergur took after her. They were alike in so many ways; the same features, the same generous smile. Bergur was invariably sunny-tempered, unlike his brother who was inclined to be irritable, overbearing and demanding. Smiling did not come easily to him either; he took after his father in looks and temperament.

The memory was accompanied by the summery scent of newly mown grass and a sultry Icelandic heatwave. Earlier that day he and Bergur had been playing down by the river, walking along its bank and dipping their hands in the water to splash its refreshing coolness on their faces.

It was the last summer the four of them spent together.

Erlendur caressed the weathered basalt. An icy breath of wind stole down the slope and pierced his padded jacket. He glanced up at the mountains, pulling his coat more tightly around him, then hurried back to the petrol station. The weather forecast had predicted a drop in temperature for the east of Iceland, and the bitter gust was confirmation that it had arrived, sweeping down from the mountains like an ill omen.

CHAPTER 27

'Why are you lying here?'

Startled by the question, he peers towards the source of the traveller's voice, lost in the gloom.

'Are you still here?' he asks.

'I'm still here,' comes the reply.

'Why? What do you want from me?'

'I'll go when you do.'

'Where do you come from?' he asks.

'From far away,' says the traveller. 'But I'm going back this evening.'

CHAPTER 28

He started awake from a deep sleep, disturbed by the sound of a car. Day was breaking. He felt bleary and disorientated, having only managed to drop off shortly before dawn. A door slammed and he heard the snow creaking under approaching footsteps. The visitor was alone. Erlendur crawled from his sleeping bag. Snow had piled up in one corner of the room and the place looked miserably uninviting.

'Anyone at home?' called an instantly recognisable voice. Bóas's face appeared outside the broken window.

'Am I disturbing you?' he asked.

'Not at all.'

'I brought you some coffee and a Danish,' the farmer announced with a grin. 'Thought you might welcome a bit of company.'

'Come on in,' said Erlendur.

'You're too kind,' said Bóas, entering the doorless house and joining Erlendur in the remains of the sitting room. He was carrying a Thermos flask and a paper bag from which wafted a delicious smell. 'I brought two mugs just to be on the safe side,' he said. 'I wasn't sure how comfortably you live up here.'

'I get by,' said Erlendur, accepting a cup of coffee.

Bóas took in his sleeping arrangements – the blankets, sleeping bag and gas lantern. His camp was neat enough, if not exactly a suite at the Hilton. Erlendur had made a giant ashtray out of a milk churn that he had found on the property. It stood in one corner, the bottom filled with water, into which he chucked his stubs. Next to it was a folding chair and a few books piled on a dry patch of floor.

'I see you've made it nice and homely,' said Bóas. 'Have a thing about tramps, do you? Thinking of becoming one yourself?'

Erlendur smiled and took a bite of freshly baked Danish pastry. The coffee was strong and scalding hot. He sipped gingerly to avoid burning his tongue.

'It's not so bad,' he said. 'Thanks for the coffee.'

'You're welcome. Seen any ghosts?'

'There are always a few around.'

'The kids used to claim this place was haunted,' said Bóas. 'Back in the days when kids could be bothered to play outside and knew what a haunted house was. Though that's many years ago now. They'd come up here, light fires and tell ghost stories. A bit of hanky-panky went on too, of course, and illicit drinking.'

'They've scribbled graffiti on the walls,' said Erlendur.

'Yes, always the same old lovers' marks. But nobody comes here any more, as far as I know. Apart from you, that is.'

'And that's not often,' said Erlendur.

'It's a beautiful spot, though. Are you thinking of staying on?'

'Not sure.'

'Aren't you cold?'

'No, not really.'

'Forgive an old busybody – I don't mean to pry,' said Bóas. 'Anyway, I mentioned that matter you asked me about to some local hunters. You know, about whether foxholes and ravens' nests might provide any clues about your brother. But nothing came of it, I'm sorry to say.'

'No,' said Erlendur. 'I didn't really expect it to. But thanks for looking into it.'

'What about your case, how's that going?' asked Bóas.

'My case? You mean Matthildur?'

Bóas nodded.

'It's hardly a case. I don't know what to say, though it appears Ezra might be able to fill me in on a few things.'

'How's that?' asked Bóas, inquisitive as ever.

'I just got that impression after having another chat with Hrund,' Erlendur said, unwilling to reveal more than was necessary. He had no intention of bringing up Ezra's affair with Matthildur, though there was a chance that Bóas already knew. Still, it was a private matter and he had no wish to encourage rumours. 'It's just an idea,' he added, hoping to put Bóas off the scent.

'Do you think there was something fishy about it?'

'It sounds to me as if you think so,' said Erlendur, turning the tables. 'Or you wouldn't have reacted the way you did to my questions about Matthildur. After all, it was you who directed me to Hrund in the first place – when I said I was from the police.'

'I don't know any more than I've told you,' said Bóas, backtracking. 'I was just giving you the story from my perspective. I've no idea what did or didn't happen.'

'So – a puzzling incident and that's all there is to it?' said Erlendur.

'That's all there is to it as far as I'm concerned,' said Bóas. 'Will you be seeing Ezra again?'

'I'm not sure,' said Erlendur, certain now that Bóas had not come bearing gifts purely out of the goodness of his heart. It amused him how the old farmer feigned a lack of interest in the case, while utterly failing to hide his avid curiosity.

'I could go over there with you if you'd like,' Bóas offered.

'Thanks, but no. I wouldn't want to take up your time.'

'Don't worry about that,' Bóas said quickly. 'It's just that I know the old boy and I might have more luck persuading him to talk.'

'Somehow I doubt that, now I've met him,' said

Erlendur. 'With all due respect. Anyway, I've no idea if I'm going to see him again.'

'Well, just let me know if I can help,' said Bóas, preparing to leave. Plainly, he was not going to make any headway with Erlendur.

'Thank you again for the coffee and pastry.' Erlendur escorted him to the door, for all the world as if Bakkasel were his home again.

CHAPTER 29

This time there was no sound of hammering
from the shed below Ezra's house and
nobody answered when he knocked. After
rapping three times, he pressed his ear to the door.
Ezra's car was there and had clearly not been moved
since his last visit, as the snow still lay in a thick
layer over the bonnet and roof. There were footprints running from the house to the drive and down
to the shed, but as far as Erlendur could work out
they were not recent. He wandered down to the
shed where he had found Ezra pounding *hardfiskur*.
Loosening the small wooden toggle of the fastening,
he pushed the door open and it swung inwards with
a chilly creaking. Nothing had changed: there was
the stone, the stool and a heap of unworked fish.
The shed was crammed with a lifetime's accumu-
lated junk: tools and gardening equipment, old
scythes, a tractor's engine block, hubcaps and the
rusty bumper of some ancient vehicle. A stack of
logs stood in one corner, and two pairs of threadbare
overalls hung from nails on the wall.

Erlendur went over to the dried fish, tore off a
small piece, put it in his mouth and chewed it

with cool deliberation as he inspected the shed. It appeared that Ezra had not left the house in the last twenty-four hours. When Erlendur arrived, he had seen no tyre tracks running up from the road. Picking up the mallet that Ezra used to beat the fish, he weighed it in his hand.

Still holding the mallet, he walked back up to the house and knocked on the door again. No response. It was locked when he tried it and he remembered that it had been open before. He shook the handle, convinced the old man was at home.

He tried calling Ezra's name at the window, again with no result. All was quiet apart from the chattering of the birds that flocked around the house. He returned to the front door. The top half consisted of small, square panes of glass, covered inside by a curtain. Erlendur was about to raise the mallet to the pane nearest the lock when the door was wrenched open and Ezra appeared in the gap.

'What the hell are you doing with that mallet?' he demanded, glaring at Erlendur.

'I . . .' Erlendur did not get any further. This hostile reception was in stark contrast to his last visit.

'What do you want?' snapped the old man.

'I wanted to talk to you.'

'And what are you doing with that? You weren't planning to break in, were you?'

'I had a feeling you were at home and was

worried you might have had an accident,' replied Erlendur. 'Are you all right?'

'I'm much obliged to you,' said Ezra. 'But clearly I'm fine. Now bugger off and leave me alone!'

'Why do you –'

Ezra slammed the door in Erlendur's face, rattling the small panes. Erlendur stood there calmly, the mallet still in his hand. Then, turning away, he walked back down to the shed and replaced it on the workbench. He had not been lying to Ezra. His police experience and the recent incident with Hrund had taught him that the elderly could get into all sorts of difficulties without being able to raise the alarm.

Glancing around the shed again, he noticed a pair of battered wooden skis with leather straps and long bamboo poles. He had not seen their like for years and realised they must be very old. He ran an appreciative hand down them.

There was a crunching outside the door and Ezra appeared, an ugly expression on his face and a shotgun in his hand. Its barrel was pointing at the ground. Ezra was dressed as he had been at the front door, in slippers, vest and trousers held up by narrow braces.

'Get the hell out of here,' he said.

'Don't be an idiot.'

'Get out,' repeated Ezra, raising the gun.

'What's happened? What are you afraid of?'

'I want you to get lost. You're trespassing on my property.'

'Who've you been talking to?' asked Erlendur. 'What's changed? I thought we could have a chat.'

'She rang me – Ninna did – and warned me about your snooping,' said Ezra. 'I don't want you poking your nose into my affairs.'

'Fair enough,' said Erlendur. 'I can understand that.'

'Good. Then you can bugger off back to Reykjavík.'

'Don't you want to find her? Aren't you even curious about her fate? About what really happened?'

'Leave me alone,' said Ezra furiously. 'Stop prying and get lost!'

'Tell me one thing first – did Jakob know about you two?'

'For Christ's sake!' shouted Ezra. 'Give over, will you? Give over and bugger off!'

Raising the gun again, he aimed it at Erlendur.

'All right, keep your hair on,' said Erlendur. 'Don't make things any worse for yourself. I'll leave. But you know I'll have to report this. You can't go around waving guns at people. I'll have to talk to the police in Eskifjördur. They'll come down and confiscate it. They may even contact the firearms unit in Reykjavík and fly them out here. Next thing you know, the press will be having a field day. You'll find yourself all over the seven o'clock news.'

'Who the hell do you think you are?' demanded Ezra. His voice, lowered now, was filled with doubt

179

and amazement at the man who was standing in his shed, bold as brass, fiddling with his skis and making threats. 'Who the hell do you think you are?' he repeated.

Erlendur did not answer.

'I'm warning you – I won't hesitate to use it.' Ezra brandished the shotgun. 'I mean it, I won't hesitate!'

Erlendur stood, unmoving, and watched the old man.

'Don't you care whether you live or die?' exclaimed Ezra.

'If you were going to shoot me, Ezra – if you thought it would solve anything – you'd have done it by now. Why don't you go back inside before you catch cold? It's not healthy to stand out here dressed like that.'

Ezra blinked at him, not yet ready to give up.

'What the hell do you think you know about me?' he asked. 'What are you implying? You know nothing. You understand nothing. I want you to go. I don't want to talk to you. Can't you get that into your thick skull?'

'Tell me about Matthildur.'

'There's nothing to tell. Ninna fed you a pack of lies. You shouldn't listen to a word she says.'

'I talked to Hrund. She repeated to me what you told her mother. I know about your affair with Matthildur. I know you deceived Jakob.'

'Deceived Jakob,' echoed Ezra scornfully. The shotgun went down a notch. 'Deceived Jakob,' he said again. 'You talk as if he was the injured party.'

'For all I know he was.'

'But you don't know! That's the point. You don't know a bloody thing!'

'Talk to me, then. Tell me about Jakob.'

'I've nothing to say to you.'

'You told Matthildur's mother everything.'

'I told her in confidence. She begged me. Wouldn't stop going on at me. I never meant it to become common knowledge. She promised she wouldn't tell a soul.'

'How did she find out?'

'About me?'

'About you and her daughter?'

'Matthildur mentioned in passing that we were good friends and she put two and two together.'

'If it's any comfort, I don't believe she told anyone except her daughter,' said Erlendur. 'Hrund, that is. I don't believe it went any further.'

'Best keep it that way.'

'Are you sure? It was a long time ago.'

'Damned tittle-tattle!' said Ezra suddenly. 'What did they say about Jakob?'

'Nothing in particular.'

'Tittle-tattle!'

'What about Jakob?' asked Erlendur, spying an opening. 'What sort of man was he? Were you and his wife really involved? Matthildur's mother swallowed your story at any rate. Is it true?'

'True?' snapped Ezra. 'Of course it is! Is that

how you're going to twist things? Make me out to be a liar?'

'Then why don't you just tell me?'

'Are you implying I lied to Matthildur's mother?'

'I'm asking you: did you play a part in her disappearance?'

'Me?!'

'Is that such an unreasonable question? You were seeing her on the sly. She was married to your friend.'

'Now, look here –'

'Why don't you explain it to me, Ezra?'

'So you want to hear how we deceived Jakob?' asked Ezra, outraged. 'You want to hear how we deceived that poor sod? All right, then. Come with me. I'll tell you how we *deceived* Jakob. Then you can bugger off and leave me in peace!'

CHAPTER 30

Ezra did not relinquish his grip on the shotgun but laid it across his knees as he sat down facing Erlendur in the kitchen. Keeping his finger on the trigger, he stroked the barrel as he recounted his tale in a low voice. He had difficulty putting it into words, partly because he hadn't spoken of it for decades and was reluctant to do so now, partly because he had never really got over the events, though they had happened a lifetime ago. It was all so vivid – every detail, every conversation and incident, as if it had only just taken place. His account was punctuated by long silences that Erlendur was careful not to interrupt. Slowly, painfully, the story took shape. Ezra would not be rushed and Erlendur was content to let him dictate the pace.

The old man confirmed most of what Hrund had learned from her mother about how the affair had begun. The letter had been the tipping point, though Matthildur's marriage had already been showing cracks.

'Jakob was a mate of mine,' said Ezra. 'I don't remember if I told you before or how much you

183

know. I met him in Djúpivogur shortly after I moved out here to the fjords. He helped me out during my first season. I was the new boy in a strange place and got on well with him. As far as I knew, other people liked him too. He didn't really stick out from the crowd, though he . . . he was popular with the ladies. I don't know how else to put it. He had a way with women.'

'Perhaps that explains his bad reputation.'

'He didn't care if they were married. I saw him get into a fight once because of that.'

'Was it any different from your affair with Matthildur?'

'I wasn't like him,' said Ezra sharply. 'There's no comparison.'

'Do you remember Matthildur's sister Ingunn from your time in Djúpivogur?'

'No, not at all,' replied Ezra. 'Matthildur asked me that too. She showed me a picture of her. I told her Jakob had been a hit with the ladies, but I didn't know who. I moved to Eskifjördur long before he did. By the time he arrived he was already involved with Matthildur. We joined the same fishing boat and that's how I met her, after they were married. I used to drop by to fetch Jakob early in the morning, so Matthildur and I got to know each other.'

'Several people have tried to describe Jakob to me but I can't make him out at all,' said Erlendur. 'Someone told me he suffered from claustrophobia. Does that ring any bells?'

'Well, all I know is Matthildur told me he couldn't sleep with the bedroom door shut. He always kept it open and had to sleep on the side nearest to it.'

'It must have come as a terrible shock when Matthildur heard about him and Ingunn,' said Erlendur.

Ezra had grown visibly calmer, though he was still hugging the gun tightly. His defiance had largely evaporated, as if he were reconciled to there being no getting rid of Erlendur.

'Poor girl,' he sighed.

'One can feel for her dilemma.'

'Feel for her?' said Ezra quietly, as if to himself. 'How could you begin to understand? You don't have a clue what you're on about.'

Erlendur said nothing.

'Not a clue,' repeated Ezra.

More than two months had passed since Matthildur's disappearance and the search had failed to turn up any trace of her. Ezra had been crushed with grief since the second Jakob informed him that she was out in the storm. But he was isolated in his anguish; his secret beyond sharing. He had considered talking to the vicar but he had never been religious and the local priest was a stranger. So he sat at home, weeping silently. The grief came in waves, interspersed with feelings of fear and anger, helplessness and a bewildering sensation of being adrift. But worst of all were the bouts of recrimination, for there was no one he could blame but himself. He should have taken better care of her, should have been there to save her from her fate. What role had he played in her death? He had lured her away from her husband. Was that why she had gone out in the storm? He was tortured by guilt, though he tried to assuage his remorse by persuading himself that he could not have saved her; she would have made the journey regardless. Perhaps she had been destined to die like that. But no! Her journey must have been linked to their affair, to their forbidden love, to all that furtiveness and deceit. Why, oh, why hadn't they come clean straight away and simply moved in together? Why?

Jakob was the only person who could conceivably provide him with answers, but he couldn't for the life of him summon up the courage to approach him. He didn't trust himself. Perhaps he was afraid to hear the truth.

It was March, the days were growing longer and spring was in the air when their paths finally crossed. Until now, Ezra had avoided all contact with Jakob. He still mourned Matthildur desperately and thought about her every day, about the few, all too brief hours they had shared. They had just begun to discuss their future, the possibility of moving away, because it would be inconceivable to remain living near Jakob.

'We could move to Reykjavík,' she suggested one evening when she had stolen round to see him.

'Yes,' he said. 'Though they say it's almost impossible to find rooms. Everyone's flocking there to work for the army. Have you told him you're going to leave him?'

'I . . .'

'Do you want me to be there?'

'No,' she said.

'There's never a right time,' he said. 'It would be best to give it to him straight, as soon as possible. I'd do it for you if you'd let me.'

'It would sound better coming from me.'

'Hasn't he started to suspect?'

'I don't know. I don't think so.'

'What are you frightened of? That he'll get violent?'

'Not with me,' said Matthildur. 'It's you I'm afraid for.'

'He can't hurt me,' said Ezra. 'There's nothing he can do to me. I'm not scared of him, Matthildur.'

'I know.'

'I don't like it one bit. He's never done me any harm and I look on him as a friend. We used to work together. So . . . I'm not finding this easy. But I don't believe we have anything to be afraid of by telling him. We have to talk to him – make him understand what's happened. It's not as if it's unusual. People are always falling in love with the wrong person.'

'I know,' Matthildur said again.

They lay side by side under his blanket, quietly savouring the warmth from each other's body. A

187

diffident tap at his door had sounded towards midnight. He hadn't been expecting her and was delighted by her surprise visit. They had kissed; he had broken off to stroke her face wonderingly, then they kissed again, with growing intensity, until he half carried her to the bedroom. They did not even undress properly but made love with all the hunger and passion that she roused in him. She had to muffle the cries that rose to her lips, born of a rapture that she had never experienced with her husband.

'Jakob mustn't find out before we talk to him,' said Ezra as he lay beside her. 'He mustn't hear it from anyone else. We have to be honest with him before the news gets out.'

'I'll talk to him,' said Matthildur. 'I promise.'

'Let me come too. He's supposed to be my friend.'

'No, it's best if I do it alone. I'm sure it would be. I'll talk to him and tell him I'm going to move in with you. Explain that I can't stay with him after what's happened, after the news of him and Ingunn ruined everything. And because I've fallen in love.'

'All right,' he said. 'But I still want to come with you.'

'Stop worrying so much about Jakob. Concentrate on us instead. On the two of us.'

Then she was gone.

Then came the sunny day in March, two months later, when he bumped into Jakob. Ezra was passing the cemetery when he heard a voice hail him over the wall. Looking in, he saw Jakob working there in his shirtsleeves. He was preparing for a funeral that was to be held at the church the following day. A local man had died in his prime after a short illness and a good turnout was expected. Ezra went in through the gate.

'Where are you off to then?' Jakob asked, taking a break from his labours. He did odd jobs for the church, mostly maintenance and gravedigging.

Ezra explained and added awkwardly that he was in a hurry. He felt uncomfortable in Jakob's presence, tortured by the possibility that Matthildur had confessed their affair or he had discovered it by other means. They had been extremely careful but one could never be sure.

'I never see you any more,' said Jakob.

'I've been busy.'

'Working hard, eh?' said Jakob. 'The meek will inherit the earth all right. And that's us, Ezra. Workers like you and me.'

CHAPTER 31

Ezra did not register the question. His thoughts were far away, reliving that fateful graveyard meeting with Jakob and all the repercussions that followed. The encounter could probably never have been avoided, though coincidence had decided the time and place. Until that day it had loomed menacingly, as inevitable as death itself.

Ezra had broken off in mid-sentence. The cat prowled into the kitchen and stared suspiciously at Erlendur before deciding it was safe to climb into its basket.

Erlendur put his question for the third time and was finally rewarded with a reaction. Ezra looked up from his reverie. 'What did you say?'

'What happened next?' asked Erlendur.

'He invited me round to his house.'

'Did you go?'

Ezra did not answer.

'Did you go?' asked Erlendur again.

'There was an ugly note in his voice when he said it,' Ezra continued at last. 'But then Jakob was an ugly customer. A despicable man.'

★　　★　　★

Jakob took out a packet of cigarettes and offered it to Ezra who refused.

'Still don't smoke?' Jakob asked.

'Never got the hang of it,' replied Ezra, trying to smile.

'I buy them from the British. Pall Mall. Bloody good fags. Stjáni's kicked the bucket – I expect you've heard.'

'Yes, I'd heard. The funeral's tomorrow, isn't it?'

'Yeah. I've got to be done here by then. We're lucky with the weather.'

'Mm,' said Ezra, squinting up at the sun. 'Well, I'd best make tracks.' He turned with the intention of continuing on his way.

'Luckier than my darling Matthildur was,' remarked Jakob.

Ezra froze. 'What did you say?'

'It was good to see you,' said Jakob, with a note of dismissal, but Ezra did not budge.

'What was that you said about Matthildur?'

It was not his words that gave Ezra pause. They were commonplace, of no special significance. Jakob had every right to express such a sentiment. But it was his tone that made Ezra prick up his ears. It was not difficult to interpret, perhaps because he was alert to every nuance regarding Matthildur, especially where Jakob was concerned. There was no question: Jakob did not even attempt to disguise it. His tone was accusatory.

'There's so much I want to get off my chest about Matthildur,' continued Jakob, with the same

191

note in his voice. 'I'd like to have talked to you before but I get the feeling you've been avoiding me.'

'No, I haven't,' protested Ezra hastily – perhaps too hastily. He wondered if Jakob would pick up on his agitation, his accelerated heartbeat.

'Well, that's how it seems. All those times you were off sick. Then you suddenly quit the boat and go and get a job on shore. As if I'd offended you. As if we weren't mates any more.'

'You haven't offended me,' Ezra assured him. 'Of course we're still mates.'

Was Jakob deliberately turning the tables on him? It was Ezra who had done Jakob wrong: he and Matthildur had gone behind Jakob's back, betrayed his friendship and his trust. Perhaps keeping his distance had been a mistake. It was true he had been steering clear of Jakob. He had never once got in touch with his friend and had offered him no support after Matthildur went missing. He had quite simply vanished from Jakob's life, just as she had. On reflection, such behaviour was bound to have aroused suspicion.

'Well, that's a relief to hear,' said Jakob.

'What did you want to say about Matthildur?' asked Ezra.

'Come again?'

'You said you had a lot to get off your chest.'

'That's right,' said Jakob. 'I was thinking of holding a memorial service or – well, you can't really call it a funeral, she has to be officially pronounced dead first. And that can take ages. They have to make absolutely sure in circumstances like these, you see? But she'll never be found. Not after this long.'

'It's not out of the question,' objected Ezra. 'When the thaw comes.'

'And there's another matter I haven't told anyone about. I don't know how much I should say. It's . . . a bit awkward. I don't really know how to put it or who to talk to. There are so few people I can trust and . . .'

'What is it?'

'It's about Matthildur,' said Jakob. 'She'd been rather distant before she vanished.'

'Distant?'

'Yes, partly because of personal stuff. You know, the kind of problems that crop up in any marriage. Maybe you'll understand one day, if you ever get a woman of your own, Ezra.'

Again, Ezra detected that tone. And the choice of words: 'a woman of *your own*'.

'And partly for other reasons,' Jakob continued. His words were followed by a significant pause.

'What do you mean, other reasons?' asked Ezra at last, when it seemed Jakob did not intend to continue.

'I don't have any proof – nothing concrete, that is. But then I don't suppose men in my position ever do until the evidence is shoved under their nose. Right under their nose – you get me?'

'Men in your position?'

'Cuckolds, Ezra. I'm talking about cuckolds. Do you know what that means? To be a cuckold?'

Ezra was speechless.

Jakob flicked away his cigarette. 'It's when someone sleeps with your wife behind your back. Other people might be aware, but you, no, you're completely clueless. Then one day your wife decides to up and leave, just like that, like it's none of her husband's bloody business.'

Ezra was trying to hide his turmoil but had no idea if he was successful. He wanted to run away but was not sure his legs would carry him; his knees had turned to jelly. He was completely unprepared for this conversation and could not think how on earth to react.

'Are you saying that Matthildur . . .?' Ezra could not finish the sentence.

'I have my suspicions, that's all. They prey on my mind, day in, day out, but I'll probably never find out the truth. Not after what's happened. Not now.'

Jakob ground the cigarette butt under his heel.

'No, she certainly won't be found now,' he said, his eyes fixed on Ezra who again read blame in the other man's gaze, his words, his entire manner.

'Come round and see me,' Jakob said. 'There's something you should probably know.'

'What's that?'

'Drop by,' said Jakob. 'I have to finish up here.

Then we'll have a chat. I'm usually alone at home in the evenings.'

Ezra rocked in his chair, becoming distressed again. The memory was still so sharply etched. He could recall every word Jakob had said.

'I didn't know what to say. I didn't want to go and see him but of course I couldn't admit that, so I slunk off with my tail between my legs.'

Erlendur merely watched the old man. He noticed how choked with emotion he was, how gruelling it was for him to relive this. It may have been ancient history but it had shaped his life, perhaps more than he realised. It took a stranger, a detached onlooker, to recognise the paralysing impact of those long-ago events.

'Didn't you find the conversation a bit odd?' asked Erlendur eventually.

'I did at first,' said Ezra. 'I was confused. But it dawned on me later that he must know – must know about me and Matthildur. He dropped all those hints because he knew everything there was to know. Because she'd told him!'

'Did you go and see him?'

'Yes,' said Ezra, speaking almost to himself. 'In the end. I went to see him. And found out the whole truth.'

CHAPTER 32

The doubt, fear and dread that had tortured Ezra ever since Matthildur's disappearance assailed him with renewed vigour in the days following his bizarre conversation with Jakob. Sooner or later he would have to go and have it out with him. A dirty secret lay unacknowledged between them, and he must confront it however much he shrank from the thought. Uncertainty about how much Jakob knew had tormented him ever since Matthildur went missing back in January. There was no way of finding out what she might have said to Jakob except by asking him straight out. Perhaps he knew nothing; perhaps everything. Ezra's deepest fear was of learning that their affair had been to blame for Matthildur's rushing off. That it had caused a quarrel. During the months after she vanished the thought haunted him.

Three times he set out to see Jakob, only to turn back. The man's behaviour in the cemetery had disturbed and alarmed him. Ezra paced ceaselessly around his house, brooding endlessly on the question of why Jakob's words should have been uttered in that tone, why he had gone on about cuckolded husbands and insisted on explaining what the word meant, as if mocking him.

One evening he resolved to bite the bullet. He walked down the hill, just as he used to every morning when he collected Jakob for work; when, in spite of his shyness and inexperience, he had lost himself to Matthildur. He had been delighted and astonished by her response. She had made his timid fumbling so effortless that it had seemed as if their love was natural and predestined. Not a day had passed since when he had not been visited by her smile, by the movement of her hand, the look in her eyes, her walk, the sound of her laughter. He missed her desperately and wept over her fate – over both their fates – through the long, lonely evenings.

Seeing a light shining in Jakob's sitting room, he knocked at the door. The wind had changed and a cold, dry gust buffeted the village from the north. He rapped again and Jakob opened up.

'Why, hello, mate,' he said, inviting Ezra inside. 'I've been expecting you.'

The word 'mate' immediately struck Ezra as false. Jakob ushered him into the sitting room, picked up a bottle of *brennivín* once they were seated and filled two shot glasses. Downing his in one go, he refilled it straight away. It was evident that he had been drinking and Ezra remembered how obnoxious and aggressive he could get. Ezra drank sparingly, immediately regretting his decision to come. He should have chosen another time of day, when Jakob was less likely to be boozing. Glancing around, he noticed that the house was much messier than it used to be, the room strewn with dirty clothes, leftover food and unwashed dishes.

'Nice to see you,' said Jakob.

'How have you been?' asked Ezra.

'Shit,' replied Jakob. 'I'm in a hell of a state, let me tell you, Ezra. Life's no fun any more.'

'I can believe it's been a rough time.'

'Rough? You can't begin to imagine how rough it's been, Ezra. So damned rough. Let me tell you – let me tell you, Ezra, it's not exactly a laugh a minute losing a beloved wife like Matthildur.'

'I'm sorry if I've turned up at a bad time. Perhaps I should come back later. I need –'

'What? Leaving already? Relax. Drink up. I wasn't doing anything, just sitting here listening to the wireless. It's not a bad time.'

Ezra was silent.

'I'm not drunk,' said Jakob. 'I'm just a bit lonely.'

'Of course,' said Ezra.

Jakob pulled himself together, straightened his shoulders and started to speak, picking his words with care.

'I'm actually a bit surprised you were willing to come here,' he said. 'To see me.'

'Willing?' Ezra was wary. 'I wanted to give you my condolences –'

'Oh, really? How kind of you.'

'I wanted to know how you're getting on.'

'But that's not all, is it?'

'I . . .'

'You're curious about Matthildur, aren't you?'

'About Matthildur?'

'Don't play the fool.'

'I wouldn't dream –'

'Do you think I didn't know?'

'Know what?'

'Do you really believe, Ezra, that I didn't know about you and Matthildur?'

Jakob was suddenly sober. His expression was hard and unforgiving. With extraordinary bluntness and no real warning, Ezra's suspicions were confirmed. He had been dreading this news for so long that now, when the truth was finally out, it almost came as a relief.

'I wanted to talk to you,' said Ezra. 'That's why I'm here. We didn't want to hurt you. It just happened.'

'Didn't want to hurt me?' echoed Jakob. 'You didn't want to hurt me?'

'We kept meaning to tell you.'

'But you never did.'

'No. But Matthildur was planning to.'

Ezra realised how pathetic it sounded, as if it had been her responsibility. 'She wanted to do it alone,' he corrected himself. 'Didn't want me with her.'

'Do you know how I found out?' demanded

Jakob. 'Do you know how I found out I was a cuckold?'

'No.'

'How do you think that feels, eh? How do you think it feels when your wife's fucking another man? Your friend, for Christ's sake! How the hell do you think that feels?'

Ezra's mouth was dry.

'You were my friend, weren't you?'

Ezra still could not speak.

'Weren't you my friend?' persisted Jakob.

Ezra nodded.

'Oh, I noticed how you two used to behave when you came to fetch me in the morning,' Jakob continued. 'Do you think I didn't see how you gawped at her? I saw you mooning over her and I saw how she liked it.'

'She told me about her sister and the baby,' said Ezra. 'She was upset –'

'That was nothing but a pack of lies!' shouted Jakob. 'That kid wasn't mine! Her sister was lying. I screwed the bitch, that's true. I screwed her in Djúpivogur, maybe a couple of times. But it wasn't my child. And I had no idea they were sisters.'

'Matthildur was heartbroken,' said Ezra. 'That's one reason why she turned to me. She was angry.'

Jakob looked a mess – unshaven, unkempt and wearing only one sock, his checked shirt hanging out of his trousers. Realising that he was not in his right mind, Ezra felt it was unwise to carry on

200

talking to him. He was relieved to know where he stood at last but Jakob's current state could only make matters worse. He rose to leave.

'Maybe we should discuss this another time,' he said.

Jakob scowled at him. 'You're not going anywhere till I've had my say,' he snarled.

'I'm not sure this is the right –'

'Shut up!' shouted Jakob. 'Shut the fuck up and sit down!'

They eyed one another until Ezra finally gave in and sat down facing him.

'Do you know how I got proof of your dirty little affair?' Jakob asked. 'Have I told you?'

'No, you haven't.'

'I had my suspicions, of course. We'd quarrelled, me and Matthildur, about her sister and that bloody brat. I won't deny it. It changed our relationship but I thought we'd got over it. That is, until she saw some something in you. You! The reason it took me so long to twig what was going on was because it was you. Christ, Ezra! No woman's ever given you a second glance. What the fuck did she see in *you*?'

He probably deserved whatever Jakob threw at him. That was why he had come, after all – to hear the accusations and insults, to bear the brunt of his rage.

'It could have been any old shit, just not you. Anyone but you, Ezra. What would people think of me if she jumped into bed with a freak like you, who'd never been near a woman in his life? What would that say about *me*?'

Ezra did not dignify this with an answer.

'I went to Reydarfjördur and pretended I was going to stay overnight. Remember? Viggó, Ninna's husband, offered me a lift.'

Ezra still did not respond.

'Remember, you bastard?' Jakob yelled at him.

Ezra nodded. 'Yes, I remember.'

'Well, I went,' said Jakob, 'but I got a lift back later that evening and saw her sneaking off to your place in the dark. I saw you together, Ezra. I hung around outside your house like a fool and saw it all. Everything!'

'Why didn't you interrupt us? Why didn't you speak up?'

Jakob hung his head as if in defeat. 'Ezra . . . you think it's so easy,' he said, his voice gradually rising again. 'So cut and dried. Why didn't you interrupt us? Why didn't you speak up? What kind of questions are they? What was I supposed to say? Don't fuck my wife?' He was shouting now. 'Was that what I was supposed to say to you, Ezra?'

'I can understand that you were angry.'

'Angry?' whispered Jakob, more composed now. 'You haven't a clue, have you? But I bottled up my anger. Bottled it up till I needed it. I sloped off home and let my rage boil and churn till I thought it would choke me. No one gets away with treating me like that, though. I won't have it. I told her – I told her in plain words that I would not be treated like that.'

'Was that why she went to Reydarfjördur?' asked Ezra hesitantly, terrified of the answer. 'Was it because of us?'

'That's right, Ezra. That's why she had to go,' said Jakob, tipping the bottle down his throat. 'That's why she had to go on a long journey.'

CHAPTER 33

Ezra had put down the gun while he was relating the story. Erlendur was not sure if he was even conscious of having done it, so absorbed was he in the memory of that meeting with Jakob more than sixty years ago. He listened in silence to the old man's tale. Dusk was gathering in the kitchen. Erlendur was worried Ezra would catch a chill, sitting there in his vest, his slippers still wet from the snow outside. He asked if he had a jumper he could put on or if he wanted a blanket, but the other man did not respond. So Erlendur got up, found a blanket, draped it over Ezra's shoulders and took away the shotgun, placing it at a safe distance. It contained a single round which he removed. Ezra made no comment.

The minutes ticked away as they sat in silence, broken by nothing but bursts of grateful cheeping as flocks of sparrows discovered the seed Ezra had scattered on the snowy ground behind the house. Erlendur asked if he should put on some coffee, to no reply.

The pause became prolonged.

'I don't know if I should go on,' Ezra said at last, his voice tinged with melancholy. 'I've no idea why I'm raking this up now.'

Erlendur was about to remark that it might do him good to unburden himself of these long-suppressed memories but bit his tongue. He was in no position to judge.

'Because of Matthildur?' he suggested.

Ezra had been gazing out of the window at the moors but now he turned to Erlendur.

'Do you think so?'

'All these years you've never stopped thinking about her.'

'No, that's right. But there's a reason for that.'

'She disappeared.'

'Yes, she disappeared. But I've never got over the circumstances, and I never will.'

'People go missing all the time,' said Erlendur.

'People go missing,' Ezra repeated. 'If only it were that simple.'

He suddenly seemed to return to the present and notice that Erlendur had removed the gun and spread a blanket over his shoulders.

'Jakob may well have lied,' he said. 'I don't know. It's too late to tell now. Matthildur was never found. There's that. I've thought about it since. Maybe he was just torturing me. Maybe he enjoyed seeing me suffer. Got his revenge that way. He threatened to do the worst if I didn't keep my trap shut, and I believed him. I did as he said. I kept my mouth shut.'

Jakob banged the bottle down, keeping his eyes fixed on Ezra, and wiped his mouth with the back of his hand.

'Do you want to know what happened?'

'Yes.'

'Of course, you have a right to.'

'What happened? What are you on about?'

'I'm talking about Matthildur, Ezra. My darling wife Matthildur. Isn't that why you're here? You've hardly come to give me your condolences. Well, I'll tell you. Just be patient and I'll tell you the whole story. Because I want you to know. You've just as much right as I have. Maybe more. I was only her husband: you got to sleep with her! You got to fu—'

'I won't listen to any more of this filth!' exclaimed Ezra. 'Don't you dare talk about her like that.'

'Filth?' queried Jakob.

He started to relate, in meandering fashion, how their marriage had gradually come unstuck after Matthildur received her sister's letter. He had never succeeded in convincing her that he was not the child's father or that he had been ignorant that she and Ingunn were sisters. Now she pounced on his earlier behaviour as evidence that he had wanted to avoid all contact with her family from the outset. Jakob had not wanted any fuss over their wedding – no church service or reception.

They had got married quietly at the vicar's house in Eskifjördur. She accused him of being unfaithful to her as well and swore she would not be outdone.

'Next thing I know she's cheating on me with you,' said Jakob.

'Did you know Matthildur and Ingunn were sisters when you started seeing her?' asked Ezra.

Jakob sniggered. 'I tried to tell her.'

'What?'

'Her sister would have given the whore of Babylon a run for her money. There's no way the kid was mine! And I'll never acknowledge it.'

CHAPTER 34

The night he had pretended to be staying over in Reydarfjördur Jakob had waited up for Matthildur. He had come home late that evening and, noticing a light on in the kitchen, decided to lurk near the house. He had begun to suspect her of wanting to get even with him. Over the last few months her behaviour had changed: she had become colder and more distant, showed little interest in him, hardly bothered to answer when he spoke to her.

It had taken him a long time and a great deal of effort to persuade Matthildur that he had done nothing wrong; he maintained that he barely knew her sister and had been completely unaware that they were related; he had no part in the child she claimed was his. Matthildur had seemed to accept his explanation, albeit reluctantly, helped by the fact that she and Ingunn were not close. He took care never to refer slightingly to her sister, whom he remembered all too well from Djúpivogur. He had slept with her, but, not content with that, she had pursued him relentlessly until he told her to get lost; he was not interested in her.

Seeing the kitchen light go out, he wondered if the simple trap he had prepared for his wife had misfired. He was ready to abandon all hope of catching her out when he noticed the back door opening. Matthildur stole out into the garden and melted into the night. He followed at a discreet distance until she reached Ezra's place, where she tapped on the door. Ezra opened it and she slipped inside. The house was in darkness. Jakob knew the layout of the rooms. After a lengthy interval, he crept over to the building and peered warily through the windows, one by one, until he reached the bedroom. In the dim light he could just glimpse the shapes of two bodies writhing on the bed.

The rage did not come immediately. Instead he coldly registered the proof of what he had suspected. He should not have been surprised that it was Ezra's bed she sought out. He was a frequent visitor to their house, worked with Jakob, had no wife or children. So far as Jakob knew he had never been with a woman. Whenever he had pressed Ezra on the subject, his replies had been evasive. He had tried to tease him about it during the long days when the fishing was slow, but Ezra had refused to rise to it. Jakob regarded him as a good friend: the man he trusted with his life at sea.

No, the rage did not come straight away. Quite the opposite. He left Ezra's house and walked home slowly, more deeply preoccupied than burning with resentment. It did not occur to him to burst in on them and drag Matthildur away or attack Ezra. In some strange way he felt such behaviour would be beneath his dignity. He had no intention of crawling to them, begging for any favours. He didn't want to hear any grovelling excuses; didn't want to listen to any bloody whining.

Instead, he waited up. He took a seat in the sitting room, and the later it became, the longer Matthildur spent in Ezra's bed, the more his anger grew. In his mind he went over and over a hundred different scenes of what he would say, how he would act, and all the time his fury intensified. A wave of heat passed through him and he realised what it meant when they described a person as burning with rage. The blood seemed to boil in his veins. He leapt to his feet, paced the floor, then dropped into a chair again, trying to get a grip on himself, but more furious accusations erupted inside him against Matthildur for betraying him, for betraying their marriage, their life together. Springing to his feet again, he stormed around the room. Then there was Ezra. He didn't know how he would achieve it but he would make sure that Ezra would remember this betrayal for the rest of his life.

He was in such a frenzy of hatred that when she finally crept home the following morning, quietly closing the door behind her, he did not hear. She spotted him immediately and nearly jumped out of her skin. As soon as their eyes met she realised he knew. Quick as a flash, she turned and tried to open the door to run away to Ezra and to safety, but he caught her and knocked her down.

'Where do you think you're running to?' he whispered, hoarse with venom, slamming the door.

Matthildur tried to get up but he prevented her. Straddling her stomach, he put his strong workman's hands round her slender neck and squeezed, shaking her with all his might, so her head banged on the floor.

'To him?' Jakob snarled. 'Were you running to him? Do you really think he can help you now?'

Matthildur never managed to utter a single word in the face of his overpowering rage and a tirade of abuse. He tightened his grip until finally he sensed her body go limp. Her head dangled, strangely heavy and lifeless, and hit the floor with a dull thud. Loosening his hold, he stared down at her motionless body, oblivious to the passing of time. Little by little his blind frenzy abated and he came back to his senses. Rising to his feet, he looked at Matthildur, panting as if he had been running a race. At first he did not fully comprehend what he had done. He spoke to her and prodded her with his foot. Then gradually it dawned that she was dead. Her head lay at an odd angle. He was not sure whether he had strangled her or broken her neck. All he knew was that she was no longer alive.

In a state of shock he felt for a chair and sat down, trying to catch his breath. He didn't know how much later it was when the roar of the wind roused him from his trance. Going to the window, he looked up at the moors and began to work out a plan.

'Murderer!' exclaimed Ezra, jumping up and stumbling away from Jakob in revulsion. 'I didn't want to believe it. I didn't believe you could do a thing like that. That you had it in you.'

Jakob regarded him steadily. 'It's your fault, Ezra,' he said coolly. 'If you hadn't stolen her from me, she'd still be alive.'

'That's a damned lie!' Striding to the door, Ezra flung it open.

'Don't do anything stupid,' shouted Jakob after him. 'You'll only make it worse for yourself. For yourself, I said, Ezra!'

Ezra slammed the door behind him. Jakob sat unmoved in his chair. He pictured Matthildur's body on the floor and remembered how heavy she had felt when he lifted her. He waited, his eyes on the door. After a considerable time, it opened again and Ezra reappeared. Stepping into the house, he closed it carefully behind him.

'Why did you tell me?' he asked, walking towards Jakob. 'Why confess to me? How can I make it worse for myself? And why the hell are you so calm?'

Jakob's face wore an ugly smirk. 'You pathetic bastard,' he said.

'What have you done?'

'It would be the easiest thing in the world to pin it on you, Ezra.'

'What do you mean?'

'If you ever tell anyone it'll be worse for you,' said Jakob. 'I'll accuse you of murdering her. I'll tell them about your antics and how Matthildur was planning to end your sordid little affair, how she'd been anxious because she knew you'd make trouble. She was going to do it when she got back from Reydarfjördur but now I'm not sure she even made it as far as the moor. Maybe she ran into you and gave you the news, and you turned on her and beat her to death.'

Ezra gaped at Jakob. 'Nobody would believe you,' he said in a low voice.

'What about you, Ezra? Who'd believe you?'

Ezra eventually managed to force out the question: 'Where is she?'

'None of your business.'

'How could you do that to her?'

'No, Ezra, how could *you* do that to her?' said Jakob. 'It was your doing. You'd better remember that next time you try and steal another man's wife.'

'Where is she?'

'Get out.'

'Tell me what you did with her.'

'Get out – I've told you all I'm going to.'

'Tell me where she is, you piece of shit!' shouted Ezra.

'Out!' yelled Jakob, standing. The unnatural

self-possession had gone. 'Get the hell out of here and never let me see your fucking face again!'

Suddenly Ezra had charged him and the two men crashed to the floor, Ezra raining down blows on Jakob, who tried in return to claw his face. They thrashed to and fro until Jakob finally managed to get the upper hand. He landed a vicious punch in Ezra's face.

'Remember that, you shit,' he hissed breathlessly. 'It's all because of you. And don't you ever forget it, you bastard!'

He stood up. Ezra clambered to his feet, wiping the blood from his mouth and feeling his jaw tenderly. His whole face ached.

'You won't get away with it,' he said.

'You're a joke,' said Jakob. 'Get out of here. Go on. Fuck off.'

'You won't,' whispered Ezra again, backing out of the door. 'You'll never get away with it.'

CHAPTER 35

A hollow silence fell: the birds had departed from the garden. Dusk deepened around the two men in the kitchen while the cat slept on in its basket. Ezra's strength seemed to have dwindled with the daylight, his body to have shrunk in the chair.

'So you kept your mouth shut,' Erlendur said.

'Yes,' said Ezra. 'I never told anyone. That's the sort of lily-livered coward I was.'

'You shouldn't have kept quiet about a crime like that, however involved you were. A cover-up does no one any good.'

'I don't need you to tell me that.'

'And so the years passed?'

'Yes, they passed.'

Erlendur realised how traumatic this must have been for the old man after a lifetime of guarding his secret. For sixty years he had concealed Jakob's crime, even after the man died, for fear of being incriminated. He had chosen the easy course and saved his own skin, and yet Erlendur felt some sympathy for his plight. Had Jakob followed his threat through, things might have gone badly for

Ezra. He was, after all, in a vulnerable position, having betrayed his friend and stolen his wife. A vengeful man like Jakob could have pointed the finger at any time and forced Ezra to defend himself against serious charges.

'I lost my nerve,' Ezra said. 'I was frightened. Terrified, I should say. I couldn't bear the thought of our affair being exposed and judged as dirty and squalid. I was so scared Jakob would spread stories about me, accuse me, brand me a murderer. He bullied me into silence. He told me the truth, but only after making sure I'd feel so guilty I'd hush it up. Well, he got what he wanted.' Ezra broke off briefly. 'He won. He defeated us both.'

'What did he do with her body?'

'He wouldn't tell me. Claimed he'd planted something on Matthildur to frame me and said he could notify the authorities any time he liked. I didn't know what it was and still can't work out if he was lying. But that's what he said and I was in such a state that I believed him.'

'So you still don't know where she is?'

'I've never known.'

'So first you lose Matthildur, then this is flung in your face?'

'Jakob . . . was an evil bastard.'

'And you had to go on living so near him.'

'Yes, it was hard. Of course I had nothing to do with him, or as little as I could help, and he moved away for a while. Perhaps he was just as scared that I'd go to the police as I was that he'd spread lies about me. It was like a Cold War between us. He said . . .' Ezra hesitated.

'What?'

'He said he'd make sure I suffered too. Make sure I was punished. And he succeeded.'

'You weren't tempted to move away, back to the west, or to Reykjavík? It would have been easy during the war. You could have lost yourself in the crowd – as far as that's possible in this country.'

'I couldn't bring myself to move.' Ezra's voice had sunk to a mumble again. 'Not while I knew Matthildur was here somewhere. I couldn't bear to leave her. Because her body was never found, it's as if she never really left. Can you understand that? I know it sounds like gibberish but it feels as if she's still here with me. I sense her presence every time I go about the streets, or look out to sea or up at the mountains. She's everywhere. She's all around me.' He paused, then added: 'I'll be dead soon anyway, and then it'll all be over.'

'You have no inkling where she is?' asked Erlendur again.

Ezra shook his head.

'Are you sure?'

'You think I'm lying?'

'No,' said Erlendur. 'I don't think you're lying. But since you said yourself that Jakob threatened to frame you, it would be in your interest that she was never found.'

'You policemen!' exclaimed Ezra. 'You're so used to suspecting everyone, doubting everything. I bet you think I've been lying all along – that I did away with Matthildur myself and I'm just using Jakob as a scapegoat. Is that what's going through your mind? That I've turned the story on its head?'

'You're reacting –' began Erlendur, but got no further.

'There was nothing I could do,' interrupted Ezra. 'Until Jakob died it hung over me like a death sentence. But what he'd done couldn't be undone. Matthildur was dead, gone. Involving the police wouldn't have changed that.'

'So you accepted Jakob's story?'

'Yes.'

'You told me earlier that you were sure he could never have harmed Matthildur. Was that part of the deception?'

Ezra nodded.

'And you've never doubted his account?'

'Doubted? Doubted what? That he killed Matthildur? Not for one second. I know he told the truth about that at least.'

'But you never had any proof. Maybe she died in the storm and he used the fact to torment you for the affair. Has that occurred to you?'

'I'm certain he told the truth,' repeated Ezra obstinately, scowling at Erlendur.

'You felt guilty. Did you have your eye on Matthildur before she made a move? Was that why?'

'My eye on her?'

'Did you drop hints?'

'What do you mean?'

'Did you flirt with her? Let her know you were interested?'

'Certainly not.'

'So you did nothing about it?'

'No,' said Ezra slowly. 'If she sensed it –'

'But you weren't exactly averse when she did turn to you?'

'No.'

'Was that it? You had a guilty conscience about enticing her away from her husband and Jakob played on that?'

Ezra did not answer.

'It must have come as quite a relief when he died,' said Erlendur.

Ezra refused to be provoked.

'Or perhaps the opposite? Because he was the only one who knew where Matthildur was?'

'Exactly.'

'And he took the secret to his grave.'

'That's right.'

'Were you here when it happened – when Jakob drowned?'

'Yes, I remember it well.'

'His body was stored in the ice house in the village.'

'Yes, before he was taken to Djúpivogur for the funeral. Then it was over.'

'Did you see his body?'

'Yes, I was working at the ice house at the time.'

'And you never found out what he did with Matthildur?'

'I couldn't get it out of him. That's all I ever wanted to know, but I don't suppose I will now.'

Erlendur looked in the direction of the moor, now shrouded in darkness.

'At the end of the day it was my fault she died,' whispered Ezra. 'I'm to blame. I've had to live with that ever since.'

CHAPTER 36

The day they are due to move to Reykjavík, he comes down from the moors for the last time and helps his father with the packing. For once he has not been searching for clues but saying a private goodbye to the world that contains both his happiness and all his sorrows. He set out early that morning, at first light, taking care not to wake his parents. It is a beautiful summer's day but his mother dislikes him traipsing around up there on his own, as she calls it. Only two years have passed since she lost her younger son and the elder must not be allowed to go the same way. But that is not the only reason for their move; there are others.

His father is uncommunicative as he carries their belongings out to the small pickup. It is a newish vehicle which has been sold to a buyer in Reykjavík. They have agreed to deliver it on condition that they are allowed to use it to move house. Only the bare essentials are going south: beds, tables, chairs and family heirlooms. The rest has been given away or thrown out. Some odds and ends can be replaced once they reach town. The small number of livestock has also been sold, along with the mower and hay wagon, but his mother is taking her treadle sewing machine on the grounds that it will come in useful wherever they end up. As ever it falls to her to try and lighten the atmosphere. But he senses that she often finds it an effort, and there are times when it is beyond even her, like when the young couple came to pick up Bergur's bed. They had decided to donate it to a needy family, and his mother kept herself busy in the kitchen when the shy and diffident couple arrived to collect it. 'There's no point taking it with us,' his mother had said. 'Anyway, their need's greater than ours.' But there are other belongings of Bergur's that she will refuse to part with for the rest of her life.

Erlendur is in the dark about exactly when the decision to move was taken. The first time he heard his parents discussing it was about six months ago. It was his mother's idea. She wants to get away from the village, but it is not enough to go to the next fjord or county – every feature of the landscape reminds her of the son she has lost. She wants to go as far away as possible, preferably to a place where she can shake off her torpor and start living again, a life that is fresh and stimulating and unlike anything they have experienced before. That place is Reykjavík.

His father has little to say on the subject. He agrees to the move almost without comment. He is a changed man since he came down from the moors, and it is not only because he lost his son. He has looked death in the face and this near-miss has had as profound an effect as the loss of his son, as if he has become reconciled to the fact that he must die.

The couple talk to Erlendur, who is deeply opposed to the plan. He feels they are betraying Bergur by leaving, as if they would be abandoning him. His mother dismisses this as nonsense; he will always be with them, never out of their thoughts. She tells him that they need a change, a new environment, without loss as their daily companion.

He really has no choice. What does a twelve-year-old boy know about Reykjavík? That there are more cars and bigger shops than he can begin to imagine, and huge houses called blocks, where people live all crammed on top of one another. There are more buildings than he can count and slums where the poor live in rat-infested Nissen huts left behind by the occupying army. But there are broad streets too and policemen directing the traffic. And lots of cinemas and theatres, and a throng of jostling people, and what his mother refers to as fashion boutiques. And schools that stay open all winter with as many as a hundred pupils. It is a terrifying prospect. The city holds no allure for him. He has heard that some dream of moving there but he is not among them.

Then the summer's day arrives when they are to close the door of their home for the last time. His mother says her final farewell to the place by making the sign of the crucifix, then they climb into the pickup and jolt off down the drive. He sits between his parents, who do not exchange a word as Bakkasel recedes into the distance behind them. The silence accompanies them all the way to Egilsstadir where his father stops at a garage and announces in an unnaturally loud voice, 'I need to top up the oil.' His mother says she will stretch her legs in the meantime. Erlendur follows her a few paces behind, too old now to hold her hand in the sight of others. She stops by the side of the road and contemplates the River Lagarfljót where it broadens into a milk-white lake before flowing down to the sea in the course it has followed for the last five thousand years. Eventually she begins to cry, so quietly that he hardly notices.

He slips his hand into hers.

'Please don't cry.'

'It's nothing,' whispers his mother.

These are their last moments in the district. Soon they will have left for good. Best say it now.

'I think we're doing the right thing,' his mother says, pulling a small handkerchief out of her pocket. 'But you can never be sure. I don't really know what I'm dragging you two into.'

'We'll never forget him.'

'No, of course not,' she says. 'Of course not.'

They stand there together, looking out over the milky water, and his thoughts return yet again to the words he uttered to his father before they set off for the moors. All because of those stupid toys and the squabble over the little red car. He has not told his mother what he said and the guilt has been gnawing away at him ever since, overwhelming all other sorrows, even after all this time – two whole years of his short life. His father seems to have forgotten that it was Erlendur who gave him the idea, who insisted on it. Or perhaps he remembers but does not want to speak of it. He is a man of few words and never refers to what happened.

Far beyond the lake, further than Erlendur's eye can see or his imagination can stretch, lies his future.

He turns to his mother and casts his mind back to their home, remembering every detail. Music was playing on the radio in the kitchen. His father had begun to pull on his outdoor clothes. The evening before, his father had said that he needed to find those ewes before they froze to death, because they were not going to bring themselves home. Now, in the morning, he was standing in the bedroom doorway, putting on his coat, when he announced that Erlendur was to accompany him. He would have to dress up warm as it was chilly outside.

Erlendur looked up from what he was doing.

'Then Bergur must come too,' he said automatically.

His father paused. Obviously it had not occurred to him to take his younger son. He had so much else on his mind.

'All right, he can come.'

It was settled. Nothing further was said. Their mother's objections were overruled: both boys were going with their father. Erlendur was pleased.

His pleasure did not last long. The words had been echoing in his mind ever since he was brought down from the moors and discovered Bergur was missing. He could hardly believe he had said it. Was it all his fault? A crushing sense of guilt oppressed him, mingled with a strange feeling that first crept up on him then grew relentlessly: that he did not deserve to be saved instead of Bergur. His body turned rigid and started to tremble and he was helpless to stop it. He went into shock. The doctor was called out.

Then Bergur must come too.

His father calls to them – he is ready to set off again – and his mother signals that they are coming. She is about to turn when Erlendur grips her tightly, holding her back.

'What's the matter?' she asks.

He fixes his eyes on her. His heart pounds in his chest; he is terrified of the consequences of what he is about to say. He has wrestled with it over and over again during the dark winter days and long sleepless nights but still cannot predict how she will react. The enormity of the problem is too much for his young mind.

'Come on,' she says. 'We've got to go.'

But he clings onto her hand for dear life. She doesn't know that it is his fault Bergur went with them. The words are on the tip of his tongue; all he need do is utter them. Tears well up in the corners of his eyes. His mother, sensing that something is wrong, brushes the hair from his forehead.

'What's the matter, my darling?' she asks.

He doesn't know what to say.

'Don't you want to move to Reykjavík?'

His father is sitting in the cab with the engine running, watching them through the window. The attendant who filled up the oil is standing by the pump, looking their way as well. The whole world seems to be staring in their direction.

'Erlendur?'

He catches the look of profound anxiety on his mother's face. The last thing he wants, the very last thing, is to add to her worries. Just when their life has regained a degree of peace, of acceptance.

His father honks the horn.

The moment has passed. He pulls himself together and dries his eyes.

'It's all right,' he says. 'Just a bit of grit.'

They walk back towards the pickup. The pump attendant has vanished and his father is facing straight ahead with both hands on the wheel. It will be a long drive on bad roads.

Erlendur sits quietly between his parents as they cross the bridge over the river.

From now on he will bear his guilt in silence.

CHAPTER 37

Ezra had told him about a farmer whom Bóas had neglected to mention when listing the locals who knew the foxholes in the area. The reason for this oversight, according to Ezra, was that Bóas hated the man so much he could hardly utter his name. The animosity dated back to a boundary dispute over a piece of land that Bóas had inherited. The dispute had ended up in court where, having lost ignominiously, Bóas had sworn he would never speak to his adversary again, a promise he had kept for at least a quarter of a century.

The farmer, Lúdvík, a man of around Erlendur's own age, gave him a surly welcome, though whether because of the long-standing feud with Bóas or because he had interrupted him at work was unclear. Lúdvík was in one of his sheds, toiling over a dismantled hay baler. He explained that it had broken back in the summer but the replacement part had only arrived in the post a few days ago. What kind of service was that? His wife had directed Erlendur to the shed, asking him to remind her husband about choir practice later that day. Erlendur passed on the message.

'Choir practice!' snorted the man. 'I'm not going to any bloody choir practice!'

Erlendur had no answer to this and couldn't tell if the man expected him to report his intentions to his wife. Lúdvík embarked on a tirade against choirs in general, but especially male-voice choirs, with their ridiculous demands on one's time for rehearsals and tours. It was all very well for the rest of their members who were old sods with nothing better to do than organise endless meetings, but he had a farm to run.

'Sing in a choir yourself?' he asked Erlendur. 'You look the right age.'

'No, never have,' said Erlendur.

'Here for the fishing?' Lúdvík asked next, changing the subject seamlessly.

'God, no,' said Erlendur. 'I . . . As a matter of fact, I wanted to pick your brains about foxes. I gather you're an experienced hunter.'

'Foxes? You'd do better to talk to a man called Bóas. Have you come across him?'

'I've already spoken to him actually.'

'Barking, isn't he?'

'You could put it like that,' Erlendur said diplomatically, 'though he's been very helpful to me.' He didn't want the man to bad-mouth Bóas any further in his hearing.

'Bóas is a prat,' said Lúdvík contemptuously.

'Well, that's not how he struck me.'

'So what do you want to know about foxes?' asked Lúdvík, putting down the part that he had detached from the baler and wiping his hands on an oily rag. 'You're not from round here, are you? Reykjavík?'

Erlendur nodded. He had been wondering in vain how to phrase his request without either sounding completely ignorant or revealing too much.

'Not many foxes there,' commented Lúdvík.

'No, and I know next to nothing about them myself, so Ezra suggested I have a word with you.'

'Ezra?' Lúdvík seized on the name. 'Know him, do you?'

'Pretty well,' said Erlendur, feeling this was no exaggeration. He probably knew more about Ezra than anyone else in the world.

'Oh, right, so *he* directed you to me?' said Lúdvík, in a mollified tone. 'How is the old boy?'

'All right, I believe.'

'Salt of the earth, Ezra. Always willing to help out, however big or small the problem. So, what do you want to know?'

'I wanted to ask if you'd ever found any interesting objects in a fox's earth or heard stories about other people finding things . . . things the animals might have dragged home with them. You know, the kind of stuff they might pick up around farms and villages or up on the moors.'

Lúdvík gave him a quizzical look.

'Of course, you can find all sorts in earths,' he said. 'You know the old saying: "The fox lurks in its hole, gnawing the whitened bone."'

Erlendur nodded.

'Are you after anything in particular?'

'I'm interested in objects with a connection to humans – remnants of clothing, shoes or boots, maybe; the kind of rubbish we leave lying around.'

'It happens,' said Lúdvík, 'though the fox isn't as big a thief as the raven.'

'Have you ever found a boot or anything like that in a fox's earth?'

'A boot? What kind of boot?'

'Well, not necessarily a boot,' said Erlendur. 'But that sort of thing.'

'A specific type of object?'

'No, nothing specific. Anything a person might drop and a fox pick up. I just wanted to ask on the off chance, in case you'd heard of any unusual bits and pieces from other hunters. I've recently developed an interest in foxes, you see. If you remember any examples, it might be useful. Even unusual bones.'

'Can't think of any in recent years,' said Lúdvík.

'What about in the past?'

'Nothing springs to mind. But you could try talking to Daníel Kristmundsson. He lives in Seydisfjördur – an old rascal who used to do a lot of guiding for hunters in the area.'

'Daníel?'

'Yes, he might be able to help. Assuming the old bastard hasn't croaked yet.'

'Well, that was all,' said Erlendur. He thanked Lúdvík for his help and said he wouldn't bother him any longer. Feeling relieved to have got the conversation out of the way, he edged towards the door. He felt uncomfortable discussing the subject with a stranger.

'There's one fact not everybody knows about foxes,' said Lúdvík, becoming suddenly preoccupied. 'I don't know if you're thinking along the same lines.'

'What?' asked Erlendur, pausing.

'The fox is a scavenger.'

'Really?'

'It's not fussy when it comes to carrion and can drag bits back to its earth, if that's what you're getting at. It can carry pretty heavy loads – I've seen a fox running along with the forequarters of a lamb in its mouth.'

'You mean lambs or ewes or . . .?'

'Whatever. Birds too. But the fox isn't a true scavenger. It doesn't leave all the hunting and killing to other animals – it's an incredibly skilled predator in its own right. But it'll eat carrion. We often find the bones of lambs, even of fully grown sheep, that it's brought back to its hole. Though I'm not quite sure what you're driving at when you say unusual bones,' said Lúdvík. 'Do you mean the bones of animals – or humans?'

Erlendur shook his head. 'That was all,' he repeated, making for the door. He had heard enough and the visit had lasted too long already. He didn't want to hear another word: the thought of scavengers was too gruesome.

'I haven't found any arms or legs, if that's what you're asking,' continued Lúdvík, 'though it's not out of the question that a fox would go for that sort of food – if a person had died of exposure in the mountains, which used to happen a lot around here in the old days. I've even heard tales –'

Erlendur fled, leaving Lúdvík with a puzzled expression. He hurried back to his car. With those few, brief words the farmer had summoned up a picture so horrible that Erlendur would have given anything to be able to expunge it from his mind.

CHAPTER 38

That evening he sat in the derelict farmhouse, warming himself at the gaslight, slurping at a mug of hot coffee and taking half-hearted bites at a smoked-lamb sandwich from the convenience store. He had little appetite and soon abandoned the sandwich and lit a cigarette instead. He pushed the meeting with Lúdvík to the back of his mind, telling himself it would do no good to obsess about the habits of foxes.

Meanwhile, Ezra's story would not leave him alone. Erlendur felt inclined to believe the old man's account: one only had to listen to Ezra for a minute to feel his torment, the terrible uncertainty he had lived with so long, the deep guilt that had plagued him for most of his life. It seemed certain that Jakob had killed Matthildur and taken the knowledge of her body's whereabouts to his grave. For Ezra, there had never been any sort of closure and it was only too apparent that his wounds were still raw, even after the passing of more than sixty years. He was old now and, judging by his constant references to his imminent death, no longer expected to live to hear the end of the story – should Matthildur ever be found. Ezra admitted he had given up searching for her decades ago.

Erlendur refilled his mug and drank slowly. Jakob had got away with murder, there was little doubt. What's more, he had arranged it so that he could confess it to Ezra, torture him with the knowledge, accuse him and tie his hands at the same time. He had taken advantage of the lucky circumstances – the storm and the disaster that had befallen the British servicemen. He had shown incredible audacity in the way he lied about Matthildur's movements. And he had known just how to apply pressure to Ezra's vulnerable point: his affair with Matthildur and the betrayal of his friend.

The most obvious flaw in Ezra's testimony was that he could not call on anyone to confirm it. There were no witnesses; he had never shared what happened with anyone and he was now the only living person who knew the facts. His statement would stand or fall by his own credibility. Erlendur considered calling a halt at this point: he supposed he had been fairly successful in his inquiry, though, strictly speaking, he was not really investigating Matthildur's disappearance; rather, he was satisfying his own curiosity, aware that no one could be held to account at this late stage. The case had been subject to a conspiracy of silence for a lifetime.

Yet Matthildur's story had touched a nerve with Erlendur; he felt he could relate to her fate and this feeling had given him a sense of connection to the case – though he didn't really know what was driving him on. Perhaps it was the thought of Ezra's dismal plight: doomed to live on in the wreckage of his lost love. If what he said was true, he had only ever learned half the story. And Erlendur knew how unbearable life could be on those terms.

He thought about Jakob's revenge; how he had trapped Ezra and made him an accessory to his deed, though Ezra had done little to deserve it. Jakob had committed a crime of passion, probably performed without premeditation. These crimes were generally committed in a fog of madness. But what had followed had been a calculated act of vengeance: Jakob had arranged it so that the person he believed bore all the blame would never experience another day of happiness.

Or perhaps it was the love story that had caught Erlendur's imagination. The love between Matthildur and Ezra denied a chance to blossom, cut short with such brutality.

During the afternoon the wind had picked up and was now making a low keening in the eaves. Erlendur reviewed all that he had uncovered by tracking people down and asking questions about Matthildur, Ezra and Jakob. His thoughts did not follow any coherent path: the individuals he had met, their stories and circumstances became mingled with the East Fjords fog and the blizzard, with his sojourn in the ruined farm, his journeys on foot and by car, the freighters sailing into Reydarfjördur and the astonishing, ever-present signs of industrial development. All these elements

236

coalesced in his mind until, abruptly, he was brought up short by three minor details to which he had paid scant attention at the time. One was the reference to Ezra's former workplace. The second was a comment, uttered during a conversation, which Erlendur had hardly taken in. But for the wind moaning in the roof he would have forgotten it completely. After he had been listening to the noise for a while, puzzled as to what it reminded him of, a memory suddenly surfaced: someone had heard a noise coming from Jakob's coffin. The third detail was a remark that Ezra had let fall when they were talking about Jakob's death and how his body had been stored overnight in the ice house where Ezra worked. It was an innocent statement about Matthildur's whereabouts that held no significance at the time: *I couldn't get it out of him.*

'Is it possible?' Erlendur whispered into the gloom.

He rose from his camp chair in sudden agitation.

'Was he talking about the ice house?' he asked aloud.

Oblivious to the passing hours, Erlendur wrestled with these three ostensibly trivial threads, trying to find a link between them and growing ever more perplexed until finally he stubbed out his last cigarette and decided that he would have no choice but to impose on Hrund one more time.

CHAPTER 39

In the middle of the night he wakes with a jolt from a dream and blinks at his surroundings. He sees only darkness beyond the lantern's ring of light but can still sense the presence of the boy in his dream. At first he isn't sure whether he has been asleep and dreaming, or whether it was something else. A sudden dread seizes him, followed by a flood of relief when he realises it was only a nightmare. Curiously, it had felt like the re-echo or revisiting of a dream he'd had in the most wretched period of his youth, which he has never forgotten.

In the dream, which shocks him so violently awake, he is lying on his side, alone in the house in his sleeping bag, covered by a blanket. The house is open to the elements. It is dark and eerie. All at once he feels a presence behind him. Turning deliberately, he peers blindly into the blackness, until a vision materialises of a dejected-looking boy whose eyes meet his.

The vision vanishes.

Erlendur lies in the darkness, meditating on the dream that had woken him once long ago with such a terrible start. He recognised the boy in the vision: it was himself.

238

CHAPTER 40

When he arrived at lunchtime to see Hrund in the hospital at Neskaupstadur, she was asleep. Unwilling to disturb her, he took a seat by her bed and waited for her to stir. He couldn't entirely shake off the chill that had gripped him when he woke early that morning and drank the dregs of the cold coffee in his Thermos. He had resorted to hurrying to the car and using the heater to thaw out before driving into the village to visit the swimming pool. It had been his morning routine for most of his stay, but he only used the showers, never set foot in the pool itself. The staff respected his privacy, wishing him good morning but never displaying any curiosity or trying to strike up a conversation. This time he stood for longer than usual under the jet of hot water, trying to restore the circulation to his body. Then, having dressed again, he went and ate breakfast at the petrol station and refilled his Thermos before heading off to Neskaupstadur.

Through it all he had been wrestling with the theory that had taken shape during the night. He had been quite excited when it first occurred to

239

him, but the more he thought about it, the more implausible it felt. If it were true, it would mean abandoning several of his preconceptions, including his instinct about Ezra. On the other hand, he knew enough about cold and its impact on the bodily functions, particularly the heart and circulation, to appreciate that they could slow down almost to a standstill without resulting in death or damage, so long as intervention was made in sufficient time.

Hrund opened her eyes and saw that she had a visitor. She pulled herself up a little in bed.

'You again?' she said.

'I won't bother you for long,' Erlendur assured her.

'It's all right,' she said. 'People aren't exactly queuing up to see me.'

'My visit isn't entirely altruistic,' he admitted.

'I guessed as much. I haven't lost my marbles yet. What is it now?'

'Various ideas I've been mulling over.'

'I don't suppose they'll be the last,' Hrund said.

'I met Ezra again and we had a long talk. He's not a happy man – hasn't been for a very long time.'

'No, I can imagine.'

'We spoke a lot about his friend Jakob.'

'Could he tell you any more about Matthildur?'

Erlendur paused. Ezra had confided more in him than he ever had in anyone else and Erlendur had no intention of betraying his trust. It would be better to massage the truth or evade the questions, regardless of who was doing the asking.

'He said a great deal about Matthildur. How much he misses her and always has. He was desperately in love with her. Was there ever another woman in his life?'

'No, never,' said Hrund. 'Ezra's always been a lone wolf. Does he know any more about what became of my sister?'

'Nothing that we can be sure of just now,' said Erlendur. 'Though things may become clearer in time.'

'Well, if you don't intend to fill me in, why did you come?'

'Because of Ezra,' said Erlendur. 'Was it you who told me he worked at the ice house in Eskifjördur after quitting the sea? After he stopped crewing the boat with Jakob?'

Hrund puckered her brow. 'It may well have been. I know he was employed there after the war, if that's what you're asking.'

'So he'd have been working there when the accident happened? When the boat went down with Jakob and his companion? There were two of them, weren't there?'

'Yes, that was in 1949. They were shipwrecked on their way home in a hell of a gale. They both drowned.'

'And their bodies were taken to the ice house?'

'Yes, that sounds likely.'

'Where Ezra was working?'

'Yes. Anyway, you can read about it in newspaper reports from the time if you want to check. There's a decent library here. What's got into you?'

'Nothing.'

'What do you mean, "where Ezra was working"?'

'And there's another thing,' said Erlendur hastily.

'What?'

'Jakob was buried in Djúpivogur.'

'Yes, that's right.'

'Where can I get hold of the names of his pall-bearers?'

'You what?'

'I need their names.'

'Why?'

Erlendur shook his head.

'What on earth do you want with their names for?'

He continued to regard Hrund in silence.

'You're not going to tell me?' she said.

'Maybe later,' he replied. 'Right now I'm not even sure myself what I'm doing.'

Half an hour later he was seated at a desk in the town library, leafing through old newspapers brought to him by the helpful young woman librarian. Erlendur checked both the national and local papers around the time of the accident. He found two fairly detailed reports of the shipwreck in the local papers, which confirmed what he knew already but added little. The men who died were both described as single; one was from Grindavík, the other from Reykjavík, though his family originally came from the East Fjords. His funeral had been held two days after the accident.

The second account was accompanied by a grainy picture of Jakob's coffin being lowered into the ground. Erlendur couldn't make out any of the faces, only the indistinct outlines of the four pall-bearers who were identified in the caption under the picture. Hrund had recalled the name of the relevant man correctly. Erlendur consulted the local records with the help of the librarian and soon tracked his family down.

'His daughter lives in Djúpivogur,' announced the librarian, after a quick search on the Internet.

Erlendur started out immediately. The road followed the shoreline, threading in and out of one picturesque fjord after another, past endless ranks of mountains characterised by the distinctive sloping rock strata of the East Fjords. The small village of Djúpivogur was the southernmost settlement of any size in the region and when he reached it, after two hours' driving, he had no difficulty finding the right house. He drew up outside a beautifully maintained period villa and switched off the engine. A light shone over the front door and another in a window that might belong to the kitchen, but he could see no movement inside. He decided to have another cigarette before disturbing the woman. He had been smoking far too much over the last few days: this was his third of the drive.

As he walked up the short flight of steps and

knocked at the door, he wondered how to explain his business or indeed how to introduce himself, deciding it would be best to stick to the local history story which had served him well so far.

No one answered. Discovering a doorbell, he tried that instead. He could hear it competing with the sound of a television. He pressed the bell again and the volume of the TV was lowered. The door opened and a man in a red-checked shirt stood looking him up and down.

'Is Ásta in, by any chance?' asked Erlendur, wondering if this was her husband.

The man looked bemused by his visit. It was not that late, thought Erlendur, surreptitiously checking his watch.

'Hang on a minute,' said the man and disappeared inside. The volume was turned up again and soon a small woman appeared. From her appearance, Erlendur assumed she must have nodded off in front of the television. Her plump figure was dressed in a comfy tracksuit and her sleepy eyes registered surprise at receiving a visit from a strange man at this hour of the evening.

'Are you Ásta?' asked Erlendur.

'Yes.'

'Daughter of Ármann Fridriksson, the fisherman?'

'Yes?' There was hesitation in her voice. 'My father was called Ármann.'

'I was wondering if I could take up a few minutes of your time?' said Erlendur. 'I wanted to ask if you'd ever heard your father talk about a shipwreck that happened in Eskifjördur in 1949.'

'A shipwreck?'

'And also about the funeral of one of the victims that took place here in Djúpivogur. I gather your father was one of the pall-bearers. The dead man was called Jakob Ragnarsson.'

CHAPTER 41

After a second's indecision, Ásta Ármannsdóttir invited him in, mainly out of curiosity. She suggested the sitting room but he said the kitchen would be fine and took a seat at the table. The flickering light of the television could be seen from the other room where Ásta's husband, one Eiríkur Hjörleifsson according to the plaque on the front door, was ensconced on the sofa, glued to a British crime drama. Ásta made some good strong coffee for her guest and put a raisin sponge cake on the table. Erlendur took a slice to be polite, though he didn't have much of a sweet tooth.

He apologised for turning up unannounced and explained that he had a particular interest in shipwrecks in the East Fjords. One had occurred in 1949 when the vessel *Sigurlína* from Eskifjördur had gone down with all hands. On researching the story he had noticed that Ásta's father Ármann had known Jakob, one of the men who died, and helped to carry the coffin at his funeral. Ásta recognised the name.

'Did he ever discuss the incident with you or

your brothers?' asked Erlendur. He knew from the records that Ásta had two brothers.

'They both live in Reykjavík,' she said. 'You can ring them if you like but I don't know if it'll help. As far as I can remember, Dad didn't talk much about the accident. At least, not to us kids. Actually, I wasn't even born at the time. He might have discussed it with his friends but he wasn't much of a talker.'

'How did your father know Jakob? Any idea?'

'They crewed a boat here in Djúpivogur for several years. Then Jakob moved away but they still caught up from time to time.'

'Do you know if your father was badly affected by Jakob's death?'

Ásta shrugged. 'The fishermen here often used to go out in bad weather. Some of them didn't come back. That's life in a fishing village. I don't think my father allowed himself to get sentimental – it wasn't done in those days. Is it my father you're interested in?'

'No, not particularly,' said Erlendur. 'But do you remember him mentioning any unusual details about the incident?'

'I can't say I do.'

'Nothing about the funeral?'

'No, I don't know. What are you getting at?'

'I was discussing all this with some people from Eskifjördur, including a woman who dimly remembered your father saying he'd heard – or thought he'd heard – a noise coming from the coffin as it was being lowered into the ground.'

The woman studied Erlendur. 'Nobody's ever told me that,' she said eventually.

'No, I'm not surprised. It sounds like an old wives' tale that got going after what happened to Jakob. He lost his wife, you see, and there were rumours that she haunted him. So that's probably how the story started.'

'Well, it's the first I've heard of it. I knew Jakob's wife had died but Dad never said a word about this. Not as far as I know, anyway. Are you sure it was Dad?'

'I expect the story's got a bit garbled. It could have been somebody else, or more likely pure invention.'

'But you don't think so?'

'Oh, of course I do,' said Erlendur quickly. 'It's just a minor detail of the incident. I thought I'd ask you in case it sounded familiar.'

'Well, it doesn't.'

'Did he ever talk about Jakob and his wife Matthildur?'

'Not really.'

'Are any of your father's friends still alive?'

'Not these days. Well, apart from old Thórdur.'

Thórdur lived with his son and daughter-in-law about two minutes' walk from Ásta's house. After obtaining his address, Erlendur rose to his feet and said a hasty goodbye, adding, in a belated attempt at courtesy, that he didn't want to keep her. He was keen to avoid sowing any unnecessary seeds of suspicion. Her husband was still sitting in front of the TV. There was a noise of gunshots and shouting. Unfortunately, Erlendur's clumsy departure only served to make Ásta more curious about the purpose of his odd visit and request, and he was forced to answer or else dodge a barrage of questions about her father, Jakob and his wife Matthildur, about the shipwreck and exactly why Erlendur was so concerned about the incident and those involved. He sensed she was having misgivings about talking to him and before he knew it her suspicions were being directed specifically at the connection between Matthildur and her father. He couldn't work out where this development had come from and tried unsuccessfully to clear up the misunderstanding as he paused in the doorway. But he left the woman standing at the entrance to her house, wearing a baffled expression.

Thórdur was eighty-five years old and existed in a world of silence. He was deaf as a post and no hearing aid could help him now. All he could hear was his own internal monologue, which he did not hesitate to share. In fact, he wasn't in the least shy about talking and had a tendency to shout, as if he wanted to be sure no one would miss what he said, even if he couldn't hear it himself. He lived in a small basement flat that his son had converted for him in his house. The son showed Erlendur downstairs and left them alone together. Erlendur had explained about his research into shipwrecks and repeated this to Thórdur who seemed pleased by the unexpected visit. His flat was nothing more than a large room containing a decent-sized bed, a TV, a desk and a washbasin. Books were piled wherever there was space.

Communicating with the deaf old man turned out to be perfectly simple. On his desk were paper and pencils, and anything Erlendur wanted to say or ask had to be written down and passed to Thórdur who answered instantly.

'I see you're a reader,' was the first comment Erlendur wrote once he had established who he was and the reason for his presence.

Thórdur smiled. Apart from his deafness, he gave the appearance of being fighting fit and sharp as a tack. His head was totally bald, his nostrils were black with snuff and he pronounced his 'r's in a strangely throaty manner.

'Quite right,' he boomed. 'I've collected them for years. But I doubt anyone'll care to keep them after I'm gone. Most of them will probably end up at the dump.'

'Pity,' wrote Erlendur.

Thórdur agreed. 'I remember the accident clear as day,' he added. 'And I remember other much worse ones more recently.'

'Do you remember the funeral in '49?' wrote Erlendur, keen to keep Thórdur on track.

'No,' said Thórdur. 'I wasn't around. I was

crewing a boat out of Höfn, where I lived at the time. But of course I heard all about it. The weather must have been appalling – a northerly gale and bitter frost. They were sailing so close to land that people could see the terror on their faces. If I remember right the engine of that rust bucket cut out at the worst possible moment and the boat was smashed to smithereens. The two men were thrown overboard. I doubt they could even swim – not that it would have helped them. People must have been able to hear their cries for help from the shore. Of course they did everything in their power to save them but conditions were so bad they had to give up. In the end, the cries stopped.'

Thórdur picked up a tin of snuff and offered it to Erlendur, who pinched a few grains between his fingers and sniffed them up his nose. Thórdur sprinkled a thick line on the back of his hand and snorted it up both nostrils.

'It must have been ghastly to watch,' he said, fiddling with the tin as if he liked to keep it nearby. 'Utterly horrible. I mean, not being able to help in any way.'

Erlendur nodded encouragingly.

'Anyway, the bodies were washed up on the beach, as you'd expect when a boat goes down, and they were taken to the ice house in the village. They were laid out on planks like stretchers, I believe. The idea was to keep the bodies straight when rigor mortis set in. At least, I think that was why.'

'And they were certified dead?' wrote Erlendur.

'Oh yes. I gather there was some locum in the village at the time. He only had to look at their eyes to confirm they were dead. Then they were put in coffins and one of them was buried in the churchyard.'

'Where did you learn all these details?'

'Fellow named Ármann. Used to live here in Djúpivogur. Good friend of mine. Died years ago. Lung cancer. We both knew one of the men – Jakob – though Ármann knew him much better than me.'

'How did you know Jakob?' wrote Erlendur.

'Used to bump into him out on the town when we were young. Though I never got to know him well. Never had much time for that sort, frankly. He was born in Reykjavík. Thought a lot of himself too. Quite the womaniser, and used to brag about it like young men do. Got into trouble over some of the girls he seduced. Didn't want anything to do with them once he'd had his wicked way. But woe betide them if they dared look elsewhere. Then he could turn very nasty.'

'Ármann was one of his pall-bearers,' wrote Erlendur.

'Yes, that's right. They clubbed together for a gravestone later on. One of his friends, Pétur I think his name was, organised a whip-round among the fishermen and boat owners in the village.'

'Ármann's supposed to have heard a noise,' wrote Erlendur, 'from the coffin.'

'Ah, so you've heard about that, have you?' said Thórdur, suddenly lowering his voice. 'It wasn't widely known. People found it embarrassing. Ármann stopped talking about it after a while, but it gave rise to all sorts of ghost stories linked to Jakob's late wife. That she'd got into his coffin with him and so on.'

'People said she haunted him.'

'That's right. Caused the accident too. I don't know why she was supposed to have wanted to take revenge on him, though.'

'What exactly did Ármann hear?' wrote Erlendur.

'I'm really not sure,' said Thórdur. 'He was a bit vague.'

'I gather it was some kind of moaning.'

'No, that's nonsense. It was nothing like that. I asked him once, shortly before he died, but he was very unwilling to say. I have a feeling he regretted ever mentioning it. No, it was more like gas.'

'Gas?'

'As if the body had some gas left inside, which is quite possible given that the man was buried so soon after he died. That's what Ármann thought he'd heard. Not moaning. That's a ghost story that was invented later on. And there were others who claimed the body had shifted in the coffin.'

Erlendur frowned. 'Ármann's daughter didn't seem aware of any of this.'

'Ármann told me he'd have done better to hold his tongue at the time,' said Thórdur. 'Of course she doesn't want to admit it. She wants to hush it up.'

'Maybe,' wrote Erlendur.

'I've never heard about any moaning,' said Thórdur. 'It would've taken inhuman strength to survive all that.'

'Yes, it would,' Erlendur blurted out aloud.

'Mind you, there are stories of people surviving in cold like that,' said Thórdur. 'I once heard of a shipwreck out west, not unlike this one. Three men fell overboard from a rowing boat close to shore. The bodies were hauled out of the sea and locked up overnight in a warehouse in the village. The weather was freezing, but when they went to check on the bodies next day it turned out that two of the men had managed to climb down onto the floor during the night, though that's as far as they got. But the third, who'd lived longest, had made it all the way to the door before he'd finally frozen stiff.'

CHAPTER 42

Erlendur drove slowly back to Eskifjördur. He was so preoccupied that he soon pulled over and stopped on the side of the road, where he sat in the car contemplating what to do. He lit the inevitable cigarette and drank some tepid coffee from the flask. It was virtually the only sustenance he had taken all day but he was not hungry. Instead, he was filled with a restless tension that he knew he would have to satisfy sooner rather than later.

There was one obvious course to take. He didn't like it, but however much he racked his brains for an alternative, he always came to the same conclusion. He wanted clear answers but he also wished to protect the interests of those who had put their trust in him. He had seen no reason so far to involve the local authorities in his investigation, in spite of the evidence of blackmail and murder he had uncovered. Erlendur had always felt that some crimes might remain hidden, so long as this was not contrary to the public interest, and this was one such occasion. He would avoid making his findings official for as long as possible. After all, it was not a formal inquiry. Innate curiosity and an obsession with missing-persons' cases had led him to delve more deeply into an ancient incident than he had ever intended, but he hadn't been seeking out a crime: in this instance the crime had found him. If he hadn't gone around following up suspicions and rumours, the long-accepted story of Matthildur, Jakob and Ezra would have stood unchallenged, a closed book, to himself and others. Erlendur was only too aware that if he wanted to act on his suspicions and do what he believed was necessary, he would have to pursue the matter through official channels, which would mean persuading one authority after another of what he knew, without any substantive proof. His request would be put before innumerable committees and judges, he would be forced to attend endless meetings and engage in the sort of persistent wrangling that he simply couldn't face. Even if he informed the local authorities of everything he had uncovered and his request passed unhindered through the system, he was convinced that he was still unlikely to receive an official go-ahead.

Gradually it had dawned on him that he was investigating not one crime but two, and that they differed in two significant respects. Of course they were related, there was no doubt: the first had given rise to the second. The first was based purely on the testimony of one man, Ezra, and would be nigh on impossible to prove. There was no witness to confirm his claim, no tangible evidence, no body had been found and no one knew its whereabouts. The second case was different in that there was no witness testimony, no certainty that a crime had in fact been committed; only a vague suspicion. But in this instance Erlendur believed he knew where the evidence was buried. All he had to do was lay hands on it.

Turning the car round, he headed back to Djúpivogur along the deserted road. As he drove, Erlendur recalled reading about a woman who had been certified dead and sealed in a body bag, only to revive and have to be rushed to A & E. He had heard of people in South America who asked for their wrists to be cut after death, for fear of waking up in their coffin. There was even a medical term for the fear of being buried alive: *taphephobia*. They called it the Lazarus syndrome when someone regained consciousness after being certified dead. People had even been known to wake up during their own post-mortem.

Erlendur parked by the graveyard in Djúpivogur and contemplated the tranquil scene, now barely visible in the gloom. He had brought along the gas lantern and a spade, on the off chance. The cemetery was fairly small, so he knew it wouldn't take him long to locate Jakob's grave and he couldn't think of a better time to tackle the job than now, tonight. His earlier scruples had been laid to rest. He had come too far to start having reservations now.

Little snow had fallen here in the southernmost

part of the fjords. The weather had been mild and dry for most of the autumn and the ground was still frost-free which would make his task easier. He looked at his watch. The sooner he started, the sooner he would be finished. And he must finish before first light, and be sure to leave behind as few traces of his deed as possible.

He stepped out of the car with the lantern in his hand, fetched the spade from the back seat and started walking towards the graveyard. He didn't want to light the lamp until it was needed. The cemetery lay beside the main road, some way above and mercifully out of sight of the village. It was past twelve. Erlendur prepared himself for a long night.

Hearing a dog barking in the distance, he froze for a second and listened, then carried on. The cemetery was surrounded by iron railings, accessed by a lychgate with a bell hanging above it. He glimpsed a tool shed to his right. Tall, handsome conifers stood vigil over the graves, most of which had raised mounds, marked out with headstones or crosses. The plots from the middle of the twentieth century lay towards the back.

Having lit the lantern, he walked along the rows, shining it on the graves to read the inscriptions, and soon came to a small stone lying flat on the ground that was engraved with Jakob's name and dates. Turning down the flame to leave just enough light, he peered about cautiously, straining for the sound of any more barking, then set to work, driving the spade into the damp turf.

He had disinterred a body once before, in very different circumstances. On that occasion he had gone through all the correct channels and had the services of a small mechanical digger to excavate the grave, in a cemetery on the south coast. What had emerged was the coffin of a very young girl who had succumbed to a rare disease. His thoughts had often returned to her over the years. Countless other investigations had left their mark on him, in differing ways, but none had driven him to visit a graveyard secretly, under cover of darkness, armed with a spade.

With great care, Erlendur laid the turves he had cut to one side, intending to replace them as unobtrusively as he could. The ground offered little resistance, the soft damp earth yielding easily to his shovel, and he worked steadily for around an hour before taking a cigarette break, leaning on a neighbouring gravestone.

Another bout of digging followed before he took a second break. There was enough coffee left in his Thermos for half a cup, but it was insufficient to satisfy the hunger pangs that were now becoming acute. The night was overcast and there was no moon, which was fortunate in the circumstances. He had no idea what excuse he could possibly give if someone were to discover him halfway down the grave but he carried on digging regardless, trying to create as little mess as he could. All of a sudden, the blade of the shovel struck wood with a dull thud. The grave was shallower than he had expected and he dug with increased vigour until he was straddling Jakob's casket, hurriedly scraping off the dirt. It was a plain wooden box, cheaply made from unpainted timber, but in the weak illumination of the lantern it looked fairly intact.

The lid consisted of four broad planks. Erlendur inserted the blade of the shovel under one and tried to lever it up. The wood gave easily, splitting under the strain. He slid the spade under the next plank and forced that up as well. The nails had loosened over time and the timber was rotten, so the hole in the lid was soon large enough to see inside.

Grabbing the lantern from the lip of the pit, he turned the flame up and shone it into the coffin where Jakob's skeleton sprang into view. He was struck immediately by the odd attitude of the bones. Judging by the way it was tilted, it looked as if the dead man's head had been craned back, and the lower jaw had fallen away from the skull as if he had died with his mouth gaping. The upper teeth jutted out but the two front incisors were missing. The skeleton's hands lay against its head, the fingers clenched and crooked, the bones twisted in different directions. Moving the lamp nearer, he examined them more closely. From what he could see, the middle finger of the right hand had broken off. Moving the lamp down the length of the skeleton, he saw that the legs were splayed apart, rather than lying neatly aligned, side by side.

Bending lower, Erlendur shone his lantern down the inside of the coffin and ran a hand over the wood. Did any of this count as evidence to confirm his suspicions?

Straightening up, he played the light over Jakob's remains again. His gaze rested on the twisted hands and missing finger. He remembered hearing that Jakob had suffered from severe claustrophobia.

Next he picked up one of the wooden planks of the lid, which had snapped when he broke into the coffin. Turning up the gas flame still higher, he inspected the section that had lain directly over Jakob's face. His fingers detected grooves in the surface, score marks that should not have been there. Elsewhere, the plank was unmarked. As he peered closer at the strange scratches he could have sworn that some were teeth marks. He illuminated the broken finger again and grimaced as he pictured the desperate battle that had been fought in that little churchyard: the futile scratching, the screams that nobody heard, the air gradually dwindling to nothing.

CHAPTER 43

Less than two hours later, soaked to the skin and covered in mud from head to toe, Erlendur put the spade back in the car and sat down behind the steering wheel. Although he had done his best to hide all signs of despoliation, it was still obvious that the grave had been tampered with. Even after he had shovelled all the earth back into the hole, the small mound had defeated his efforts to beat it flat. It would take time for the soil to subside to its former level. He replaced the turves on top of the heap, hoping that no one would visit the cemetery for a while. With any luck the villagers would remain in the best of health and the snow would fall heavily on Djúpivogur all winter long, lying in deep drifts far into the spring. Ashamed now of what he had done, he didn't want anyone to discover it, and yet he didn't really regret it.

He headed back to Eskifjördur. Few people were about that early, so he only met a couple of cars. In some places small drifts had formed over the road but otherwise the going was reasonable. He relished the warmth from the heater and listened to soothing music on the radio while mentally reviewing the grisly tale he had uncovered in the graveyard.

The sky was turning grey when he arrived back at the ruined croft and crawled into his sleeping bag, wrapping the blanket carefully around himself before lying back, exhausted. He didn't anticipate having any difficulty in getting to sleep, despite the twinges of pain and stiffness from his exertions with the spade. He had worked like a man possessed, terrified of being caught in the act, not easing up until the last sod had been replaced. His arms and legs ached and he had blisters on his palms. It was years since he had last engaged in such intense physical labour.

Yet for all that, sleep would not come. He grew agitated every time he thought about Ezra in the ice house where the bodies were laid out; about Jakob in his coffin, and the mystery of Matthildur's whereabouts. He was uncertain what to do with the information he had obtained in such a macabre manner. When he woke up, he resolved, he would go and have it out with Ezra, and perhaps that would settle his next move. There were many questions he wanted to put to the old man about what had gone on in that ice house long ago. After all, the indications were that Ezra had known full well Jakob was alive when the lid of the coffin was nailed down.

Cases where people revived after being certified dead could often be put down to negligence. But it was not from any suspicion of neglect that Erlendur had developed his hunch about Jakob and felt compelled to disinter him. Ezra's words had played a part, along with Ármann's tale of the noise he had heard during the funeral. Added to this was Erlendur's own experience and knowledge of hypothermia. The fact that Ezra had direct access to the ice house had only served to fuel his suspicions. Then there was Thórdur's story of the three men in the west of Iceland who were written off as dead but had risen from their biers and tried in vain to raise the alarm. Finally, Erlendur's conviction had been so strong that he had felt compelled to act. Whatever the cost. He wasn't trying to excuse his action but to find an explanation for what he had done.

And what had he uncovered? What had all his toiling in the cemetery achieved?

He had found an answer to the question that had troubled him most: Jakob had indeed been buried alive. A shudder had run down Erlendur's spine when he realised what he was seeing, recognised the evidence of desperation, the terrible suffering in the skeleton's attitude – the raised hands, head arched back, mouth gaping. Even though he must have been more dead than alive after his immersion in the icy sea and night in the freezing warehouse, Jakob had found the strength to score splinters from the wood of his coffin lid. His hold on life must have been phenomenal; his death an indescribable ordeal.

But what Erlendur could not read from the coffin, and would have to seek an explanation for elsewhere, was why Jakob had been buried alive. Had it been accidental or deliberate?

Although it was never possible to know a person completely, Erlendur reckoned he was pretty well acquainted with men of Ezra's type. He was confident that the old man had nothing in common with the many criminals who had crossed his path. Ezra was neither amoral nor violent. He was like the vast majority of ordinary citizens Erlendur had encountered, people who had never so much as incurred a parking fine. Was it possible, though, that somewhere inside him lurked the will to commit an atrocity like the one Erlendur had just exposed?

If all Ezra had said was true – if Jakob had killed Matthildur and consistently refused to reveal where he had hidden her body – then he'd certainly had a grievance to avenge. Seven years later Jakob's fate had been sealed, quite literally. But what role had Ezra played? Had he known Jakob was alive? Had they exchanged any words? Had Jakob told Ezra what he did with Matthildur's remains?

Only one man could lay these questions to rest and Erlendur had every intention of speaking to him at the earliest possible opportunity.

CHAPTER 44

Why are you lying here?

Relentlessly, at intervals, the question is repeated. But then he forgets it until it is asked again, becoming so insistent he can no longer ignore it. He has formed an image of his persecutor, based on the idea that he must be a traveller who has lost his way and by an odd coincidence stumbled onto the strange shores where he himself has washed up. Like Bóas by the crags at Urdarklettur.

Yet this is not Bóas but a stranger. He has no answers that will satisfy the traveller and is angered by his prying. Moreover, he senses once again the presence of another figure standing in the man's shadow, hanging back. He feels the presence ever more strongly, without being able to work out who can be lurking there.

All he knows is that he fears the presence.

'Should you be lying here?' asks the voice.

'Why not?'

'Do you really think you should be lying here?'

'Yes.'

'Why?' asks the man.

'Because . . .'

'What?'

'Who's that with you?' Erlendur asks.

'Do you want to meet him?'

'Who is it?'

'It's up to you. If you want to meet him, then of course you can.'

'Who is it? Why's he hiding?'

'He's not hiding. It's you who's keeping him away.'

The traveller is fading, receding, and only then does he remember where he has seen him before.

'Is it you?' he asks warily.

'So you remember me?'

'Don't go,' he says, though the man frightens him. 'Don't go!'

'I'm not going far.'

'Please stay! Tell me who's with you. Where does he come from? Who is he?'

Little by little he surfaces into consciousness and becomes aware of the iron grip of the cold. The faint echo of his own silent cries still rings in his ears. It takes him a long time to remember where he is. Not only is his whole body numb but the cold has affected his brain; his thoughts are wandering and irrational. This causes him no particular concern, however. He has ceased to feel concern.

The cold drives him to seek out warming thoughts. He calls to mind old methods of restoring heat to one's body, methods he has read about in his books. The most common and effective means, when no other was available, was to use one's own body heat to warm the victims of hypothermia, whether they were sailors rescued from the sea or people lost in snowstorms. The rescuers would take off every scrap of clothing and lie down beside the victims, sometimes one on either side, using their body heat to revive them.

His mind goes in search of heat.

He thinks about balmy sunshine.

His mother's smile.

Her warm touch.

Hot summer days by the river.

He turns his face to the sky and basks in the midsummer sun.

Suddenly he remembers the traveller and recalls where he has seen him before. A memory returns of the day at Bakkasel when they received an unexpected visitor, a passer-by who broke his journey with them before continuing on his way. That spring it was so cold that the hay harvest was almost ruined and the snowdrifts lay far down the slopes well into summer. He recalls the peculiar thing the man said to his mother about Bergur. Recalls her startled reaction.

He never knew where the man came from or where he was going, though doubtless he had told his parents. After his brief stop, he had vanished from sight over the moor. Perhaps he was heading for Reydarfjördur over the Hraevarskörd Pass, or taking the old path that skirted the glacier, ran northwards under the foot of Mount Hardskafi and from there over to Seydisfjördur. Unexpected guests would turn up at Bakkasel every now and then, passers-by who looked as if they had come a long way. They were always invited to rest and enjoy his parents' hospitality. Some were alone, like this man; others travelled in twos or threes or larger groups, often in high spirits, bringing an atmosphere of good cheer. Occasionally people would request a night's lodging and they would be offered a bed in the boys' room. They even had foreigners turn up, trying to make themselves understood with sign language, asking for a drink of water or permission to camp on their land.

From his manner and outfit, Erlendur had gathered that this man was an experienced hiker, an impression reinforced by the handsome walking stick he left propped outside the house. He wore thick-soled boots, laced up to the calf, plus fours and a leather jacket buttoned up to his neck. His hands were clad in fingerless gloves and he stroked his beard with his strong fingers as he spoke.

He seemed curiously at home as he took a seat in Erlendur's parents' kitchen and accepted coffee and a bite to eat. He chatted about the weather, especially the bad spring they were having, about the district and the scenery, and enquired after the names of various places as if he had never been there before. Perhaps he came from down south, perhaps even all the way from Reykjavík, the big city that felt as remote as any of the world's great metropolises. Erlendur didn't dare speak to the visitor but loitered by the kitchen table, eavesdropping on the conversation. Bergur stood at his side, hanging on the guest's words and gazing at him as he drank his coffee and ate the sandwich their mother had prepared.

Every now and then the man would send a glance and a smile in the boys' direction. Bergur, unabashed, met his eye, whereas Erlendur was shy and looked away each time, before finally leaving the kitchen to take refuge in the bedroom. He could remember the man's kindly expression, his sincere eyes, the wisdom in his broad brow. He was as amiable as could be, and yet there was some quality that frightened Erlendur, that meant he could not be comfortable in the same room as the stranger and that eventually drove him from the kitchen. He wanted him to leave. He couldn't fathom why but he found the man menacing.

By the time Erlendur emerged the traveller was getting ready to leave. He had thanked them for their hospitality and was now out in the yard, walking stick in hand. He had been talking briefly with Bergur, who was standing with his parents in the crisp air, and in parting the man let fall those peculiar words, addressing them to their mother; smiling at her even as he pronounced Bergur's fate.

'Your boy has a beautiful soul. I don't know how long you'll be allowed to keep him.'

They never saw the man again.

He is convinced that the traveller who visits him intermittently in the cold is the same man who came to Bakkasel and delivered that incomprehensible verdict about Bergur, so true and yet so cruel. As his consciousness gradually fades, he begins to have his suspicions about the presence accompanying the man, about who it is that follows him like a shadow but will not come forward into the light.

CHAPTER 45

Erlendur could hear hammer blows coming from the shed below Ezra's house. He had slept unusually well, until past two that afternoon, then made his routine trip to the swimming pool and afterwards enjoyed a late lunch of fresh poached haddock, potatoes and dark rye bread at the cafeteria. He had slathered the fish and potatoes with generous knobs of butter and spread a thick layer on the bread, as if piling on calories would banish the chill that still lingered in his bones after his night's work.

He sauntered down to the shed. The door stood wide open and Ezra was sitting inside with his mallet, beating *hardfiskur* with the same unvarying rhythm. He didn't notice Erlendur, who was at leisure to watch him for a minute or two. There was no sign of the shotgun. The old man appeared serene, yet his movements betrayed a certain firmness of purpose – unless it was simply force of habit.

'You again?' he said, without looking up. Although he had sensed Erlendur's presence, he didn't seem put out. 'I have nothing else to tell you,' he said.

'You tricked the whole story out of me. I should never have told you any of it. I can't understand why I did – you've no claim on me.'

'No, neither can I,' said Erlendur. 'But the fact remains that you did.'

Ezra looked up. 'Do you take me for a fool?'

'No,' said Erlendur. 'If anyone's a fool around here, it's me.'

Ezra had raised his mallet to flatten a new fillet of fish that he had hooked out of the plastic bucket, but now he paused, lowered his hand and studied Erlendur.

'How do you mean?'

'I'm talking about your friend Jakob.'

'What about him?'

'I'm not sure,' said Erlendur. 'Is there any further detail you'd like to add to your story?'

'No.'

'Positive?'

'Of course I am.'

'I'm afraid that won't do.'

Ezra put down the mallet, dropped the fish back into the bucket and stood up.

'I have nothing to add,' he said. 'And I'll thank you to leave me alone.'

He pushed past Erlendur out of the door and trudged up to the house with heavy steps, his shoulders bowed in his scruffy anorak, the ear flaps on his hat hanging loose. Erlendur hesitated, unsure if he wanted to open any more old wounds, doubtful that it was his place to do so. Ever since he had left Djúpivogur last night, he had been wondering whether he or anyone else would be the better for knowing what secrets Ezra was concealing about his dealings with Jakob. Erlendur had satisfied his own curiosity but this was none of his affair, even if he was a policeman. If Ezra was to be believed, the only crime that had been committed was Matthildur's murder. What had been done with her body was a mystery that would probably never be solved. The case was not subject to a criminal investigation, nor was it likely to become so. It was up to Ezra whether he informed anyone or not. Erlendur would not insist that he did. Anyway, who would benefit if the truth came to light so many years after the event? Why rake up what was better left undisturbed? Best let sleeping dogs lie.

Erlendur had often wrestled with such questions over the years, but seldom reached a conclusion. Each case had to be considered on its own merits. He almost wished he had never started to pry into Ezra's affairs, but it was too late now. He was in possession of knowledge that he could never forget, and it was natural that he should at least look for an explanation. It was not his aim to punish or to fill the prisons with unfortunate souls. His sole intention was to uncover the truth in every case, to track down what was lost and forgotten.

It was this goal that impelled him now to follow Ezra, with leaden feet, into the house. Ezra had not locked the door, and this ignited a spark of hope in Erlendur. He knew he could never provide the old man with absolution, but he could listen and try to understand. Unburdening himself about Matthildur appeared to have done him good. Ezra had allowed himself to talk, perhaps because Erlendur was a complete stranger, or because he sensed that he wouldn't judge him.

'Why did you follow me?' Ezra asked. He was standing by the kitchen sink. 'I asked you to leave me alone.'

His tone lacked conviction. Ezra turned his back on Erlendur and leaned over the sink to stare out of the window that overlooked the shed.

'I wanted to talk some more about Jakob,' said Erlendur.

'Well, I have nothing more to say about him.'

'Let me repeat my question: is there any further detail you'd like to add to your story?'

Ezra turned and met Erlendur's eye.

'Would you please leave?' he said. 'I beg you. Go away. I have nothing more to say to you. I've told you everything I'm prepared to say.'

'Did Jakob have buck teeth?'

'What?'

'I haven't seen any pictures of him but my impression is that his teeth stuck out.'

'You could put it like that,' Ezra said, nonplussed. 'You want to discuss dentistry now?'

'Maybe. What happened when he died?'

'What do you mean?'

'Was he dead when they brought him to you at the ice house?'

Ezra gaped. 'Of course he was.'

'Are you sure?'

'Absolutely,' said Ezra. 'Both men were certified dead.'

'The doctor wasn't local.'

'No, he wasn't from round here.'

'He did a short stint as a locum for your GP. He didn't bother to examine the bodies very closely, did he?'

'I'm not a doctor,' protested Ezra. 'And you seem to know much more than me. Look, I've no idea what you're on about and I want you to leave.'

'Then let me explain,' said Erlendur. 'It suddenly struck me that you were at the ice house the day Jakob was brought in. They assumed he'd drowned, like his companion. Perhaps the doctor was lousy at his job. Perhaps he thought he could get away with examining only one of them properly, since they were both in the same condition. Perhaps he didn't listen carefully enough for Jakob's heartbeat. I don't know if you're aware but at very low temperatures the heartbeat slows right down. All the bodily functions slow down and respiration becomes very shallow. An inattentive doctor could have failed to notice that Jakob was still alive.'

'I don't follow you,' said Ezra.

'That's why I went over to Djúpivogur yesterday. Because Jakob was buried there. I spoke to a nice old bloke, Thórdur – maybe you know him? Thórdur told me about an extraordinary case of survival in freezing temperatures and it occurred

276

to me that you might remember the story of the three men from the west, whose bodies were pulled from the sea. They froze to death in a warehouse that night because no one had realised they were still alive.'

Ezra regarded him in silence.

'I also spoke to the daughter of the man who believed he heard a noise coming from Jakob's coffin when it was lowered into the grave. Sound familiar?'

No response.

'Still don't know what I'm talking about?'

'No.'

'Her father got into a hell of a lot of trouble for mentioning it and later regretted ever having made such a foolish claim. But when I put all these facts together, it came to me that I ought to stop by the cemetery and take a look at Jakob's grave.'

Ezra did not react.

'The story about you and Matthildur really got to me, Ezra – what Jakob did to her; what he did to you. I can imagine the torment you've been through. So my mind started running on how even the best of men can commit terrible acts of retaliation, can find themselves capable of appalling crimes.'

Ezra turned away and stared out of the window at the shed again. The door was open and swung a little in the breeze, the rusty hinges squeaking.

'They justify it to themselves as revenge,' continued Erlendur.

'I don't understand why you won't leave me alone,' said Ezra in a low voice.

'*I couldn't get it out of him.* That's what you told me.'

'I don't follow.'

'When I asked you if he'd told you where Matthildur was. We were talking about Jakob's body being brought in after the shipwreck. You said: *I couldn't get it out of him.* Was that in the ice house?'

'I haven't a clue what you're on about.'

'Was he still alive?'

No answer.

'I dug up Jakob's coffin,' said Erlendur.

Slowly, Ezra turned from the window, looking as if he was not sure he had heard right.

'I opened it up.'

Ezra looked aghast.

'I had to know,' said Erlendur. 'I had to know what happened. I couldn't help myself.'

'Are you out of your mind?' Ezra gasped. 'Do you think I'd believe such a crazy lie? Get out of here right now and stop persecuting me! This is the final straw.' He raised his voice. 'I thought I could trust you but this is madness. Madness! Stop it at once.'

'I knew you wouldn't believe me so I brought you a pair of little objects that I found in the coffin,' said Erlendur, reaching into his pocket. 'I don't know if you'll recognise them.'

He walked over to where Ezra was standing and placed the contents of his pocket on the worktop.

At first Ezra's gaze seemed riveted to his, then he looked down. He frowned, unable to work out what Erlendur had placed there.

'What . . . what are they?' he whispered.

'Look closer,' said Erlendur.

Ezra bent and examined the minute objects. There were two of them: small, grey and somehow familiar, yet he couldn't think what they were. They looked like small, oddly shaped pebbles.

'What are they?' he repeated.

'He tore at the coffin lid with all his strength,' said Erlendur.

'What do you mean?'

'Don't you recognise them?'

'No,' said Ezra, 'I don't. Please, tell me what they are.'

'His teeth,' said Erlendur. 'Jakob's front teeth. They were lying beside him in the coffin.'

CHAPTER 46

Ezra's reaction did not surprise Erlendur. He stumbled back from the sink, lost his footing and fell to one knee, knocking over the kitchen table in the process. Erlendur made a move to help him but Ezra pushed him off.

'Get away from me!' he yelled.

Erlendur righted the table instead and went to pick up the glass and plate that had fallen on the floor.

'Get out!' shouted Ezra, averting his eyes from the teeth that lay side by side on the worktop.

Erlendur picked them up and put them back in his pocket. He had known he would need proof to convince Ezra that he had really dug up Jakob's body. Spotting the teeth lying on the base of the coffin by the weak light of the lantern, he had decided to take them with him. He didn't believe in ghosts but even so he had felt uneasy about bringing them into the farmhouse and had left them in the car overnight.

'What kind of sick behaviour is this?' Ezra shouted at Erlendur when he had recovered from the worst of his shock. 'How dare you?'

'I examined what was left of Jakob and it wasn't a pretty sight,' said Erlendur. 'Head wrenched back. Jaw gaping.'

Ezra had slumped into a worn wicker chair in the corner, where he sat with bowed head. It seemed he no longer trusted himself to meet Erlendur's eye. He was chalk white.

'Do you want to know my theory about how his teeth fell out?' asked Erlendur, pulling up a chair and sitting down.

'Who are you?' groaned Ezra, raising his hurt, angry face. 'Who would do such a thing? You must be sick.'

'So I've been told,' said Erlendur. 'I want to know what happened in the ice house when Jakob was brought in.'

Ezra remained mute.

'I suspect the reason his teeth fell out was connected to the marks I saw on the coffin lid. Do you want to know what I think?'

Ezra sat with his head buried in his hands.

'Can you face the truth?' asked Erlendur.

'Those teeth could have come from anywhere,' protested Ezra unconvincingly.

'No, they couldn't,' Erlendur contradicted. 'And you know it.'

'I beg you. Please, for God's sake, go and never come back. I don't know why you're persecuting me. I haven't done you any harm, I don't even know you. You bullied me into telling you about Matthildur. Isn't that enough? Just leave me to die in peace.'

'Did Jakob tell you what he'd done with her?'

'No, he never told me. Have pity on me and get out. Leave me alone.'

'If there's the slightest chance, I want to help you find her,' said Erlendur. 'You ask why I won't leave you alone and I can understand your question. I hope you understand my answer.'

Ezra's face remained hidden.

'It's very simple,' said Erlendur. 'I want to help you, Ezra. That's the only answer I can give. And I think that's what I'm doing, though it may be hard for you to recognise, especially now. But I want to find Matthildur. If you know where she is, Ezra, I want you to tell me. If you don't know, I'll do what I can to see that you find her.'

'I don't know where she is,' said Ezra. 'And you'll never find her.'

'I'm not after a culprit,' Erlendur continued. 'I'm not looking for crimes or trying to mete out punishment. This is not a police matter. You needn't be afraid that it'll go beyond these four walls. Eventually, someone will notice that the ground has been disturbed in Djúpivogur cemetery. I don't know when – it might take days or weeks, even months. I asked two of the locals about Jakob. They might make the connection but they don't know who I am or where I come from, only that I'm researching shipwrecks in the East Fjords. And even if the disturbance is discovered, no one would dream that the coffin had been disinterred. It'll just look like a spot of vandalism to a small area of the graveyard. At least that's what I'm banking on.'

Ezra did not interrupt Erlendur's speech.

'All I want is to find Matthildur,' he said. 'We have that in common, if nothing else.'

'Why?' asked Ezra.

Now it was Erlendur's turn to be lost for words.

'You've never found your brother,' suggested Ezra softly.

'That's right.'

'But you think you can find my Matthildur?'

'I don't know,' Erlendur admitted. 'You'll have to tell me about Jakob. I understand how hard it is, especially after all these years. But you must tell me.'

'There's nothing to tell.'

'Ezra, help me find her.'

The old man was stubbornly mute. But Erlendur was not prepared to give up and proceeded to explain how he had come to the decision to dig up Jakob's remains. How his suspicions had been roused by his conversations with Ezra and Hrund. How they were fuelled by his interest in the human ability to withstand extreme cold; an interest derived from his professional experience. He told him about the spade that had come with the hire car and had proved invaluable during his night-time visit to the graveyard. That he had been terrified some passer-by would see what he was doing and raise the alarm. Erlendur wanted to win back Ezra's trust, to come across as scrupulous and credible. He described the wooden planks from which the coffin was constructed, how solid it had been despite the passing of more than half a century and yet how easy it had been to break open.

'I don't want to hear,' protested Ezra.

'But you will though,' said Erlendur. 'And don't claim there's nothing to tell. I believe you committed a terrible crime, Ezra.'

'I wanted to know about Matthildur – that was my only thought. The only thing I'd cared about since she disappeared. I wanted to know where she was.'

'I understand.'

'All I was thinking about, or could think about, was what she suffered at his hands.'

'That's to be expected.'

'I wanted revenge.'

'I'm sure you did.'

Ezra's eyes dropped again. 'What marks on the coffin lid?' he mumbled.

Erlendur didn't grasp what he was asking.

'You said you saw marks on the coffin lid.'

'I realised Jakob must have been alive when he was buried. He still had the strength to claw and bite at the lid, but that can't have lasted long because he'd have suffocated fairly quickly. But I imagine he realised he was shut in a coffin, though that's only a guess. His death must have been hideous. Indescribably horrible.'

Ezra straightened up in his chair and looked

Erlendur in the eye, as if he had made up his mind.

'He was alive,' he said. 'The other man died in the sea. His crewmate. But Jakob survived. And . . .'

'And what?'

'I didn't tell anyone. I kept it secret. I was the only person who knew.'

Ezra smothered his face in his hands again.

'My God,' he groaned. 'I still have nightmares about what I did.'

CHAPTER 47

A storm had blown up that morning and most of the fishing boats had returned to harbour shortly after midday. The bad weather was not supposed to have extended that far north – the forecast had been for a strong breeze and light precipitation – but not long after lunchtime conditions deteriorated dramatically and a gale began to lash the coast, whipping up a blizzard. The storm affected the entire region as far north as Vopnafjördur, the wind measuring hurricane-force twelve during the worst squalls and temperatures plummeting.

Ezra had been working at the ice house for several years, though there was no ice there these days. Its original function had been superseded by the new fish factory that had opened two years previously. Instead the building was used to store equipment for the fishing fleet and processing plant, under Ezra's supervision. He had been tidying away boxes of bait when he was told that one of the boats that had gone out that morning was missing, and that Jakob was on board with another man. People were becoming increasingly concerned and phoned round neighbouring villages to see if the men had put into harbour there, but no one had any news of them. The wind was so ferocious by now that it was barely possible to walk the short distance to the next-door building.

The two men had rarely encountered each other in the years since Jakob had informed Ezra of Matthildur's fate. From what Ezra heard, Jakob had moved away from Eskifjördur for a period, spending time in Egilsstadir and Höfn in Hornafjördur. According to rumour, he had even made a bit of money in the post-war boom that Reykjavík was enjoying. Then, two years ago, he had moved back to Eskifjördur and rented the same house that he had lived in with Matthildur. He had been offered his old job on the *Sigurlína* and been going out with the village fishing fleet ever since. On the few occasions he had cause to drop by the ice house, the men had ignored one another. Although he had never remarried, Jakob had been involved with other women. Ezra, single until he met Matthildur, remained alone.

Twice following that first cataclysmic meeting he had visited Jakob to plead with him to reveal what he had done with her body. Both times Jakob had refused, mocking him and humiliating him as a 'womaniser'. But when it came to reporting the matter to the authorities Ezra lost his nerve, and instead spent his time trying to think up schemes to force Jakob to tell him the truth. He was not by nature violent and knew he could never beat the information out of the bastard. Nor did he have any money with which to bribe him. Besides, it was in Jakob's interest to protect himself – a fact he did not deny. When they last spoke he had repeatedly pointed out that if Ezra knew where Matthildur was he could use the information to have Jakob charged with murder. But where there was no body, there could be no trial. 'It would be best for both of us if she was never found,' he had said. 'Best for both of us that she died on the moors.'

Ezra locked up the ice house and was plodding home against the wind along Strandgata when a man raced past him, yelling that a boat had gone down on the other side of the fjord. 'They reckon it's the *Sigurlína*!' He vanished into the falling snow. Ezra didn't know where the man could be heading and wondered if he should run after him. Then he lowered his head into the storm again and continued on his way. When he got home he took off his outer clothes, which were plastered with snow, and hung them up to dry. He put the coffee pot on the range. It would take time to warm up the house and restore the feeling to his limbs. Sitting by the stove, he began to cram dried fish into his mouth, his thoughts dwelling on the wrecked boat and the fate of her crew. If what he had heard was right and the *Sigurlína* had gone down, had they lost their lives? Was Jakob dead?

He had finished the *hardfiskur* and was just beginning to thaw out when he heard a loud

288

banging on the door. When he opened it, a boy called Valdi who worked with him stepped inside, caked with snow. Ezra forced the door shut behind him.

'You have to open up the ice house,' the boy told him. 'They want to put the bodies in there.'

'The bodies?'

'Both men from the *Sigurlína* are goners,' Valdi said. 'Drowned.'

'Jakob's dead?'

'Him and Óskar. The engine cut out. There was nothing they could do. Or that's what I heard.'

Ezra clambered back into his coat, thick gloves and hat as Valdi repeated what little he knew. Later Ezra extracted the whole story from two eyewitnesses who were waiting with the bodies. They had been driving over the ridge from Eskifjördur with a couple of other men when they spotted a light at sea beyond the Hólmaborgir cliffs, at a spot called Skeleyri. In difficulties themselves, they had been about to turn back but guessed immediately that the light meant a boat was dangerously close to land. The men made their way as near as they could to the shore and through the swirling veils of white glimpsed a boat drifting directly towards the rocks by Skeleyri. They could make out two figures on board, who looked as if they were frozen, drenched and fighting for their lives. Then the boat appeared to lose power – at least they could hear no sound of an engine – but by then the screaming of the wind was so deafening they could hardly hear their own voices calling. The boat moved swiftly but inexorably towards land until it crashed into the cliffs and though the men had a rope which they tried in vain to throw to the sailors, it was impossible to get near enough as the cliffs were taking a pounding from tremendous gusts of wind and massive breakers. All at once, the boat, which had begun to break up on the rocks, was snatched away by a wave, raised on high, turned over and flung back at the cliffs where it was broken to matchwood before their eyes. The two men were thrown into the water, hurled against the rocks, then vanished in the retreating wave. A long interval passed before they saw a limp body cast up, first onto the wreckage and then onto the rocks. They reached it by tying the rope round one of their party, who inched his way down, seized hold of the lifeless man and hauled him back up to his companions. He had been so badly battered that there was hardly a bone left unbroken in his body. They judged him to be dead. After this they shouted at length to the other man but received no answer. There was no way he could survive long in a sea that cold. The wreckage of the fishing boat was strewn over the surface. The minutes passed and, wet and shivering themselves now, they had given up all hope of finding the other sailor when one of them noticed a shape at the bottom of the cliffs. The man was lying prone, his face covered in blood and a large gash in his head.

By the time Ezra reached the ice house quite a crowd had gathered, though they could hardly stand upright in the wind. A nervous young locum from Reykjavík had already signed death certificates for both men. The four witnesses had taken the bodies straight to his house and, once he had heard their account, the matter had seemed simple. The owner of the *Sigurlína* had ordered that the bodies should be kept in the old ice house until the dead men's next of kin could be informed. Jakob was known to have relatives in Djúpivogur, but his companion, Óskar, came from the other side of the country, from the village of Grindavík in the south-west. He had been an itinerant fisherman, working the seasons in various parts of the country, including Eskifjördur, where he had only recently been taken on. The owner had no idea who to contact.

Ezra immediately set about arranging a place for the bodies. He erected trestles, laid a couple of old filleting boards across them, and had the dead men placed there side by side. They felt like blocks of ice. One man's face was masked in blood: it appeared to be Jakob.

The crowd soon dispersed, leaving Ezra alone in the now quiet building. It was nearly midnight. He was tired and chilled to the bone after a long day. Should he keep vigil over the bodies, he wondered, or go home and try to sleep? It had not yet sunk in that Jakob was dead. That the man he hated with such passion, the man he had so often plotted vengeance against, was no longer alive. He didn't know what Jakob's death would mean for him or for Matthildur's fate. But one thing was certain: there would be no question of recovering her body now. Slowly the full implications became clear as Ezra stood over the bloodied corpse on the filleting board. He might as well abandon all hope of ever finding her.

'Hell,' he whispered.

The storm had lost some of its force but the wind was still raging around the building, whining in the roof and making the rafters creak. The naked light bulb swung on its wire.

'Hell,' Ezra whispered again. 'I should have killed you myself.'

He decided to go home, persuading himself it was not for him to keep vigil: one of the men he didn't know from Adam; the other he had loathed more than words could express.

When he returned to work early next morning after a short, restless night, he was shocked to see that Jakob had rolled off the filleting board and onto the floor. Ezra hurried over, sat him up and with considerable difficulty hauled him back onto the board. He simply couldn't understand how he could have fallen off. As he lifted Jakob back up his head banged on the board and Ezra thought the body emitted a faint moan. He examined the other fisherman and tried to move his leg, but the limb was stiff and unyielding: rigor mortis had taken hold of his entire body. He had the feeling Jakob should be equally rigid but he was not. Although he was very cold, there was no sign of stiffness.

Again he thought he heard a faint moan from Jakob. Startled, he put it down at first to the wind. Stooping over the man's body, he tried in vain to detect any sign of breathing, then pressed an ear to his chest but could hear no heartbeat.

Straightening up again, Ezra stared at the body.

He thought he saw the face twitch. One eye was closed by a clot of blood, and Jakob's hair was sticky with it. He also had an open wound on his cheek and a deep gash on his chin. Ezra guessed he had sustained these injuries when he was beaten against the rocks at Hólmaborgir.

He must have been mistaken about the movement. But he wasn't certain.

Ezra was turning away when he glimpsed it again – the slightest twitch around the mouth. This time there was no doubt. As he concentrated on Jakob's face he clearly saw his lips move.

It looked as if Jakob was breathing.

The door opened.

Ezra's heart missed a beat: he thought he would die of fright.

The *Sigurlína*'s owner came in out of the storm and looked Ezra up and down.

'Hell and damnation,' he said, stamping his feet to shake the snow from his galoshes.

CHAPTER 48

Ezra rose from his chair: the memory was too much. Unable to sit still any longer, he began to pace around the kitchen. As he listened to his tale, Erlendur noticed that the old man was finding it increasingly difficult to describe events so vivid in his mind's eye that they might have taken place yesterday. The pauses between his words became prolonged, his voice gruffer. He wrung his hands and avoided Erlendur's gaze. Erlendur pitied him, as he did all those who could not escape their fates.

'Would you like me to make some coffee?' Erlendur asked, standing up too. 'It looks as if you could do with a cup.'

Ezra was in another world. He didn't respond until Erlendur had asked him twice. Finally he paused his pacing.

'What was that?'

'Coffee?' asked Erlendur again. 'Should I make us a cup?'

'You have some,' Ezra said. 'Go ahead. Help yourself.'

He retreated back into his own world, where

it was still the frozen, stormy depths of winter. Erlendur had no wish to hurry him. He knew the story would emerge eventually but he had an ever stronger sense of what it cost Ezra to tell it. He had never spoken of these events and wanted to give a conscientious account. It was plain from the way he spoke that far from trying to wipe it from his mind he remembered everything in minute detail. It was too early to judge if he felt unburdened, but Erlendur knew from long experience that the time would come when he did.

Neither man spoke while Erlendur made a strong brew and hunted out some reasonably clean mugs. He handed one to Ezra who took a cautious sip of the scalding black liquid.

'I can see it's not easy,' Erlendur said.

'It's not a pretty story.'

'I realise that.'

Ezra hesitated. 'Did I show you a picture of Matthildur?'

'No, I'd remember if you had.'

'Would you like to see one?'

'That would be –'

'It's in my bedroom,' said Ezra. 'Just a minute.'

While he was gone, Erlendur stepped over to the window that faced onto the moor. The ground was completely white. From this angle he couldn't see up the valley to Bakkasel, and he was just craning his neck to catch a glimpse of the old farmhouse when Ezra returned.

'She gave me this,' he said. 'It's the only one I've got.'

He handed the photo reverently to Erlendur, as if it were a priceless treasure. Erlendur took it carefully. It was very creased, having once been folded in the middle, and appeared to be half of a larger picture which had been cut in two.

'It was taken here in Eskifjördur,' Ezra said, 'one summer. A photographer came through the village and gave them the photo. Matthildur cut it in half. Jakob was next to her. It was taken outside their house.'

Erlendur looked at the image. Matthildur was standing in front of her home, eyes screwed up against the sun; a lovely smile; dark, shoulder-length hair; arms by her sides; head slightly tilted; her face wearing a friendly but determined expression. Her shadow fell on the door behind her.

'We hadn't started seeing each other then,' said Ezra. 'That didn't happen until a year later. But I'd already begun to have feelings for her.'

'What did you say to the boat owner when he came into the ice house?' asked Erlendur, passing the picture back.

'I don't know why I lied,' said Ezra. 'I hadn't even planned what I was going to do, but after the first lie, the rest came easily. At first all I wanted was to force Jakob to tell me about Matthildur – if he really was alive, that is. I wanted to take advantage of his predicament to make him tell me how he'd disposed of her. But later . . .'

'The desire for revenge got the better of you?'
Erlendur suggested.

Ezra's eyes dwelt on the photo.

'I wanted justice,' he said.

The boat owner, a man in his late seventies, was well kitted out in a thick winter coat, scarf and woollen hat. He lingered by the door as if he did not wish for any closer contact with death. He had lost not only two of his men but his boat, and the personal cost was obvious from his demeanour. Ezra knew him to be a decent fellow. After all, he had worked for him not so long ago, and had nothing but good to say of him. The man owned two other, much larger vessels with bigger crews, and would hang about on the docks if his vessels were out in dirty weather, waiting for their safe return. He had been at sea himself for many years and his luck had for the most part held – he had only once before lost a man overboard, during the herring season. The man had drowned.

'They're in good hands, Ezra,' he said.

'There's nothing more anyone can do for them now,' Ezra replied, trying to pretend all was well. He was still so stunned at seeing Jakob's lips move that he could scarcely control his features and voice. He tried to appear as relaxed as he could but felt beads of sweat pricking his scalp.

'I still haven't got hold of the Grindavík lot,' the owner said, averting his eyes from the bodies. 'I don't know much about the lad. Jakob's easier.

His parents in Reykjavík are both dead and he had no brothers or sisters. His mother's brother from over Djúpivogur way asked me to have a coffin knocked up for him. He's going to pick up the body later today. They want to get the funeral over with as quickly as possible. He says there's no reason to delay, which is fair enough, I suppose. They're going to dig the grave this morning before the ground freezes any harder.'

'It . . . I . . . suppose they're right.'

'They don't want any expense either,' said the owner with a shrug. 'He made that quite clear. I offered to help out but he wouldn't hear of it.'

'No, right,' said Ezra, struggling for something to say.

'Neither of them was a family man,' added the owner, 'which is a small mercy.'

Ezra was at a loss. It was slowly sinking in that Jakob might still be alive. Under normal circumstances he would have raised the alarm, hurriedly moved him to a warmer place and tended to him until the doctor arrived. It was his duty to save a life, whoever was involved. He knew that.

But this was Jakob.

If there was one person in the world he truly hated it was this man. Ezra wasn't sure how he would have answered if someone had asked him yesterday whether he would be prepared to save Jakob's life. Now the power to do so lay in his hands. His conscience urged him to report what he had seen and seek help for Jakob that instant.

He almost expected him to rise up from the filleting board. But the minutes passed. He said nothing, did nothing. He made no attempt to help the man lying there at death's door.

'Hell and damnation,' repeated the boat owner. 'You could knock up a simple coffin for Jakob, couldn't you? You can use some of the timber over at the new building. Try and do a decent job, mate.'

Ezra nodded.

'Then wait for the Djúpivogur lot to arrive. The uncle didn't want any fuss. He's going to transport the coffin by sea. Said it wouldn't do for me to attend the funeral. They're a rum lot. I'll go anyway, of course. You knew him quite well, didn't you?'

'Er . . . quite,' stammered Ezra. 'We worked together on the *Sigurlína* for several seasons.'

'Of course you did,' exclaimed the owner. 'Silly me. He had a fine wife in Matthildur. Such a shame that.'

'Yes.'

The idea crystallised when Ezra heard the owner utter Matthildur's name. He would just delay alerting people. He wanted to take a better look at Jakob first. Then he would ask him. If Jakob refused to tell, he could refuse to help him. Or at least threaten to leave him to his fate.

The owner took his leave and Ezra stood rooted to the spot, watching him disappear through the door. It was several minutes before he turned back

to Jakob. Going over to the filleting table, he scru-
tinised him minutely. No sign of movement. Ezra
crouched over him for a long time. Had he been
wrong? Hadn't he seen Jakob's lips move after all?

Ezra had begun to believe it was all a strange
trick of the eyes when Jakob's lips quivered again.
He seemed to be trying to speak, but the movement was almost imperceptible.

Ezra bent close, putting his ear to Jakob's
mouth. He could hear very faint breathing now.
And every time Jakob exhaled it was like a prayer
for help . . .

Help.

Help.

CHAPTER 49

Ezra raised his head in consternation. The man's resilience was incredible. He had lived through shipwreck and raging seas, the transfer to the ice house, and, despite being battered and wounded, had managed to survive a freezing night.

'Jakob?' he whispered, glancing nervously at the door. 'Jakob!' he repeated more loudly. 'Jakob?'

One eye opened a slit. The other was covered by the clot of blood from the wound to his head.

'Do you know where you are?'

Ezra put his ear back to the other man's lips.

'. . . *Help* . . .' he heard Jakob breathe.

It was not his imagination. Jakob was alive.

'Can you hear me?' Ezra asked but received no response. He pressed his mouth to Jakob's ear and repeated the question.

The eye opened slightly wider.

'I'll help you, Jakob,' whispered Ezra in his ear. 'I'll get you out of here, fetch a doctor, bring you a blanket. I'll do all that, Jakob.'

The slit narrowed.

'Jakob!' Ezra hissed.

The slit opened again.

'I'll save you, Jakob, if you tell me where Matthildur is. If you tell me what you did with her.'

Jakob's lips moved and Ezra moved his ear closer.

'. . . co . . . ld.'

'I'll save you right now if you tell me. What did you do with Matthildur?'

The eye opened wider and Ezra thought Jakob was looking at him. His skin was blue with cold, his lips dark. The teeth protruded from beneath his upper lip. His hair still had lumps of sea ice in it, and there was more on his thick, black woollen jumper and oilskin trousers. But his eye was half open and Ezra thought he saw his pupil quiver.

'Where's Matthildur?'

'. . . col . . .'

'I know you can hear me. Tell me where Matthildur is and I'll help you.'

'C . . . can . . .'

'You can't? You can't tell me where she is? Is that what you're trying to say?'

The eye closed again. The lips had stopped moving. Ezra thought he had given up the ghost. For a minute he dithered. Was it too late? Should he run for help? Should he do everything in his power to save this man? Jakob had killed his beloved. He had choked the life out of Matthildur and hidden her body. What mercy did he deserve?

Ezra's old hatred for Jakob, unleashed now from

its bonds, began to course through his body, bringing a hectic flush to his face. He saw Matthildur in Jakob's hands, saw her fighting for her life, slowly suffocating, her eyes pleading for mercy. Jakob had shown none. He'd had no pity.

Ezra stood there and contemplated Jakob on the filleting table.

Then he went out to fetch the materials for the coffin.

Having locked the ice house, he took a wheelbarrow and set off to get the timber. He did not meet or speak to anyone on the way. Following the boat owner's advice, he found some nails on the site of the new fish-processing building, then marched home to fetch his own hammer and saw. As he knocked the coffin together in front of the ice house he tried not to let his thoughts stray to Jakob by concentrating on Matthildur instead, on the times they had shared. On the life together that might have been. He often daydreamed about their future, how it might have turned out if only she had been allowed to live. Perhaps they would have had a family by now, children to say goodbye to in the morning and come home to in the evening, to read to, tell stories to. Jakob had destroyed all that when he strangled Matthildur with his bare hands.

Ezra laid out the planks lengthwise, nailed them to crosspieces, and soon had a rough-and-ready box. The weather was still bitterly cold and snowy, and only the odd passer-by stopped to ask for news. Ezra told them that Jakob's body was going to Djúpivogur, while the Grindavík man would be taken home to the south.

Jakob had few friends in the village. Only one man came expressly to pay his respects. His name was Lárus and he approached Ezra from behind, almost giving him a heart attack as he materialised without warning through the veil of snow.

'I hear they're taking him to Djúpivogur today,' Lárus said. He was a short man in his early fifties, who used to sail out to the fishing grounds with Jakob. His face was deeply furrowed, his teeth stained yellow from tar, and his shoulders rounded by hard labour. Ezra had met him about the village and knew his life had not been easy.

'That's right,' Ezra replied, stopping to stretch, the hammer still in his hand.

'And you're making his coffin?'

'Yup.'

'I just wanted to see him one last time,' said Lárus, nodding at the door of the ice house.

Ezra hesitated. 'He's a bit of a mess,' he said, groping for excuses. 'Doesn't look too good.'

'I'm sure I've seen worse,' said Lárus, taking the cigarette he had been shielding in the palm of his hand, pinching the glowing end between finger and thumb, and putting the stub in his pocket.

'Come on then,' said Ezra reluctantly.

They went inside and crossed the shed to the filleting tables. To Ezra's intense relief, Jakob had not moved. He lay flat on the board, arms at his sides, face to the ceiling. Lárus walked right up to him and made the sign of the cross over his body, then stood there. He appeared to be saying a prayer over the dead man. Ezra looked frantically from Jakob's eye to his lips, then to Lárus standing over him. Time stood still.

'He was all right,' said Lárus suddenly, turning to Ezra. 'A mate.'

'Yes,' said Ezra. 'I know.'

'His number must have been up,' said Lárus. 'He was meant to go. Everything has its time and place.'

Ezra's attention was fixed on Jakob and he could have sworn he had opened his eye again. Lárus, whose back was turned, didn't notice.

'I expect so,' he heard himself reply automatically.

Lárus glanced back at Jakob. Ezra dropped his gaze to the floor. Surely he must notice that Jakob had half opened one eye. He kept expecting to hear Lárus exclaim in horror but nothing happened. He raised his head slowly. Lárus was still looking at Jakob.

'He could be a bloody menace as well,' he said loudly.

Ezra was silent.

'A bloody menace,' Lárus repeated, giving Ezra a significant look, before striding briskly out of the building.

When Ezra had finished constructing the coffin, he took hold of one end and dragged it into the ice house. The wood scraped over the concrete floor and he dropped the casket with a crash beside the filleting board where Jakob lay. Jakob didn't move, although Ezra studied him for some time. He went back outside for the coffin lid.

Then he went and fetched the nails.

CHAPTER 50

Ezra had come to a decision. It had been reached while he was collecting the planks and building the coffin, but had germinated during the years after Matthildur vanished. Jakob must pay for his crime. Ezra would try and force him to reveal Matthildur's whereabouts. If he was successful, all well and good; his long ordeal would be over. But that would not alter Jakob's fate. His days were numbered. He should have died when the boat broke up on the rocks. The only way Ezra could justify his deed was to convince himself that he was merely finishing what a higher power had begun.

After it was over, Ezra was perturbed to realise that his decision to deny Jakob help had been reached without a struggle. On the contrary, it seemed the logical consequence of what had gone before. He hardly even stopped to think that he was commiting murder, a criminal act, a sin. Perhaps he had suppressed the thought deliberately, avoiding giving the correct name to his intention, because it sounded sordid, merciless, brutal.

When he came back, he discovered that Jakob had opened his uninjured eye fully and was looking around as if he sensed danger. One of his arms that had been at his side now lay across his chest. A puff of breath, so tiny as to be hardly visible, emanated from his nose and mouth. Jakob had been teetering on the brink of death for an eternity but he had turned a corner. His tenacity defied belief.

'Tell me about Matthildur,' Ezra stooped and hissed in his ear. 'What did you do with her?'

The eye stared at him. Under the clump of dried blood the other was now trying to open.

'Where is she?'

Jakob's eye, wide open now, was fixed on him. His lips trembled. Ezra put his ear to them.

As he did so, Jakob's deathly cold arm hooked round his neck and weakly tried to drag his head down as he gasped out:

Go

to

hell

Ezra tore himself free and Jakob's arm fell back lifeless to his side as he lost consciousness again.

Ezra found two fairly large crates to put under the coffin, then hauled the man off the filleting table and let him fall into the casket. There was a heavy thud as he landed on the bottom.

Then he fetched the lid and, taking one nail after another from his pocket, hammered it down. He avoided thinking about what he was doing. The fact that he was killing a defenceless man. He would have to fend off that thought for the rest of his life.

Ezra was hammering in the final nail when he heard approaching voices. Jakob's uncle had arrived with the boat owner to fetch the body.

The owner rebuked Ezra for nailing down the lid before the uncle had had a chance to see the dead man and ordered him to go for a crowbar immediately.

'Wouldn't you like to see him?' the owner asked Jakob's uncle, an elderly man, inadequately dressed in an old leather jacket and rubber boots. He did not seem notably troubled by his loss.

Ezra gaped at him. It had not crossed his mind that he might want to view his nephew's body.

'There's no need,' the uncle replied finally, and Ezra was overwhelmed with relief. 'I didn't know him that well.'

The uncle had enlisted the help of a Djúpivogur neighbour who owned a boat, and with Ezra's assistance they carried the coffin on board and tied a tarpaulin over it.

It was over. The wind had dropped considerably and the boat set off across the choppy fjord, bearing the coffin. The owner clapped Ezra on the back and thanked him for taking such fine care of Jakob. Ezra mumbled a reply. They said goodbye and went their separate ways.

CHAPTER 51

Now that Erlendur had got what he wanted, he was no longer sure if he had been justified in putting such pressure on Ezra. Or whether he had really needed to hear the whole truth. He had sat quietly through the old man's account, noting that Ezra had decided to leave out nothing but to tell the unvarnished truth at last, however uncomfortable or painful. But it was obvious to look at him that finally confessing to his crime had been one of the most traumatic experiences of his life.

Erlendur waited for him to resume his tale but Ezra sat silently in his wicker chair in the corner, his mind no longer in the kitchen, in the house, or even in this world. He was holding the picture of Matthildur and caressing it with his finger as if he longed to touch her one more time.

'For what it's worth –' Ezra broke off. 'For what it's worth,' he tried again, 'I've been filled with remorse ever since. As soon as I'd done it I was in two minds about whether to tell. I half hoped they'd leave it a few days before burying him, so he could attract their attention. I did nothing to save him. But I prayed for him – that he wouldn't suffer. I prayed to God that he wouldn't have to suffer. I couldn't bear the thought of him writhing around in his coffin. But that wasn't on my mind when I shut the lid on him. And I never really had to wrestle with my conscience because I never knew what had happened after I closed the lid. Over the years I've become reconciled to my God. All I had left was to die. Then you appeared.'

Ezra looked up.

'You come in here claiming to have dug him up. You say you've seen scratch marks on the coffin lid. You put his teeth on my kitchen counter.'

'I'm sorry if –' But Erlendur was not allowed to finish.

'That was the first time it really hit home what I'd done.' Ezra looked back at the picture. 'You must utterly despise me.'

'It doesn't matter what I think,' said Erlendur.

'You say that now. But if you hadn't haunted me like a ghost from the past, I'd never have dredged all this up.'

'I can believe –'

Ezra interrupted again. 'You're the stubbornest bastard I've ever met.'

Erlendur did not know how to take this.

'Anyway, I'll be dead soon and that'll be an end to it,' said Ezra.

'I can believe it's been hard for you to live with,' said Erlendur. 'An honest man like yourself.'

'Yes, well, so much for honesty,' said Ezra. 'I've

tried to do my best, tried to atone for it in my own way. And you mustn't forget what Jakob did to Matthildur. There are times when I justify my crime. I blame Jakob. Then I feel better for a while. But it never lasts.'

'As I said, it's not the first extraordinary story of survival I've heard,' said Erlendur. 'People who've been written off as dead. Man has a phenomenal instinct to live.'

'I've often wished he'd simply died in the ship-wreck,' Ezra went on. 'It would have been . . . it would have been simpler, purer.'

'Life's never simple,' said Erlendur. 'That's the first thing we learn. It's never straightforward.'

'Are you going to take action?' asked Ezra.

Their eyes met.

'Not unless you want me to.'

'You'll leave it up to me?'

'It's not my concern. I just wanted to get to the bottom of the mystery.'

'But you're a policeman. Isn't it your duty . . .?'

'One's duty can be complicated.'

'Not that it really matters to me what you do. Though a few people around here would revise their opinion of me, not that I really care. But I'd be grateful if the story of Matthildur's fate could be left unchanged. There's a certain poetry to it. Though it's a damned lie, there's something in the idea of her striding over the Hraevarskörd Pass that I'd like to be allowed to live on in people's memories. Unless they're all dead by now.'

312

'I don't suppose anyone's asked after Jakob in all these years?'

'No. You're the only one.'

'And he never told you what he did with her?'

'No.'

'So you still have no idea?'

'No.'

'If you'd been able to save his life, might he have told you then?'

'No, it wouldn't have made any difference,' said Ezra. 'I'm convinced of that. Even if I'd helped him, he'd never have let on.'

'Jakob seems to have been rallying when you put him in the coffin,' Erlendur continued, choosing his words with care.

'He was dead as far as everyone else was concerned,' said Ezra. 'I just put him in his coffin.'

The justification sounded as if it had been rehearsed countless times in the intervening years. Ezra got to his feet and looked out of the window at the moor which loomed against the sky, pristine and untouched.

'I sometimes wonder,' he said. 'Don't get me wrong, I didn't mean him to live, but if he'd shown any remorse, the slightest hint of remorse or regret . . . would things have gone differently? Would I have saved his life?'

Erlendur didn't know what to say.

'I've had to live with it ever since,' Ezra whispered to the window. 'At times the shame's been almost more than I could bear.'

CHAPTER 52

Hrund had been discharged from hospital. It was evening as Erlendur drove up to the house and spied her back in her habitual place at the window. She smiled at him and this time came to the front door to welcome him. Joining her in the sitting room, Erlendur asked after her health. She said she had come home that morning and had nothing to grumble about.

'Any new discoveries?' she asked, bringing him some freshly made coffee. 'Any news about Matthildur?'

Erlendur was uncertain how much to share with her about the fates of Matthildur and Jakob, or Ezra's act of vengeance after the shipwreck of 1949. He would rather gloss over the business of his grave robbery as well. And since he was concealing these facts, he might as well keep quiet about others too. So he gave her a heavily edited account of his meetings with Ezra. Hrund sat and listened without comment until it came to what concerned her most.

'I hope we can keep this between us,' said Erlendur. 'So it doesn't go any further.'

'Of course.'

'Ezra's convinced Jakob killed Matthildur.'

Hrund regarded him impassively.

'He has no proof,' said Erlendur. 'But he told me that Jakob had confessed to the killing in his hearing. Jakob acted out of jealousy and a desire for revenge. Some would call it a crime of passion. Matthildur was going to leave Jakob for Ezra, but he began to suspect they were up to no good and followed her to Ezra's house one night. He saw everything and couldn't take it – couldn't take the betrayal.'

Hrund's expression was still unreadable.

'Jakob invented the story about Matthildur going to your mother's house in Reydarfjördur and getting caught in the storm. As it was, she never left home.'

'Oh my God!' whispered Hrund at last.

'I have no reason to disbelieve Ezra,' said Erlendur.

'The evil bastard.'

Erlendur described how he had gradually coaxed Ezra into telling him what he knew, how he and Matthildur had been in love, how time had stopped for Ezra when she went missing. He told her about Ezra's encounters with Jakob after she vanished, first in the graveyard, then at Jakob's house, where he had confessed to killing her.

'How did you get him to talk?' Hrund asked.

Erlendur shrugged. 'He seemed ready to

unburden himself,' he said, hoping this was not too great a lie.

He wouldn't dream of admitting the pressure he had put on Ezra to make him cooperate. Indeed, he rather regretted it, especially given the cost. Erlendur was not proud of the lengths he had gone to. He was worried about digging up Jakob's grave but even more about how he had treated Ezra. He had bludgeoned the old man into confessing and now he could only pity him. He might himself be driven by an insatiable compulsion, an obsession with uncovering the truth, but why couldn't Ezra have been left in peace with his secrets? He was no hardened criminal, no danger to his community. When they parted, Ezra had said it didn't matter to him what Erlendur chose to do with his discoveries, but Erlendur knew better.

Hard on the heels of revelation came anger.

'It's hardly possible to imagine a worse end,' Erlendur said.

'Do you think I don't know that?' Ezra snarled back. 'Do you think it hasn't preyed on my mind every day? You needn't start preaching to me on that score.'

He turned to glare at Erlendur.

'You can leave now,' he said. 'Bugger off and leave me alone. I never want to set eyes on you again. I don't have long left and I don't want to have to see you.'

'I can understand –' Erlendur was not permitted to finish.

'Out!' said Ezra, raising his voice. 'Get out, I say! For once in your life do as I ask. Get out!'

Erlendur stood up and went to the kitchen door.

'I don't want us to part in anger,' he said.

'I don't give a damn what you want,' said Ezra. 'Just bugger off!'

So they parted. Erlendur retreated, though he was unhappy leaving him in such a fragile state. There was nothing he could do for Ezra right now, yet in spite of the old man's pleas he intended to come back the following day to check if he had recovered.

It had taken Hrund some time to grasp the full implications of what Erlendur had said.

'You mean Jakob admitted this to Ezra?' she said, aghast. 'That he'd killed her?'

Erlendur nodded.

'How?'

'With his bare hands,' said Erlendur. 'Apparently he strangled her.'

Hrund inadvertently clasped her hands over her mouth, as if to stifle the cry that rose to her lips when she pictured her sister's end.

'But why didn't Ezra tell anyone? Why didn't he go to the police?'

'It was more complicated than that,' said Erlendur. 'Jakob had a hold over Ezra. He fixed it, or at least claimed to have fixed it, so that Ezra would be framed for the murder if he ever told anyone what he had heard. Ezra chose not to take that risk. It wouldn't have restored Matthildur to him and he was convinced anyway that Jakob would never reveal how he'd disposed of the body. As indeed it turned out.'

'What did he do? What did Jakob do with her body?' asked Hrund.

'He always refused to tell.'

'So nobody knows?'

'No.'

'Not even Ezra?'

'No.'

'And you haven't found out?'

'No.'

'So she'll never be found?'

'Probably not.'

Hrund reflected on what Erlendur had said. She was profoundly shaken. All the wind seemed to have been knocked out of her.

'The poor man,' she said at last.

'Ezra's life has been pretty wretched ever since,' said Erlendur.

'He's had to live with this uncertainty all these years.'

'Yes.'

'Who would do that – what kind of man?' she said, rising to her feet in her anguish. 'What kind of monster was Jakob?'

'You said he had a bad reputation.'

'Yes, but this! Who could do such a thing?'

'He got his just deserts.'

'Not just enough in my opinion,' snapped Hrund.

'Perhaps he had an opportunity to reflect on the suffering he had caused others before he died,' said Erlendur.

Her gaze sharpened. 'What do you mean?'

'That would have been punishment enough,' said Erlendur.

CHAPTER 53

At the end of that long day Erlendur drove up to a small, wooden house, clad in corrugated iron, situated in the town of Seydisfjördur. After leaving Hrund, he had driven straight along the Fagridalur Valley, pausing briefly in Egilsstadir to replenish his supplies of petrol, cigarettes and coffee, before taking the road east over the high mountain pass to Seydisfjördur which lay at the head of the fjord of the same name. He had one remaining call to make and wanted to get it out of the way that evening. He had found the address in the phone book. The man he was on his way to visit was called Daníel Kristmundsson and his name had cropped up in conversation with Bóas's nemesis, Lúdvík. Daníel used to work as a guide for hunters from Reykjavík. 'An old rascal,' Lúdvík had called him.

There was a faint gleam of light in one window of the house, which stood on a secluded, badly lit street at the eastern end of the little town. After vainly fumbling for a bell, Erlendur knocked on the door. Nothing happened. He knocked again. After a long interval he finally heard movement

320

within. He waited patiently until the door opened and a man in his early fifties, unshaven and tousled, squinted at him dubiously.

'What can I do for you?'

He could hardly be described as an old rascal, so assuming he was the wrong man, Erlendur asked if this was Daníel Kristmundsson's house.

'That Daníel's dead,' said the man.

'Oh?' said Erlendur. 'Has he been dead long?'

'Six months.'

'I see,' said Erlendur. 'Well, that's that then. He's still listed at this address in the phone book.'

'Yes, I suppose I should give them a call.'

The man inspected him. A glint of curiosity appeared in his eyes. 'Why did you want to see him? Are you selling something?'

'No,' said Erlendur. 'I'm not a salesman. I'm sorry to have bothered you.'

He said goodbye and was about to return to his car when the man came out onto the step.

'What did you want with Daníel?' he asked.

'It doesn't matter,' said Erlendur. 'I'm too late. Did you know him?'

'Quite well,' the man replied. 'He was my father.'

Erlendur smiled. 'I wanted to talk to him about fox-hunting – in the old days. Specifically about fox behaviour, and about their earths. That was all. I was told he was an expert.'

'What did you want to know?'

The dim light spilled out into the darkness where they stood. Erlendur felt awkward and unsure about his errand now it transpired that the man he had come to see was dead. But his son's interest had been piqued by the visitor who had disturbed his nap.

'Nothing important,' replied Erlendur. 'Just whether he'd ever found any unusual objects on the moors to the south of here. In the mountains above Reydarfjördur or Eskifjördur – on Andri or Hardskafi, for example. I don't suppose you'd know?'

'Are you working on the dam?' asked the man. 'No.'

'The smelter, then?'

'No, I'm just passing through,' explained Erlendur. 'I'm not working out here.'

'He found all sorts of stuff, my dad,' said the man. 'All kinds of rubbish. Kept some of it too.'

'Objects found in nests or foxholes, you mean?'

'That's right. And from the shore. He used to beach-comb for shells, pebbles and animal bones. I expect you'd have enjoyed meeting him.'

'I'm sorry to hear he's passed away.'

'Ah, well, he'd had a good innings. Bedbound towards the end. It didn't suit him. He was glad to go. Maybe you'd like to see the junk he collected? The garage is bursting with it. I haven't got round to throwing any of it away yet though I've some-times thought of setting light to the lot.'

Erlendur paused. It had been a gruelling day.

'Well, it's up to you,' the man said, waiting for an answer.

'It wouldn't hurt to have a look,' said Erlendur. The man was so eager to help that he didn't want to appear ungrateful.

'My name's Daníel too,' said the man, offering him his hand. 'Daníel Daníelsson. There aren't many of us around.'

Unsure how to take this, Erlendur followed him in silence round the back of the house, where the darkness was even more impenetrable, to a concrete building that might once have been intended as a garage. Daníel opened the door, felt for the light switch and turned on the naked bulb that hung from the ceiling.

Unfortunately, no one could have claimed that the old rascal had been tidy or arranged his collection in any sort of order. The garage was crammed with objects, some useful, others worthless, that old Daníel had evidently picked up and then put down wherever he happened to be standing. Erlendur hung back in the doorway: there was no point going any further.

'See what I mean?' said Daníel. 'Wouldn't it be simplest to torch the lot?'

'I'm afraid I don't think there's anything here for me,' said Erlendur politely. 'I shouldn't take up any more of your time. I'd better be going.'

'You mentioned foxholes,' said Daníel.

'Yes, but it's all right. I'm a bit pressed for time actually.'

'I know there are some crates in here somewhere – three of them, I think – full of smaller boxes and envelopes that he kept his bones in. He often used to show them to me in the old days, tell me where he'd found them and so on. He had quite a collection. Foxes' bones too. A fair number. Is that the kind of thing you had in mind?'

The man forced a path through the piles of junk, pushing aside the spare parts of cars, tyres, a broken bicycle frame. A collection of plumbing materials, including pipes and joints, hung from the ceiling. Erlendur spotted two ancient shotguns that must have been defunct: one was missing the trigger; the barrel and stock were facing in opposite directions on the other. A stuffed raven and the hide of an animal he didn't recognise graced one corner. Daníel bored further into the garage and Erlendur regretted ever having dragged him out of bed. He was about to succumb to the urge to tiptoe away without saying goodbye when Daníel uttered an exclamation. 'Here's one.'

Erlendur saw him straighten up with a large cardboard box in his arms.

'Take a look in here, if you want,' Daníel said, bringing it over. 'I'm going to check if the rest are over there.'

'Really, there's no need,' protested Erlendur, but the man either didn't hear or didn't want to listen.

Accepting the box, Erlendur placed it on a heap of carpet offcuts. It turned out to be full of turnip-coloured bones that he found hard to identify, though they might have included the skulls of birds and cats, a fox's jawbone with needle-sharp teeth, and assorted leg bones and ribs. Among them were what appeared to be the skeletons of mice. None were labelled in any way, either with the name of the species or the site of discovery. Erlendur glanced up from the box to see Daníel cradling an old wooden crate which had once contained bottles of some long-discontinued Icelandic fizzy drink called 'Spur'. Erlendur had never tasted it.

The contents of this one were better organised. Some of the bones were in brown paper envelopes, with the name of the animal and the find site written on the front. Erlendur guessed that Daníel had started out with a system but eventually abandoned it. Perhaps he had amassed the bones quicker than he could catalogue them.

'He knew a whole lot about bones,' Daníel's son remarked from the other end of the garage. He sounded proud. 'Specially of birds. He trained as a taxidermist when he was young, though he never practised. It was just a kind of hobby. I've got a white fox indoors that he stuffed. Did a good job too. And a falcon, if you're interested.'

'Would I be right in thinking he did the raven?' asked Erlendur, gesturing at the black bird stowed up among the rafters.

'That's right,' said the younger Daníel. 'Are you from Reykjavík, by any chance?'

'Yes, I live there,' said Erlendur, going through the envelopes in the crate. He was engrossed now. One was marked 'Arctic tern, Lodmundarfjördur'.

He opened it, tipping a near intact skeleton into his palm.

'He used to talk about putting these bones in a display case with proper labels and donating the collection to the local college. He had a case built ages ago, with a glass front, but I can't find it anywhere. I spotted it in here once, so I can't understand what's become of it.'

Erlendur replaced the skeleton in the envelope. Daníel was holding yet another crate which he now passed to him. Inside were numerous smaller containers which were clearly labelled. Old Daníel had been very systematic about organising this part of his collection.

Erlendur picked up one of the smaller boxes. The white label glued to its lid read 'Foot of Mount Snaefell, Golden plover'.

Erlendur took out several more and examined them. One had a question mark scribbled on the lid. He read the label: 'Hardskafi, North flank'.

The words were written in pencil. The question mark gave him pause.

Opening the lid, he saw immediately that the small bones it contained were human. He had after all once dug up the skeleton of a four-year-old girl. A shiver ran like cold water down his spine.

'What have you got there?' called Daníel from the back of the garage. He had noticed that his visitor was standing as if turned to stone, with one of his father's boxes in his hands.

'Did your father ever mention someone going missing on the moors around here?' asked Erlendur, not taking his eyes off the bones.

'Missing? No.'

'A child from Eskifjördur, lost on the moors forty years ago?'

'No, he never mentioned it,' said Daníel. 'At least not in my hearing.'

'Are you sure?'

'Yes, I'd remember that. But I don't.'

Erlendur stared at the question mark on the lid. Old Daníel hadn't known what it was that he had found on the northern slopes of Mount Hardskafi, but he had shoved the bones in his pocket anyway because of his collecting mania. Perhaps he had intended to find out what they were, maybe even send them to an expert, but never got round to it. If he had, he would without a doubt have discovered what he had in his possession. Then someone would have heard about his find and made the connection with the boy who went missing.

He searched for a date on the box but there was none.

There were two bones. He didn't dare touch them but was convinced he was right. One was part of a chinbone, the other a cheekbone.

They were not fully grown.

They belonged to a child.

CHAPTER 54

Erlendur walks in silence behind his father as they slog up the hill to the moor. He pays little heed to where they are going. Bergur, lagging behind, breaks into a jog to catch up. Soon the distance between them opens once more and Bergur is forced into a trot again. Erlendur himself is walking hard on his father's heels, trying to tread in his footprints, though this is tricky because they are too far apart. At times he has to quicken his pace to avoid being left behind like Beggi.

They continue like this for a good while, until their father decides it is time for a rest. Not for him; for the boys. The higher they climb, the deeper and more of a hindrance the snow becomes, especially for short legs. Raising a pair of binoculars to his eyes, their father scans the landscape for the lost sheep.

'Wait for me, Lendi,' Beggi calls. He pretends not to hear.

Beggi calls him 'Lendi', 'big brother Lendi'. His mother occasionally addresses him as 'Lillabob', which infuriates him, though she only uses it nowadays to tease him. But his father only ever calls him by his given name. 'Erlendur,' he will say, 'pass me that book, will you?' Or, 'Time you were in bed, Erlendur.'

Beggi catches up. He notices that Beggi is struggling with his gloves and discovers that he has brought along his toy car. He has freed his hands so he can extract the car from his pocket to check if it's all right. Then he pushes it inside one of the gloves and tries to put his hand in after it, so that he can hold the toy.

'I can't see them,' their father announces. 'We'll climb a bit higher and see if we can find their tracks.'

They resume their journey, their father in front, Erlendur in the middle and Bergur bringing up the rear, fiddling with the little car inside his glove and trying to keep up. Their father sets a steady pace, lifting his binoculars from time to time and heading first one way, then another. Before they know it they have reached the high moors. To a half-comprehending child's eye, everything then happens very fast. Events arrange themselves into a series of brief snapshots. Their father glances at the sky. Beggi is lagging behind. Snow has been falling for some time but now heavy, black storm clouds pile up with alarming speed over the mountains. The sky grows dark. Their legs sink into the snow and Erlendur, who has paid scant attention to the weather, now feels a cold breath of wind on his cheek. He can no longer see down to

Eskifjördur Fjord through the thickly falling flakes. Bergur is some distance behind and Erlendur calls out to him but he doesn't hear. Erlendur goes back to fetch him and loses sight of their father when out of nowhere a blizzard strikes, reducing visibility to zero. He shouts again to Bergur, who has fallen over in the snow, then yells his father's name, but receives no answer.

Beggi gets up again but drops his glove which is immediately snatched away by the wind. He starts off after it with Erlendur in pursuit. The glove is lost in an instant in the blinding snow but they do not give up the chase. Erlendur comes close to losing Bergur who is oblivious to everything but his glove. Their mother has taught them to take good care of their clothes. He grabs hold of Bergur's jacket to slow him down. Bergur is holding the toy car in his bare, raw hand and stops to put it in his pocket.

'I want my mitten!' His cry is whipped away by the wind.

'We'll find it later,' Erlendur tells him.

He has to yell to make Beggi hear. He heads back in the direction where he thinks he left his father. Running after the glove like that has muddled him, but he is fairly sure he knows the way. It is terribly difficult to make any headway against the wind and freezing pellets that sting his face. The force seems to intensify with every step he takes until he can scarcely open his eyes. He doesn't seem to be moving at all and can see nothing but whiteness. Everything happened so rapidly that he hasn't even had time to feel frightened. It's a comfort to know his father is nearby. He shouts and Beggi joins in, but there is no reply.

He no longer knows which direction to take, can't tell if he is going up or down. He believes he is climbing towards where he last saw his father, but perhaps this is wrong? Perhaps he shouldn't look for him at all but try to get back to the farm, concentrate on saving Beggi and himself?

He begins to feel afraid now and Beggi senses it. 'Will we be all right, Lendi?' he asks. He has to shout into his older brother's ear.

'It's all right,' Erlendur reassures him. 'We'll be home soon.'

He takes off one of his own gloves, intending to give it to Beggi, but fumbles and drops it, and it disappears in the storm. Beggi takes hold of his hand.

Erlendur doesn't have a clue where he is going. He hopes he is heading downhill but is too disorientated to be certain. He tries to persuade himself that the weather will improve once they get low enough. Beggi keeps tripping over in the snow, slowing them down, but it doesn't cross Erlendur's mind to let go of his hand. Their fingers are numb with cold, yet Erlendur takes care not to lose his grip on his brother.

The blizzard pummels them from all sides, buffeting them to and fro, knocking them down into the snow and making it ever harder to stand up again. They can't even see their hands in front of their faces and before long both boys are exhausted and freezing. Erlendur keeps hoping they will bump into their father, but in vain, and they are making no progress in descending to the farmlands.

Then it happens. He can no longer feel Beggi's hand in his own frozen one, as if they had been parted some time ago without his noticing. His fingers are locked in the grip he had on his brother, but he is holding thin air. Turning round, he tries to run back but stumbles into a drift. Rising, he yells Beggi's name over and over, but is knocked down again, still shouting and screaming. He is weeping now and the tears freeze on his cheeks.

Utterly bewildered, he squats in the snow, overwhelmed with fear for himself, for his father but most of all for Beggi. He feels it is somehow his fault that Beggi ever came with them on this journey, and can't shake off the thought that if he hadn't interfered, Beggi would have stayed at home.

The roar of the storm has intensified by the time Erlendur gets up on hands and knees and begins to crawl, rather than walk, confused and aimless. He has read about people caught in bad weather and knows that an important survival technique is to dig yourself into a drift and wait for the worst to pass. And you must on no account fall asleep in the snow because if you do you may never wake up again. But he can't bear to abandon his search for Beggi. He hopes fervently that Beggi has managed to get down from the moors and is on his way home or even now in their mother's arms. When he reaches Bakkasel, no doubt Beggi will come to meet him with their father, and everything will be all right when their mother flings her arms around him. He's worried about her, knowing she must be desperately anxious.

He has lost all sense of time. It feels as if night fell hours ago. His strength is rapidly flagging. Yet refusing to give up, he toils on through the falling snow, half crawling, half walking, in the feeble hope that he is heading in the right direction. The cold pierces his clothes but his teeth have ceased their chattering and the involuntary shivering that had seized his whole body has also stopped by the time he finally topples headlong and doesn't move again.

He falls asleep the moment he hits the snow.

The last thing he remembers is Beggi battling through the storm, placing all his trust in his big brother.

'Don't lose me,' Beggi had shouted. 'You mustn't lose me.'

'It'll be all right,' he had said in reply.

It'll be all right.

CHAPTER 55

On his last morning at Bakkasel he woke up after a bad night's sleep, unable to feel his extremities, so he hurried out to the car and switched on the heater. He had brought the Thermos and cigarettes with him and once he had warmed up a little, he poured coffee into the lid of the flask and lit up. He stayed there until he had got the blood back into his limbs. The box containing the bones lay beside him on the passenger seat. Daníel had given it to him in parting, saying he had no idea what to do with all his father's junk and repeating that it would be best to set fire to the garage. Erlendur had thanked him and brought the bones back to the croft.

Judging by the label on the lid, Daníel senior had stumbled upon them while walking across the north flank of Hardskafi, a considerable distance from the spot where Erlendur had been found in a state close to death. Bergur must have strayed further north than anyone would have believed possible – assuming these were his brother's remains. But they weren't necessarily proof that he died on the mountain. The remains could have

334

arrived there in the mouth of a fox, for example. The bones themselves couldn't tell Erlendur much, lying in a cardboard box in a garage in Seydisfjördur, but it was enough. He was convinced they were the chin and cheekbone of a child, and immediately felt a powerful intuition that they could only belong to his brother.

During the night he had considered sending them off for tests. He could have them dated and get an expert opinion on how long they had been at the mercy of the elements. But the process would take time and it was uncertain what the results would show. He came to the conclusion that he didn't need the help of science. He was sure in his own mind, and soon an idea began to form about what he should do with the bones.

Having finished the coffee and smoked two cigarettes, Erlendur started the car and drove slowly away from Bakkasel along the track to the Eskifjördur road, then headed in the direction of the village. Turning off just before it, he parked by the gate of the graveyard. Once there he remained in the car for a while with the engine running, still savouring the blast of warm air from the heater. He picked up the box, opened it and inspected the two bones. If there had been any more, surely Daníel would have picked them up too? Erlendur had been plagued by such questions all night. He knew he would have to climb the north flank of the mountain, not necessarily in search of further remains, as he had no idea where the bones had been found or how they had got there. No, he must go there for other reasons.

He stepped out of the car, box in hand, and fetched the spade from the boot. He wouldn't need to dig nearly as deep this time, merely scratch the surface of his mother's grave.

He found his parents' plot and stood there in the raw air, thinking about the years that had passed since the accident, since they had lived in the east. His mother had coped well with the bustle and traffic when they moved to Reykjavík, but his father had never been happy, finding the city brash, noisy and alien. At the time new suburbs had been springing up almost overnight. These were now old and established, yet districts were forever being added to the city to cater for incomers from the countryside, who didn't all adapt easily to their new circumstances. And so the years passed, time crawling on inexorably into a future that no one from the obsolete past would recognise.

Like his father, Erlendur had never settled into the new environment, never understood what he was doing there or adjusted properly. All he knew was that somewhere on his journey through life time had come to a standstill, and he had never managed to wind the mechanism up again. When he stood there with the bones in his hands, he had experienced no elation, no sense that his suffering was at last over and he had received answers to the questions that had dogged him ever since his brother's disappearance. Any hope of happiness was long forgotten.

Erlendur raised his eyes to the mountains. Snow was falling on their slopes.

He shifted his gaze to the cemetery, to the rows of headstones and crosses. Born. Died. Buried. Beloved wife. Blessed be your memory. Rest in peace. Death above and all around.

Death in a small box.

Looking again at the bones, he knew in his heart that he had recovered two tiny fragments of his brother's remains. For years he had been trying to envisage how he would react if he ever found himself in this position. Now an answer of sorts was at hand. But he felt numb. Empty. These little fragments of bone couldn't satisfy his questions. It was impossible to say exactly where his brother had died and it would always be a mystery how his bones had ended up on the northern slopes of Hardskafi. Nothing would alter the fact that he had died in a blizzard at the age of eight. The discovery of his bones brought Erlendur no fresh insights. It was merely confirmation of what he already knew. After all these years, however, it did bring some small sense of closure, however paltry. What remained was a feeling of emptiness more desolate than anything he had ever experienced.

His gaze wandered among the graves and crosses, and somewhere in his mind a year and date registered as familiar, as significant. He went back over the inscriptions, trying to work out which was nagging at his memory. The year 1942 caught his eye.

He walked over to the headstone of weathered granite that projected a metre above the snow. It turned out to be the year that a woman called Thórhildur Vilhjálmsdóttir had died. She had been born in 1850. Erlendur did some quick mental arithmetic. She had been ninety-one when she passed away. She had been born on 7 September in the mid-nineteenth century and died on 14 January 1942, in the middle of the Second World War.

He considered the date again. She had died on 14 January in the year Matthildur went missing. Thórhildur had died a week before the storm in which the British servicemen came to grief. A week before Matthildur vanished.

He frowned down at the woman's grave. No doubt the stone had been erected some time after her death, maybe years or even decades later. It was impossible to tell. But one could be fairly confident that not much more than a week would have elapsed between her death and funeral. The storm of 21 January might have occasioned a delay but it was also possible that Thórhildur had been buried before it struck.

Erlendur stood, lost in thought, concentrating on the date. January 1942. He considered the storm that had been raging, and Matthildur's death, and Ezra. But most of all he focused on Jakob and the options that would have been

338

available to him. He realised that he would need to consult a copy of the parish register.

After receiving directions to the vicar's house from the staff at the petrol station, he drove straight round and rang the doorbell. A middle-aged woman answered and he asked to see the vicar. The woman explained that he had gone on a short trip to Reykjavík but would be back in a couple of days.

'Do you know where I could get hold of the parish registers dating back to the Second World War?' he asked, making an effort to hide his impatience.

'Parish registers?' repeated the woman. 'I'm afraid I don't. You mean the old ones? I expect they're kept at the Regional Museum in Egilsstadir. That would be my guess. Though no doubt my husband Rúnar could help you if he was here.'

Erlendur thanked her, drove back to the petrol station and borrowed their phone to ring the museum. He hadn't charged his mobile once since arriving in the east. He was informed that the Eskifjördur parish registers were indeed in their archives and he was welcome to consult them if he wished. He had noted down Thórhildur's dates before leaving the graveyard, so he got back in his car and made the now familiar journey up the Fagridalur Valley to Egilsstadir.

When he asked to see the Eskifjördur church records dating back to the war, the museum curator, who turned out to be the man who had answered the phone, couldn't have been more obliging. Having shown Erlendur to a table where he could peruse the ledger at his leisure, he went and fetched it.

Erlendur turned the pages until he reached the beginning of 1942. There had only been the one funeral between New Year and March. He recalled Ezra telling him that he had encountered Jakob in the cemetery in March, two months after Matthildur went missing, and that he had been digging a grave at the time.

Thórhildur had been buried on 23 January, two days after the storm. Nine days after she had passed away.

The vicar's brief, cryptic marginal note came as no surprise to Erlendur.

Gr. d. by Jak. R.

Grave dug by Jakob Ragnarsson.

CHAPTER 56

Two hours later he was standing beside Thórhildur Vilhjálmsdóttir's grave again. He had already dug up one coffin recently and was not at all sure he wanted to repeat the experience, but he could not confirm his suspicions by any other method. He was feeling fairly certain of his theory after turning the matter over in his mind all the way back from Egilsstadir.

This time, however, he didn't believe he would need to dig as far to find the evidence. It was unlikely he would have to disinter Thórhildur's coffin or excavate underneath it. Jakob would presumably have taken the easiest course, especially as he wouldn't have had much time in which to act. In any case, there would have been little risk that anyone would ever want to re-examine the body of a woman in her nineties. The longer Erlendur stood over her grave, the more convinced he became that he would need to dig no more than a metre to find what he sought.

The light was already failing, so he decided to wait until it was fully dark. He got back into the car, switched on the heater and settled down to

341

listen to a radio station playing modern jazz that he didn't recognise but found relaxing. He tried to unwind, tried to stop himself brooding on Ezra, Matthildur and Jakob, on his brother and the box of bones, and all that he had discovered during his few days' leave in the East Fjords. He hadn't thought about home once, so preoccupied had he been with his investigation. The case had gnawed at him for years. In fact, he had toyed with the idea of looking into Matthildur's disappearance before now, but it was that chance encounter with Bóas on the moor that had provided the impetus. He hadn't really needed to think twice before going to visit Hrund. He longed to know more. To find out why. Someone had told him it didn't matter any more, that the passing years and time's destructive power had erased all need for any investigation. It would change nothing; it only had relevance for a handful of people now. This was true up to a point. There was no danger: only one person had any interests to protect. But Erlendur knew better. When a loved one went missing time changed nothing. Admittedly, it dulled the pain, but by the same token the loss became a lifelong companion for those who survived, making the grief keener and deeper in a way he couldn't explain.

His thoughts turned to his daughter and their last meeting, when she said she had forgiven him for all the years of neglect since he divorced her mother. And his son, who never made any demands on him, and Valgerdur who simply tried to make his life easier. And Marion Briem who had died such a lonely death. His colleagues too, Elínborg and Sigurdur Óli. The cases they had investigated, the years they had worked together.

Night fell rapidly and when he felt it was dark enough to enter the cemetery with lantern and spade, he stepped out of the car. As he made his way towards Thórhildur's grave, he thanked his lucky stars that there was so little traffic in this part of the village. Putting down the gaslight, he began to shovel snow from the plot, then sliced off a sizeable patch of turf to uncover the bare earth.

He worked methodically. The question of what to say if he was caught in the act gave him a moment's pause but no more. He could always wave his police ID if all else failed. His superiors would not look kindly on a private investigation of this kind but at least his intentions were good. All he was doing was solving an old crime. That was why he had permitted himself to disinter Jakob and was now hacking his way into Thórhildur's grave.

Placing the lantern nearby, he dug carefully but was not aware of any hindrance. He picked up the light and shone it into the hole but could see nothing unusual. He stretched his back.

The village street lights lit up the harbour and the mountainsides above the highest houses. Like other settlements in the East Fjords, Eskifjördur

343

was little more than a cluster of buildings round the docks with a main street running along the seafront, yet it had a long history and over the generations its inhabitants had experienced great changes. The most radical transformation of all was taking place now, with the building of the giant dam in the highlands to provide electricity for the aluminium smelter in the neighbouring fjord. The past was once more giving way irreversibly to the present.

He resumed his excavation. Every now and then he glanced around to check for anyone who might demand an explanation. But he never saw a soul.

He drove the spade into the ground again. The hole was no more than half a metre deep. Flinging the soil over the top, he pushed the blade down again and felt resistance, as if it had struck a stone. There was a small click. He shone the lamp over the spot but could see nothing, so he started digging again and now there was no doubt of the impediment. Using the blade, he scraped away the dirt, then illuminated the pit again.

This time he immediately spotted something in the soil that he couldn't identify. By sliding the spade underneath it, he managed to lever it up, then he put down his tool, felt around with his fingers and held the object up to the light. He hadn't a clue what it was until he had cleaned off some of the dirt. Then it became clear: he was holding a knife. The blade was rusty and notched; the wooden handle had almost rotted away.

Recalling what Ezra had said about Jakob hiding some possession of his with the body, Erlendur guessed that the knife must have belonged to him.

Laying it aside, he picked up the shovel again and continued his excavation. After another spadeful, he met further resistance.

At first he could see nothing, but when he strained his eyes he began to perceive a shape in the soil, like one of those trick images that gradually reveals itself to the observer: familiar lines, an outline he recognised. Lying down, he reached into the hole to scrape more earth off his discovery. A little water had collected in the bottom but he could see no splinters of broken wood or any other trace of a coffin.

Finally he lowered the gas lantern down the hole and now at last he came face to face with what lay hidden above the last resting place of Thórhildur Vilhjálmsdóttir. The old woman was not alone in her grave. Under cover of night, an uninvited and unwilling guest had been laid down there with her and hastily covered with earth.

The first thing he made out distinctly, half submerged in the muddy water, was a row of teeth. Then a segment of skull took shape, complete with lower jaw and molars, and Erlendur knew that he had found the earthly remains of Matthildur Kjartansdóttir, who had purportedly died of exposure on her way over the Hraevarskörd Pass in the great January storm of 1942.

CHAPTER 57

He opens his eyes. That insufferable question again.

'I know who you are,' he says.

'Yes?' says the traveller.

'You once came to our house and talked to Bergur.'

'You remember.'

'You said we wouldn't have him with us for long.'

The traveller makes no reply to this.

'Because he was that kind of soul. It was you. I remember it clearly. Who are you? Why are you here?'

Still no answer.

'Where are we?'

He has been under the impression that he was lying on his sleeping mat in the ruined farmhouse and that the man has come to visit him there. But that can't be right because he now recalls leaving the house. He left behind his belongings and the car, and set out, unencumbered, for the mountain, for the north flank of Hardskafi. Although he barely surfaces into consciousness for more than a few seconds at a time, and the cold that is gradually killing him has addled his brain, he is fairly sure of this fact at least. He can't be speaking to the man in the old croft because there is nobody there, not even himself.

'Don't you know?' asks the traveller.

'Where do you come from?'

No reply.

'Where am I?' he asks.

Again he senses that the traveller who once enjoyed his parents' hospitality at Bakkasel is not alone. He is accompanied by that invisible being whose presence he has felt so strongly, never more so than now.

'Who's that with you?' he asks yet again.

'Who?'

'The person with you? Who is he?'

'You needn't be afraid of him.'

Silence.

'Do you think the time has come to meet him?'

'Who is he?'

'You're holding him at arm's length, but you know who he is. Deep down. You know who's come with me to see you. He says you have nothing to fear. Do you believe him? Do you believe him when he says you have nothing to fear?'

Silence.

'You know who he is.'

'Not . . .'

'It's you who's keeping him away.'

When the traveller disappears he thinks he hears a child's voice. Faint, remote. He can't distinguish the words. But he knows who the voice belongs to, knows now who is with the man. He hasn't heard that voice for many a long year and had believed he would never hear it again.

Briefly he recovers his wits, to find that the cold has intensified.

His consciousness fades once more.

CHAPTER 58

He had found Matthildur's earthly remains but experienced no sense of triumph, no satisfaction with what he had achieved. Instead, he was filled with sadness and an urgent desire to go and tell Ezra that his quest was over at last. He shovelled the earth back into the hole in frantic haste, replaced the square of turf and threw a few spadefuls of snow over the broken soil, praying that no one would notice immediately. Then, picking up the lantern and spade, he hurried back to the car.

Ezra's house lay in darkness. His headlamps illuminated it before he switched them off and stepped out onto the drive. No light was visible inside and the bulb by the front door was broken. Erlendur had noticed this on his first visit a few days earlier and had meant to mention to Ezra that he needed to replace it.

He knocked on the door and, receiving no response, tried the handle. The door swung open and he walked inside.

'Ezra!' he called. 'Are you home?'

There was no answer, so he groped his way along

to the kitchen doorway where he found a light switch. Nothing happened when he flicked it. He tried it several times, to no avail.

'Ezra!' he called again.

Maybe he had gone out. Perhaps a fuse had blown and he had gone to buy a replacement. Erlendur stood in the kitchen, waiting for his eyes to adjust. He could hardly see a thing apart from the outline of the kitchen table, but recalled that the sink was behind him.

'Ezra!'

He heard a creaking noise from one corner.

Peering over to where he knew the wicker chair to be, he perceived a figure rising from it, but only as a black shadow.

'Ezra?' Erlendur whispered.

A dark shape showed against the grey square of the window, advanced a step, then another, and he felt a cold object pushed gently under his chin. He didn't dare move. There was a whiff of metal and cordite. With infinite slowness, he gave way before the pressure of what he guessed was the muzzle of a shotgun.

'Have you come to arrest me?' he heard a low voice ask in the darkness.

'No.'

'Then get out.'

'Ezra?' whispered Erlendur.

'I don't want to see you here again. Get out before I do something stupid.'

'I came to . . . Ezra, I've found her.'

350

'What do you want?'

'I'm trying to tell you.'

'What are you talking about? What have you found?'

'I've found her. I've found Matthildur. I know where she is.'

'What do you mean?'

'I know what Jakob did with her, Ezra. I've discovered where he hid her body.'

His head was still tilted back by the pressure of the gun and he could only see Ezra indistinctly, as a black silhouette against the window.

'Are you making fun of me?' asked Ezra.

'I think I can prove it,' said Erlendur. 'Could you turn on the lights?'

'Prove it? How?'

'I found something with her that I believe belongs to you.'

'What? What have you found?'

'You'll have to turn on the light,' repeated Erlendur.

'That's not possible,' said Ezra.

'Have you got a torch then?'

Ezra did not answer.

'I can't show you in the dark.'

'There's a torch on the table.'

'Bring it over to the sink,' said Erlendur. 'I need to rinse the dirt off.'

Ezra didn't relinquish his grip on the gun as they made their way over to the sink. Finding the torch with one hand, he switched it on and for a moment

Erlendur was blinded as the glare struck him full in the face.

'Don't do anything you'll regret, Ezra,' he warned.

'I told you to leave me alone,' he heard Ezra mutter.

Erlendur had wrapped the knife in a small plastic bag that he had found in the car. He removed it warily from his pocket, took it out of the bag and, turning on the cold tap, washed off the soil. Ezra shone the torch on the knife as the clods of earth fell away.

'Recognise it?' asked Erlendur.

Ezra did not answer immediately.

'Do you recognise the knife?'

Still no reaction.

'It was buried on top of the body,' said Erlendur. 'Jakob wasn't lying. He put the knife in her grave to implicate you in her killing. He may even have stabbed her once or twice with it after she died. Was it yours?'

'It's my knife,' said Ezra's disembodied voice from behind the torch.

'I expect he stole it when he came round to tell you Matthildur was out in the storm.'

'Where is she?'

'In the cemetery,' said Erlendur. 'She's buried in the cemetery. Jakob worked as a gravedigger and had just dug one for an old woman whose funeral took place at around the time Matthildur went missing. He must have hidden her body at home, and after half filling the old woman's grave, sneaked back, fetched Matthildur's body and laid it on top.'

'In the cemetery?'

'Yes.'

'How do you know?'

'I noticed the woman's death date by chance and put two and two together. All I needed was to dig a small hole in her grave. I found Matthildur's remains, Ezra. I found her. The uncertainty's over.'

Ezra's hold on the gun did not waver.

'She's not coming back, Ezra. She's gone forever,' Erlendur continued. 'She's dead. I've seen her bones.'

'How can you be so sure it's her?'

'It's her all right.'

'But how can you be so sure?'

'Believe me,' said Erlendur. 'I've found Matthildur. Your knife was buried with her, Ezra. It's her.'

Ezra's reaction took him by surprise at first, but on reflection he understood. He had been overwhelmed with the same feeling when confronted by the small bones in Daníel's cardboard box. He realised that he had broken some unwritten law of immutability. He had cut its fetters and set the mechanism of life in motion again. Naturally it would take Ezra a little while to make sense of this new, altered reality. One couldn't expect it to happen in an instant.

'Can't we turn on the lights?' asked Erlendur.

'No,' Ezra said.

'What are you going to do with the gun, Ezra?'

'You've really found her?'

'Jakob hid her in an open grave in the cemetery.' Erlendur attempted again to explain. 'It was easy for him. The grave would still have been recent when you met him there two months later and he started dropping hints. Perhaps he thought he was being clever – to use that of all places. He was confident she'd never be found. He may already have dug the grave when he killed her. Then he used the storm to invent a lie about her journey and seized the opportunity to dispose of her body in the hole. It can't be anyone else. He didn't need to dig far. She's hardly more than a spade length down.'

The pressure of the muzzle eased a little against Erlendur's chin.

'The bloody bastard!' Ezra whispered.

'Jakob knew what he was doing.'

Acting quickly, Erlendur grabbed the barrel of the gun and twisted it easily out of Ezra's hands, sending the old man reeling backwards. The torch fell on the floor and went out. Erlendur laid down the gun at his feet.

'What's wrong with your lights?' he asked.

'The electricity went.'

'What were you doing sitting here in the dark with a gun?'

'Are you lying to me?'

'It's as true as I'm standing here.'

'What did you see?'

'Enough. It's up to you to decide what to do about her grave.'

'He put her in an open grave?' Ezra repeated. 'The gravedigger – I should've guessed. It's obvious once you think about it. Of course he used the cemetery. I was sure he'd sunk her body in the sea, or thrown her into a fissure. It never occurred to me that he'd used the graveyard.'

A long silence followed his words.

'Would there be any point in reburying her?' Ezra asked at last.

'Are you still afraid of being found out?' Erlendur asked. 'That the whole sad story will come to light?'

'I'm not thinking of myself,' Ezra said. 'I should probably thank you for all you've done. I've . . . I've never encountered such pig-headed obstinacy.'

'I won't tell anyone what I know. You can count on that,' Erlendur assured him. 'What you do now is entirely up to you. Now you know where she is, you know the full story of her fate and can finally say goodbye to her after all these years, in whatever manner you choose.'

'I should . . . I should probably thank you.'

'It's really not necessary.'

'I'm sorry for the way I've treated you. I've –'

'I quite understand,' Erlendur interrupted. 'It's no fun receiving a visit from someone like me. I'm well aware of the fact.'

He could sense in the lightless kitchen that Ezra was now leaning on the table.

'Would you like me to drive you over there?' asked Erlendur. 'It's pretty late.'

'Thank you, I would. Of course, I always knew she was dead. I never let myself dream of the alternative. But it's good to know where she is. It's good to know she's in a place like that.'

CHAPTER 59

Erlendur drove the old man through the night to the cemetery. Neither was in the mood to talk. Ezra slumped, shoulders hunched, in the passenger seat and Erlendur wondered what he had been doing, sitting there alone with a shotgun in the darkened house. He had asked if there was any friend he should call to keep him company, but Ezra had said no with such vehemence and resentment at his interference that Erlendur abandoned the subject. He couldn't tell how it had affected Ezra to resolve the doubt that had been consuming him for decades, for most of his life. Any relief he felt must be tempered by a profound grief over Matthildur's fate. At long last he knew the entire story, from beginning to end, but time had done little to mitigate its horror.

Erlendur parked by the cemetery and switched off the engine. The two men remained in the car for several minutes without speaking until finally Erlendur broke the silence.

'Well, shall we get out?'

Ezra was in another world.

'Ezra?' said Erlendur.

'Yes.'

'Shall we go?'

As the old man turned to him, Erlendur realised he was fighting to hold back the tears.

'I don't know if I can do this,' he stammered.

'No, of course. I can take you home again. You can come back tomorrow. Or whenever you feel up to it. As I said before, you can keep the information to yourself or tell anyone who'll listen, as you see fit.'

They sat there, unmoving. The moon, finding a rift in the thick cloud cover, cast a pale light over the graveyard. This seemed to galvanise Ezra. He raised his head to look at the serried ranks of stones and crosses, many of them belonging to people he had known. He had even attended funerals here, never suspecting how close he was to his lost love.

'Let's go,' he said at last, opening the door.

They climbed out and Erlendur escorted him through the gate and over to Thórhildur's grave.

'Matthildur is down there,' he said. 'The fresh spoil's my doing.'

Ezra squinted at the headstone, trying to make out Thórhildur's name and dates by the light of the moon. Then he got down stiffly on one knee.

Erlendur turned aside to give him privacy and strolled over to his parents' plot. There was one more task he had to perform before the night was over. He glanced out of the corner of his eye at the old man kneeling on the grave of the woman

he had loved so many years ago. He had managed
to unite them again, though death still stood
between them. He had managed to draw a line
under the story of Ezra and Matthildur.

Ezra rose and made the sign of the cross.
Erlendur walked back to join him.

'Could you take me home?' Ezra asked.

'Of course. I can't imagine how difficult this
must be.'

Ezra gave him a look. 'I suppose I deserve it
after what I did to Jakob.'

'Do you remember Thórhildur at all?' Erlendur
asked.

Ezra nodded. 'Yes, I remember seeing her around
the village – a very old lady. But I didn't really
know her. She was a good woman, though.
Matthildur's been in good hands.'

'So you're going to let her stay?' said Erlendur.

'What do you think I should do?'

'If she's in good hands . . .'

'At least I know where she is,' said Ezra. 'It's
quite a relief, a tremendous relief to know where
she is at last. I don't think I should disturb her. I
can't think who'd benefit.'

'Good,' said Erlendur. 'Fine.'

'I reckon it's best for everyone that she disappeared in the storm,' said Ezra. 'Perished on the
moors.'

They drove home without further conversation.
The moon was obscured by cloud again.

'Well, that's that,' said Erlendur as he stopped the car in front of Ezra's house.

'Yes, I suppose so.'

'How are you doing?'

'I'll survive.' Ezra held out his hand. 'Thank you for all you've done.'

Erlendur shook it.

'What were you doing sitting there in the dark with the gun?'

'Do you really want to know?'

'Not unless you want to tell me. I'm not going to interfere any further in your life.'

'Let's leave it at that then.'

'Fine.'

'Do you know what I was thinking as I knelt by her grave?' Ezra asked. 'When I'd found her at last. Do you know what struck me?'

Erlendur shook his head.

'I can die now, I thought. There's nothing to hold me here any longer. Nothing to keep me away from her.'

As Erlendur pondered his words he pictured the gun lying on the kitchen floor. He met and held Ezra's eye. The old man returned his gaze with an imploring look.

'What'll happen to the cat?' asked Erlendur.

'He'll manage.'

Erlendur looked away, into the night.

'I'm glad to have met you,' he said at last.

'Likewise.'

Erlendur watched the old man disappear into

360

his house. He lit a cigarette, then turned the car and drove slowly back along the drive.

Parking by the cemetery for the fourth time in twelve hours, he took out the spade and the small box of bones from Daníel's garage. His attempt to bury them earlier the previous day had been interrupted when he noticed the date on Thórhildur's grave. He didn't want anything else to detract from this ceremony.

Picking up the spade, he scraped the thin layer of snow off his mother's mound and cut through the grass into the soil. Having removed a small square of turf, he laid it aside and dug down to a depth of one foot. Then he put down the spade, took the box, knelt and solemnly placed it in the hole.

Afterwards, he refilled the little grave, firmly tamping down the earth and replacing the piece of turf so one could hardly tell the grave had been disturbed.

With that, the little funeral was over.

Erlendur glanced up, towards Hardskafi, then sent a long look back in the direction of Bakkasel where the ruined farm lay hidden in darkness.

Then he set off on foot for the slopes of the mountain.

CHAPTER 60

He hears the child's voice approaching from a great distance. The traveller has gone, taking with him all the feelings he stirred up, of dread and pain and cold, leaving only this little voice and the radiance that accompanies it.

It is a sunny morning and they are walking along the river together. The air is still, the sky a cloudless blue and the sun is making him hot. Bergur, who is in front, stops, dips a hand in the water and takes a drink. He senses the cool of the river on his hot face and watches his brother kneeling on the bank. He feels oddly light at heart.

'Are you ready?' asks his brother, standing up.

'Yes,' he says.

'There's nothing to be afraid of. I'm here.'

'I know.'

Behind them the house shimmers in the heat. Ahead is the welcoming moorland, with its scent of heather. He raises his eyes to the crags at Urdarklettur and the Hraevarskörd Pass, mild now and benign in their summer guise.

Then he takes Bergur's hand in his and together they walk along the river into the bright morning.